THE GIRL IN THE YELLOW DRESS

THE GIRL IN THE YELLOW DRESS

Jane A. Adams

**SEVERN
HOUSE**

First world edition published in Great Britain and the USA in 2022
by Severn House, an imprint of Canongate Books Ltd,
14 High Street, Edinburgh EH1 1TE.

Trade paperback edition first published in Great Britain and the USA in 2022
by Severn House, an imprint of Canongate Books Ltd.

severnhouse.com

British Library Cataloguing-in-Publication Data
A CIP catalogue record for this title is available from the British Library.

ISBN-13: 978-0-7278-50966 (cased)
ISBN-13: 978-1-4483-0711-1 (trade paper)
ISBN-13: 978-1-4483-0710-4 (e-book)

All Severn House titles are printed on acid-free paper.

MIX
Paper from
responsible sources
FSC
www.fsc.org   FSC® C013056

Typeset by Palimpsest Book Production Ltd.,
Falkirk, Stirlingshire, Scotland.
Printed and bound in Great Britain by
TJ Books, Padstow, Cornwall.

AUTHOR'S NOTE

As the lockdown eased in the autumn of 2020, I drove a lot, exploring the countryside just a few miles from where I lived and discovering places I had no idea existed, even though they were only a short distance away. Keeping to the back roads and making an arbitrary left/right decision at each junction, I could go for miles almost without seeing other traffic. The countryside in Leicestershire and across the border into Northamptonshire is very beautiful, but there is also that quality of containment that I tried to capture in the book. High hedges just allow for glimpses of fields and deep valleys, and the roads twist and turn so that sometimes it's hard to figure out the relationship between one village and the next, one small road and another.

I decided I wanted to set the next Henry Johnstone mystery in this part of the country – but couldn't quite find what I needed in terms of location. Anyone who knows the area will therefore recognize certain landmarks and be able to identify particular places, but East Harborough and King's Toll do not exist, except in my imagination and in this book. Having squished them into the existing topography, the surrounding area has been slightly shifted on its axis. I've taken small liberties with distances but, I hope, have lost nothing of the appeal of this rather lovely bit of the UK.

PROLOGUE

February 1930

'Do you have any final words before sentence is carried out?'

Brady Brewer cast a contemptuous look at the formally suited official. 'As it happens, yes, I do,' he said.

He flexed his substantial shoulders and straightened up to his full five feet eight inches in height. Brewer was a squared-off kind of man, bulky and solid, and even after a month of prison food, his arms strained against the fabric of the tough canvas shirt.

'I do very much have something to say.'

He took them in with a glance, the four men attending these last few minutes of his life. The executioner, a small and solemn-looking man whose expression Brewer could not read. The priest Brady had tried to send packing – along with his God – but the little man had refused to go and stood now to Brady's left, prayer book in hand and a look of professional concern on his bland, pasty face. The official in the black suit whose name Brady had not caught but who had asked him this bloody stupid question. Of course he had something left to say. A damn sight more to say than they'd likely give him time for.

And the detective who had made it his business, in Brady's view, to fit him up. Two minutes – no, less: thirty seconds alone with that bastard and Brady Brewer would show that smug bugger what violence really meant.

Out of the corner of his eye Brady caught sight of a fifth man. No doubt the executioner's assistant, hovering in the background, waiting to pull the lever that would damn him to hell.

'I've done some mean, cruel things in my life,' Brady Brewer said, 'but as God is my witness, I didn't do for that girl. Some other bastard choked the life from her. Sure as God's my witness, it wasn't me.'

He turned to look at the detective. 'And you know it. You fixed me up, good and proper.'

Anger – no, something closer to rage and despair – got the better of Brewer then. He lunged for the policeman, even though his hands were bound behind his back and he didn't think he had a chance in hell of reaching him. But for once in his life, and much to his surprise, Brady figured luck was on his side. Those with him on the platform had been surprised by his sudden action as he had hurled himself at his enemy, and Brady had reached him a split second before hands grabbed at him and pulled him down. Brady Brewer just had time to jerk his big bull head upwards. He caught the unfortunate policeman beneath the chin and heard the satisfying crack of a breaking jaw before the man fell.

'Got yer, you bastard!' Brewer's voice was gleeful even as they grabbed him and held him hard. Four men, including the priest, prayer book dropped to the floor, pinioned him as the rope was practically thrown around his neck and he was hustled with more haste than dignity to the hatch and the lever thrown. Brady Brewer was still howling with laughter as he dropped through into empty space.

ONE

Ronan Kerr didn't mind the early mornings in summer. Watching the sunrise, even when he knew that meant a long and exhausting day, was one of the little pleasures in life. This time of year, when winter had officially passed but not yet released its grip, and it was still dark when he started work and dark when he turned for home, had less appeal. He had, he reflected, seen too many winters for there to be any pleasure left in them.

The birds were up, though, the blackbird loudest and most defiant of them all, and he heard the yip of a fox close by. Off to bed, no doubt, the lucky beggar. Ronan had a sneaking liking for foxes, not that he would have admitted to such. This was the heart of fox-hunting country, the local hunt kennels not two miles distant, so it did not do to evince any liking for the russet animals.

He rounded the bend and, to his surprise, saw the red tail of the fox he had heard. From the angle of the body, it appeared to be rooting at something on the verge, close to the field gate. Getting closer, the whole of the fox came into view, as did the thing it was nosing at.

Ronan yelled in shock. The fox took off at speed. *Oh no*, Ronan thought, *not another*. The bastard that had killed that girl was already hanged, so it couldn't be . . .

Fearfully, his heart pounding, he approached what was so clearly the body of a girl lying beside the road. It was not light enough for him to make out all the detail, though his eyes, accustomed to the morning grey, confirmed that she was very dead. She lay on her back, legs splayed at an awkward angle, skirt rucked up about her waist. Her coat was muddied and open, her dress soaked through. He looked at her face, almost fearful that he would recognize her, but he did not. Her matted hair was spread out in the mud. Her dead eyes stared at him, and her throat looked red with what he realized with shock were fingermarks.

'Oh God, oh God,' Ronan moaned. 'God, you poor little girl.' And she was no more than that – a child in his eyes, no more than eighteen or twenty.

He could not help himself, even though he knew that he should leave the body untouched. He reached out and pulled her skirt down so she was covered, tucked the edges of her coat closed as though to keep her warm and then ran back the way he had come as fast as his old legs could carry him, his face wet with tears, his heart pounding fit to burst from his chest.

Inspector Walker had been summoned. Now he stood looking down on the second body he had seen in these past few months – another young woman, the method of killing and the carelessness with which she had been left so like the first. His mind and his reason rebelled against this. He had literally seen the man hanged for the first and now this. The idea that his judgement could have been wrong was more than he could deal with. A copycat killing, he thought; yes, of course, that was it – a copycat. But even as he sought to countenance this idea, the pain in his jaw reminded him of the man he had seen hanged and of his insistence that Walker had got it all wrong, that the accused was innocent of the crime. The slow realization that he might indeed have erred crept into his head, enraging him. Walker believed himself to be a good copper and a sound investigator; he worked hard, had always worked hard to get to be an inspector in His Majesty's constabulary.

He crouched down and felt for the pulse that he knew would not be there. He moved strands of hair from the girl's face so that he could see her more clearly. She had been a pretty girl, he thought, but her face was now congested, tongue protruding and eyes bulging. He knew that the whites of her eyes would be dotted with the red of burst blood vessels. At least, he thought, Brady Brewer's neck had been broken and his death had been clean and swift, but this young woman had fought and died painfully, and the time it had taken her to die must have felt like forever as the breath was choked out of her.

The sound of car tyres alerted him to the arrival of the doctor. Dr Clark was still police surgeon, even though he had officially retired. Moments later, the doctor, clad in a warm winter coat, his bright red scarf somehow out of place, had taken Walker's position by the body and death had been officially pronounced.

'If we can get her back to the mortuary as quickly as possible, I will deal with her this morning,' Dr Clark told him.

'It looks too much like the other one,' Walker said quietly. 'What if I made a mistake?'

Clark, who had known Walker since he was a boy, patted him gently on the arm. 'Mistakes can happen; there are few that would mourn Brewer's death even if he wasn't guilty of that particular crime,' he said.

Walker stood watching as the doctor got back in his car and drove away, and knew that he was right: very few would mourn Brady Brewer – yet was that a good enough reason for him to die? He looked down at the girl, remembering the other body, that of young Sarah Downham. Brewer had claimed to be in love with the young woman, and she, young fool, had claimed to be in love with him. Girls could have strange fancies, Walker thought. They could also be deceiving, and he had reason to believe that Sarah Downham was not as innocent or as inexperienced as her family reckoned.

Which is not to say that she deserved to die. Not to say that at all.

TWO

The first Detective Chief Inspector Henry Johnstone had heard about the arrest of Brady Brewer had been in a letter received in mid-February and read to him by his sergeant, Mickey Hitchens. He was, apparently, destined to hang. That Brewer should die by hanging was, Henry thought, no more than he should have expected. Whatever he had done that had finally brought such justice, it was no loss to the world. Henry rarely wasted energy or time on hating anyone, but he had long ago made an exception for Brewer.

'He is to be hanged for the murder of a young woman by the name of Sarah Downham,' Mickey told him.

'Well, for that I'm sorry, but not for the outcome as far as Brewer is concerned. The man has long deserved the rope and on many counts.'

Mickey did not disagree; he too had come first to know and then to hate the man. 'His sister – that's who this letter is from – swears he didn't do it and asks for our help in proving his innocence.'

'Innocence! Don't make me laugh, Mickey.'

'She swears that he was with her on the night the young woman died.'

'And why should I care, Mickey? Why should either of us show concern?'

Looking at his sergeant, he saw a flicker of emotion cross Mickey's somewhat wrinkled face and recognized that there were times when Mickey's moral compass pointed northward far more reliably than his own. He waited for the gentle rebuke from his old friend, but it didn't come. Even Mickey, it seemed, found it hard to scrape up any pity for Brady Brewer. With a small sigh, Mickey, as though regretting his lack of compassion, tossed the letter aside and they both turned their attention to the stack of open cases piled upon their desks. As far as Henry was concerned, the matter was closed.

Two weeks later, another letter arrived.

'It appears that Brewer was hanged three days ago and still protesting his innocence,' Mickey told him. He dropped the letter on the desk, and Henry glanced at it dismissively. He noted the address was somewhere called King's Toll, close to the border of Leicestershire and Northamptonshire, and that the sister went by the name of Elizabeth.

'The man would argue black was white and heaven was hell,' Henry said irritably. 'If not for this crime, he surely deserved death for others. You and I both know that, Mickey.'

Mickey Hitchens acknowledged that, to Henry's experienced eye, with a slightly diffident shrug. It was Henry's turn to sigh. Mickey Hitchens had ever been his conscience, but he neither needed nor wanted that pricking now. Although he was, truth be told, not quite prepared to look him full in the face. Henry muttered an excuse and went off to make them both tea. By the time he returned, Mickey was sorting through statements and evidence in preparation for a court appearance, and the matter was put aside.

For a short time.

Ten days later, another application for help arrived and this was not one they could just sweep aside. A young woman had been killed in the same fashion as Sarah Downham and barely a mile from where that first body had been found.

THREE

Truth to tell, Henry had hoped that the call for help from the Leicestershire constabulary would be passed on to someone else. He and Mickey were not first or even second on call on the board – the official rota system for the Murder Squad that hung prominently in Central Office at Scotland Yard. First on call were tasked with immediate deployment to whatever scene shouted loudest for attention. Second on the list were given a few more hours to prepare and take themselves in more civilized fashion to the back of beyond. Third on call had a full twelve hours to deploy – though most officers knew that to wait that long would be to risk disturbance of the crime scene and would do their utmost to beat the target. Others in the Central Office took cases as they arrived. At the time the call for assistance arrived from the deputy superintendent of the Leicestershire constabulary, a fatal shooting in Rickmansworth had taken the first on call. The second had gone to a stabbing in a pub not more than a few hundred yards away on the Thames embankment, and the third to the murder of a very young child down on the coast near Plymouth. Henry was glad to have dodged that one. He hated attending infanticides, especially when, as in this case, the boy's teenage mother was the chief suspect.

And so they were destined to go to the Midlands on the eight-thirty train. Packing his bag in a fit of pique, Henry found he was of the opinion that somehow Brady Brewer had arranged this, albeit from beyond the grave, irrational though he knew that thought to be.

'Maybe he was telling the truth,' Mickey had said sombrely.

'Truth and Brewer were not on speaking terms when he was alive,' Henry had told him acerbically. 'I doubt they've become acquaintances now the man is dead.'

But it irked him that Mickey might be right. Irked him more that Brewer had not been taken for one or other of the many crimes Henry knew beyond doubt he was responsible for. He was further irritated by the fact that the murder of a young woman by the name of Penelope Soper was now three days old, the local constabulary having walked all over it, no doubt trampling both actually and metaphorically on the evidence and coming up empty before thinking to call for assistance from the Yard.

Henry knew that there were provincial investigators worthy of the name, but he also knew that they could be lonely and isolated points of inspiration in a desert of mediocrity.

Henry caught the thought, held it and turned it in his mind for a moment or two, and then admitted that he was being unjust. He was angry, he realized. Unwontedly angry at Brewer and the memories that even this peripheral contact with the man had dragged to the fore. Irritated with himself for the feelings of helpless ire that thinking about Brewer always elicited. Vexed even with Mickey and his speculation about Brewer's possible innocence – even though the comment had been fully justified. Worst of all, and it disgusted him as he acknowledged it, he was profoundly angry with the young woman, Sarah Downham, who had met such a tragic end, even though she should be the last to take any blame. And now there was this other young woman, Penelope Soper. It seemed like too much of a coincidence that two murders should happen in the same area and not be connected. But how could they be?

Henry threw himself into his favourite chair and gazed down at the view of the river. The Thames was busy even at this hour of the evening, lights moving along its length, fixed to and illuminating the barges and lighters and wherries that moved their goods and passengers along the river as they had done for centuries. Usually, the slow, distant bustle of river traffic soothed him, but he was beyond that tonight. Although it was patently obvious that Brady Brewer had not been responsible for this latest murder, he was still inevitably linked to events by his having been hanged for the previous one. So perhaps his sister had been right. Perhaps when she had written asking for assistance, they should not have been so swift to dismiss the claim. Perhaps Brady Brewer need not have been hanged.

No, Henry thought decisively. The bastard was deserving of

the noose even if he'd ended up being hanged for the wrong crime.

Henry's thoughts slipped back more than a decade, to the last few months of the war. The remembered image of the young woman in the barn, the child, barely in her teens, lying at her side.

The blood, the ruined bodies. Brewer's face and arms raked with deep scratches from where the child had fought to help her sister. Brewer had laughed about it. Had laughed more as he had recounted how he had 'laid the little bitch out'. He had clouted her with his fist and she had fallen unconscious to the floor at her sister's side. Henry had hoped fervently that the child had still been unconscious when Brewer had raped her.

He closed his eyes. He should have shot the bastard then, followed through on the impulse. That he had not done so was down to Mickey, not because he didn't agree but because Brewer's cronies would have made certain it was Henry who hanged for it.

At the time of the incident, Henry had told himself that he would get even with Brewer, for this and other crimes, but within the next day or two they had been separated, posted to different sections of the line before the final push began, and he had only heard of Brewer after that in oblique references made by mutual acquaintances.

He had heard that the man survived the war, had come home and gone to live with his sister. It seemed that arrangement had continued, and he could not help but wonder what the sister thought of this man. Did she see some other side of him, invisible to those, like Henry, who had seen only his evil face?

No doubt they would soon find out, Henry thought bitterly. The sister was not exactly likely to meet them with open arms, whatever she thought about her brother, but she would have to be interviewed now. He ought to get some sleep, even though he was well aware that sleep would not come easily. The only place he ever slept well was in his sister's house. He laughed grimly, wondering if sisters possessed some magic when it came to younger siblings. Since leaving Cynthia's comfortable abode, coming back to London and returning to his job, sleep had been even more elusive, and Henry was beginning to realize that perhaps this work was no longer for him. It was an occupation that dealt only with death and destruction, and although it certainly exercised his intellect and his conscience, and he knew that he was good at it, he wasn't sure how much longer he could continue.

As he got ready for bed, Henry acknowledged that there was one more issue to do with the job that was perhaps even more pressing than simple mental exhaustion. While Henry had been off sick, recovering from an injury that still pained him and still denied him full use of his right arm and shoulder, Mickey had worked with other detectives, and Mickey's worth had quite justifiably been recognized. Mickey had finally been put forward for promotion. No doubt, before the summer came, he would be a fully-fledged inspector with a sergeant of his own to look after.

It was not before time; Henry knew this. He acknowledged also that, in part, Mickey's delayed rise through the ranks had been the result of his loyalty to their friendship, and because he was married to a somewhat itinerant actress, although Belle had now returned to London to live full-time and was performing in productions that not even the most curmudgeonly of superior officers could object to.

He got into bed and lay down, trying to find a position where his arm didn't ache. There were sleeping pills and analgesics on the bedside table, but he tried to avoid taking them, afraid of becoming dependent on them. Henry realized that he had become afraid of many things recently. His beloved niece had been kidnapped, had almost died. He had seen then, in his first case back at work, what could have become of Melissa when investigating the death of a young woman not so much older than her. It all preyed on his mind, and although he was totally in agreement that Mickey should accept his promotion, and that life should change because that was what life did and that Mickey deserved every accolade that might come his way, Henry was increasingly unconvinced that he could continue this work without his friend at his side. Perhaps it was time for his own change of direction.

As the train pulled out of the station the following morning, Henry studied the map of their destination, noting a cluster of little villages, a series of farms. 'Oh, it is close to the battlefield of Naseby.'

'I noticed that, too,' Mickey told him. 'The body of the first girl, Sarah Downham, was found on a grass verge at the side of this road' – he pointed to the map – 'close to a footpath that crosses the top of the battlefield. It's thought the young woman was taking a shortcut home that way. She had been visiting friends – the Simpsons – in Naseby itself and was returning to East Harborough, which is between there and Husbands Bosworth. You see from the map it's quite a walk, but it would seem she didn't even make it to the footpath.'

'And King's Toll is where the sister of Brady Brewer lives,' Henry said, remembering the address he had seen on the letter. He looked again at the map. 'It looks like a tiny place.'

'I looked it up in the gazetteer. It has a fine church, apparently, built in the perpendicular style, a pub and a main street, but you're right, it is a small place. The second girl, Penelope Soper, also lived there, so we might assume she knew the Brewers. She worked in the village of Selford, down here, a couple of miles from her home. But here is East Harborough, the market town where Sarah Downham lived, and that's where we will be staying. The nearest train station is a few miles away at Market Harborough; apparently, a car and driver will be made available to us.'

Henry nodded and then closed his eyes, suddenly overcome by tiredness.

'You're still not sleeping,' Mickey said.

'I sleep, after a fashion.' He opened his eyes and sat up straight, trying to shake the weariness from his bones. 'What do we know so far?'

'Very little, in fact. The girl had more than one job but for three days a week was in service at a small hotel in Selford. Apparently there is a wharf there for unloading from the canal. That will be the Grand Union, I suppose. She lives in at the inn – the Wharf – for part of the week but, as poor luck would have it, had returned home on the previous Tuesday because her mother had been ill and there was no one to look after the younger siblings. She was due to return to work the day after she died, and she took advantage of the final day of freedom to go and visit friends. And here we have some confusion. She was found close to the footpath that would have taken her back to her mother's house, but equally, if she had continued along the road, she would have reached her place of employment. Now, her friends assumed that she was going home, but the landlord assumed that she was coming back to work that day; in fact, he raised the alarm when she didn't arrive at the expected time in the evening. He sent word to her mother's house, worried that the woman might have had a relapse, then when it became obvious that she wasn't there, they went to enquire with the friends to see if perhaps she had stayed longer than expected, and that's when she was found. This was the following morning. It had rained in the night, but the earth beneath the body was dry. The young woman herself was soaked through to the skin, so she must've been lying there through the night. The rain started just after nine, so the time of death must have been before nine that evening. Her body was found just before seven in the morning.'

'If she had lain in the rain, it would be difficult to judge from body temperature when she might have died,' Henry observed. 'And the night would have been cold at this time of year, so that would have made body temperature fall more quickly. Had rigor set in?'

'That I don't know; that information wasn't in what scant details we have received so far. But here's the interesting thing. The man in charge of the investigation, Inspector James Walker, is the man who arrested Brady Brewer for the first murder. It seems he left his sick bed to take the lead on this one.'

Henry raised an eyebrow. 'And what was wrong with him?'

'Well, he attended Brewer's execution, but it seems that Brewer took advantage of the occasion to headbutt said inspector and fracture his jaw.'

Henry looked at him in surprise. 'Embarrassing for all concerned,' he commented. 'And is he healed?'

'Apparently he is healed enough. No doubt he also feels the burden of a wrongful arrest and execution.'

'If it was a wrongful execution. It might be that another man killed this second young woman. Strangulation is not such an uncommon method of killing.'

'True. The other thing we should be aware of is that Inspector Walker is not happy about our presence. It seems that his superiors decided he should have assistance as he was making very little progress on this case, and he seems to have royally misjudged the last one.'

Henry grimaced. It was almost commonplace for the local police not to welcome interference from Scotland Yard, but it never made for a pleasant atmosphere and it was often counter-productive to the investigation itself if there was conflict between the local constabulary and the incomers.

'Well, we shall just have to do our best,' Henry said.

FOUR

They arrived at Market Harborough railway station a little after ten a.m., and the police car and driver were waiting for them. The first destination was the mortuary at the local hospital, so they could view the unfortunate girl's body. Penelope Soper had been nineteen years old. She was small – not above five feet and two inches, Henry guessed – and built like a bird. She had long, dark hair and blue eyes, although, three days dead, these were sunken back and glazed over. The cheeks had lost any plumpness they might have had, and the mouth was a slack line between two pale lips. He hoped someone had a photograph of her so he could remind himself of what she looked like alive. Corpses had a tendency to take on a sameness, Henry thought absently as he examined the wounds around her neck, post-mortem bruising clearly showing the grip of fingers that had taken her life from her.

'He seems to have used the fingers and thumbs of both hands,' Mickey commented, demonstrating by placing his own around the girl's throat. 'So either he did not have the strength or the size of hand to do it with one, or he was making certain. Either way, he choked the life out of her.'

Henry was examining the post-mortem report. 'So the nearest guess at time of death is between eight o'clock, when she left her friend's home, and nine o'clock, when we know it began to rain,' Henry said. 'A short window of opportunity.'

'Which confirms our earlier speculations.' Mickey turned to speak to the mortuary assistant. 'You were present when the post-mortem was carried out?'

The young man nodded. 'I made the notes for Doctor Clark,' he said. 'Doctor Clark likes to have an amanuensis; he says it is better that everything is recorded contemporaneously as the memory does not hold detail.' He grinned suddenly. 'Frankly, sir, I don't think Doctor Clark would forget anything even if I wasn't here. Mind like a trap, he has. He said to tell you that if you wish to meet, he will be free by the middle of the afternoon.'

Henry exchanged a glance with his sergeant and then nodded. He doubted the doctor would be able to tell them more – the post-mortem notes were thorough and precise – but it would be good to speak to the man in case he could add anything.

'Did Doctor Clark also carry out the post-mortem on Sarah Downham?' he asked.

The mortuary assistant nodded. 'Doctor Clark deals with all of the suspicious deaths that might be brought to us, and any of those deaths where a doctor has not been consulted.'

'He must be a busy man.'

'He is, sir. Busier now than before he retired from his general practice. He sold his practice to a younger man, and Doctor Clark said he could now focus his attention on post-mortem examination. Doctor Clark did not believe that this had been carried out efficiently prior to his arrival and he felt that he should change that.'

Henry looked with interest at the young mortuary assistant, noting the smile that quirked at the corner of the boy's mouth. He was clearly an admirer of Doctor Clark but also clearly saw something in the man's attitude that amused him.

'And he trained you up to be his assistant,' Mickey asked.

'He said I have the skills to become a doctor, but I don't have the resources. At least I can learn here and it's better than being a general porter, which is what I was when Doctor Clark discovered me.'

There was a story here, Henry thought, but unfortunately there wasn't time to hear it. He thanked the young man for his time, and they returned to the car, having asked for an appointment to be confirmed with Doctor Clark that afternoon.

'So if the same doctor carried out both post-mortems, we should at least hope for consistency. He seems to be a conscientious man, at least,' Mickey observed.

'True, and I suspect also one who will be hungry for details of the investigation and eager for an opportunity to assist us,' Henry said with less enthusiasm.

His sergeant laughed. 'I expect we'll be able to keep him at arm's length as regards the investigation, but local knowledge is always of value, as is someone in authority who is not openly hostile.'

They had arranged to be taken to see Inspector James Walker next, and then Mickey had suggested they find somewhere to eat lunch. Mickey always told his boss that he did not operate well on an empty stomach, but Henry realized that this was also a way of ensuring that Henry himself had something to eat. He did have a tendency to forget, recollecting that his body needed nourishment only when his stomach cramped.

The Victorian police station was very like many Henry had visited over the years and the office of Inspector Walker likewise. It was small, crowded and tucked away at the back, reached by crossing the small brick-paved yard. James Walker himself was not a big man, not quite matching Mickey for height, but he had an interesting physique – broad shoulders and a narrow waist – and a way of moving that made Henry wonder if he was a boxer.

He bid them sit down and settled himself behind his desk, offering whisky which was refused, but pouring some into his own glass and chasing that down with a handful of pills that Henry assumed were painkillers. The man was clearly in pain and his jaw still showed the yellow and grey of old bruising. He had shaved, and Henry could imagine the discomfort that must've caused. His gaze, though, was challenging.

'I do not need extra assistance,' he said thickly. He was moving his face as little as possible, and Henry was reminded of a ventriloquist.

'I understand you came off sick leave to handle this,' Henry said.

'I am fit enough.'

'We've not come to challenge your authority,' Henry told him, despite the fact that, on some level, that was exactly what they were doing. 'We are, as you say, here to assist you, not to take over the case.'

Walker laughed at that, and a look of pain crossed his face as he clearly regretted the response.

'You no doubt want to see my records regarding Penelope Soper's murder,' he said.

'And that of Sarah Downham,' Henry told him.

No laughter this time, but a grimace and not just one of pain. 'What the devil for? That case is closed. The man who committed the murder is dead. He was hanged.'

'We are aware of that,' Henry told him. 'We've also become aware of the possibility the man could have been alibied for the night of Sarah Downham's death. New evidence has emerged.'

Beside him, he could feel Mickey tense as Henry pushed the truth to its limits.

'What bloody evidence?' Walker did not bother to hide his contempt. 'Brewer was guilty. He killed that girl because she rejected his advances. Every bugger knows that. If the new evidence you refer to comes from that sister of his, well, more fool you for believing it.'

Henry felt Mickey tense even further. The inspector's contempt, particularly as Henry outranked him, was unforgivable, Henry thought. A moment later, Walker found himself being dragged across his desk, the hand grasping his collar and tie also pressed painfully against his swollen jaw. 'Do you always speak to your superiors in such a fashion?' Henry said quietly. He let go, and Walker's bruised face thudded down on to his desk.

'And now, your notes, if you please. And then you may return to your sickbed.'

With bad grace, Walker removed the folders from his drawer and dropped them in front of Henry, who picked them up, turned his back and walked out of the tiny office, across the courtyard and through the building. Mickey followed in his wake.

'Why are you so keen to make enemies?' Mickey asked him as they got in the car. 'I've seen you show lack of judgement before, but that was foolish and unnecessary.'

For a minute, Henry glowered at his sergeant and seemed about to tell him that he outranked him as well. Instead, he turned to look out of the window, observing the passing scenery of the little town, his hand still clutching the folders that Walker had given him. Mickey was right, he conceded. The man was hostile and he had been disrespectful, but Henry knew he could have handled it better. Or could he?

'I do not think that Inspector Walker is a man who would respond to conciliation or gentleness,' he said harshly.

'I never said he was. But there is a vast difference between being gentle and grabbing a man by the throat and then bashing his face on the table, especially if that man is recovering from a fractured jaw.'

But Mickey was smiling, Henry noticed – disapproving, yes, but not about to make an issue of it. Another sergeant might be different, of course, Henry thought, putting his finger on one of the things that was really bothering him. At some point, there would be a last case that he and Mickey worked on together. That time was getting closer. Mickey was well overdue for promotion. That time could be now; Henry wasn't sure that he could bear the thought of it.

The car took them out of town by a back road, and soon they were passing through small villages with names that ended in 'worth' and 'ing' and 'byre', which spoke to Henry of Viking invasions and movements of ancient peoples. Then the car turned off on to an even smaller road, narrow, with high hedges on either side. Where the hedges broke and farm gates intervened, Henry could see down into a deep valley. All around was farmland with new lambs playing and crops showing spring green, hedges white with blackthorn. Sloes come autumn, Henry thought. He had grown up in the countryside, in a large and prosperous village where his father had been the general practitioner for a vast area – in truth, far too big for one man to handle. Even if his father's workload had been less, it was unlikely he would have been a better father or husband. The man showed a cheerful, benevolent face to his patients – as long as they could pay – but he was at best neglectful and at worst violent where his family was concerned. The memories tainted any joy Henry may have taken from the countryside; in any case, he knew all too well the poverty and backbreaking work that was the lot of most inhabitants of even this idyllic setting.

'Do we know anything about the sister?' he asked.

'Only that she was older. I remember Brewer mentioning her when we knew him in the war and I think there was a younger sibling that died in infancy or something like that.'

Henry nodded. Now that Mickey had reminded him, he too

remembered Brewer talking about his big sister and how she had taken on responsibility for the family, much as Henry's own sister had for him.

Their route now took them into a village that Henry assumed must be King's Toll, and the driver pulled up outside a row of four tiny whitewashed cottages opposite the village pub. A brightly painted sign declared it to be the George and Dragon, and Henry noted with amusement that the dragon was unusually large, each scale the size of the knight's gauntleted hand. As he got out of the car, Henry glimpsed the church. What was it Mickey had said – early perpendicular or some such? It looked big for such a small place, but perhaps the village had been larger when the church had been built, or perhaps it had been created for some rich landowner who would rather spend money on his soul than on his tenants.

Oh, Henry, you are in a sour mood, he told himself. He made an effort to push thoughts from his mind that did not directly relate to the case. They would undoubtedly face a cool reception from the sister, and who could blame her for that?

The door to the end cottage, furthest from them, opened, and a woman stood with her arms folded, glaring at them. There was no doubt, he thought, that this was Brady Brewer's sister. He remembered that she had never married – she was still Miss Brewer – and, mentally preparing himself for a battle, he went over to her with his hand outstretched. He was unsurprised when she ignored it and turned back inside.

'You'd best come on in, then,' she called back over her shoulder and Henry followed her inside, Mickey hard on his heels. It occurred to Henry that his sergeant was concerned in case his temper had not improved since the encounter with Inspector Walker. Henry was suddenly amused. Did Mickey expect him to grab this woman round the neck and shake her till her teeth rattled? Or bash her head against the kitchen table? Frankly, he thought, now he had a closer look at her, he might well come off worse in such an exchange. She was not tall, but she was built as her brother had been – square and solid – and had a look of immovability about her.

She pointed to chairs set beside a small black leaded range and then went across and pointedly closed the front door, which

Mickey had failed to do when he had entered. 'You might be able to afford to let the heat out, but I can't. Especially now I'm down to one wage coming in.'

Henry let this pass. He glanced at his sergeant and made a small gesture that told Mickey he was going to take the lead on this particular interview. Mickey was generally better with women, although Henry was not certain that would hold true for this one.

Elizabeth Brewer took a seat opposite and settled her hands in her lap and then, after a brief hesitation, she reached for her knitting, which was set in a basket beside the hearth. It seemed she was not a woman who liked idle hands.

'Well, I'm waiting,' she said. 'I sent you two letters and you did not even have the courtesy to reply. I fully understand that you did not like my brother, that he had given you many reasons not to like him, but he assured me that you were honest men and would not let him hang for something he did not do, despite all the things you may have believed about him.'

'Despite all the things we knew to be true,' Mickey said mildly.

The woman glowered at him, but Mickey, Henry noted, seemed sanguine.

'I will make no apology for that,' Mickey said quietly. 'I will apologize only for not responding to your letters. As you say, that was rude, and common courtesy should have demanded a reply. But you must know that there was no love lost between your brother and me, and the same goes for the chief inspector here. Frankly, Miss Brewer, we considered your brother to be an evil bastard and the fact that he had escaped the hangman's noose for this long a matter of luck rather than judgement.'

Henry held his breath. Well, he thought, Mickey was *usually* better with women than he was, but perhaps this time was the exception. To his surprise, Elizabeth Brewer nodded.

'He was aware what you thought of him and would have admitted most of it was justified. But not all. However, that's not what you've come to talk about. He never killed Sarah. He never laid a hand on her – he would never, ever have laid a hand on her. The sad thing, the tragic thing, is that he loved that girl.'

Loved! Henry thought. Another thing he didn't consider Brewer capable of.

'And for what it's worth, she loved him.'

'And did she know about his past?' Mickey asked.

'Some of it, some of it not. He felt he had to tell her some things. Other things – well, they were in the past and there was nothing he could do about them.'

'Like raping a child,' Henry challenged her.

She looked at him coldly. 'I'll not be discussing that with you just now. There are things about that incident you don't understand, and I'm not going to be drawn.'

'Incident!' Henry was outraged. 'I know he was your brother, but surely you can't—'

She held up her hand. The steel knitting needle glowed red in the light from the range. 'You are here to talk about Sarah Downham and about that poor little scrap, Penny Soper. And that is *all* I'm prepared to talk about. You understand that.'

It was not a question, Henry realized, but a simple statement of fact.

Mickey took over. 'Was your brother walking out with Sarah Downham? What did her family think of this?'

'Her family thought the same as you did: that my brother was a bastard and that she'd had her head turned. They were going to send her away. Sarah was from a respectable family and the time was when ours was a respectable family, too. Anyone can fall on hard times. She was a sweet girl, gentle as a lamb and pretty as a picture, and he would no more have laid a hand on her than he would on me. I would have welcomed her into our home had they married as he wished.'

'A woman likes her own kitchen,' Mickey said slyly.

'Indeed, a woman does, but Sarah and I would have rubbed along well enough, and I would have been a second pair of hands when the babies came.'

'And did her family know of their intention to marry?'

She snorted angrily. 'That was when the trouble started. Her father had threatened him often enough, but her aunt had said that it was just a phase she was going through, and that if they left well alone, she would soon tire of him. There are many young girls that like a rough and ready man until they learn better. She knew Sarah was far too conscious of her own welfare and position to have slept with any man until she had a ring on her finger, so she told him to have no worry on that score, and indeed I know that to be true. The aunt came here, and we chatted about it for a long time, but I told her they were serious about one another. She wouldn't believe me, of course; what could *I* possibly know?

'So the family warned them off, but Brady wanted to do the right thing – he wanted to treat the family properly, tell them that he and Sarah were going to be wed and that he hoped they would come to the wedding, like civilized folk. And that's when it all started to go very wrong. The father locked her in her room, let her out only for meals. They told us she was going to marry where *they* chose, not where she was being so foolishly led. I went round there and tried to reason with them, and, in the end, they did let me speak to Sarah. They said I was to tell her, woman to woman, that this was a ridiculous notion, that her family had her best interests at heart and that she was to give in to them.'

'But, of course, she wouldn't,' Mickey said. 'A young girl in love will not be reasoned with. As I understand it, she came from a respectable family, a family better off than yours, if you'll pardon me saying. Her family had the right surely to encourage her to make a marriage among her own kind.'

Elizabeth's eyes flashed but it seemed she realized that Mickey was goading her.

'She was a good girl, but they pushed too far. They'd arranged for her to go away and be wed to a man that they had chosen. Well, he is a good man, no mistake about that. Philip Maddison, his name is, and he's training to be a doctor. He knew Sarah from when they were both little things; they used to play together. The families always believed they would make a good match and always encouraged them to grow up thinking that one day they would marry and be together. Sarah was content to do that until she met Brady.'

She sighed and set the knitting down in her lap. 'Look, I am not going to say that the girl might not have changed her mind. It's true what they say – girls are often foolish when it comes to their choice of men. They are drawn to the wild and the unknown and the bad boys of this world.'

'Brady was hardly a boy,' Mickey said.

'No, he was not. He had never even had the chance to be a boy. He'd grown up far too fast; we both had. And yes, he was a good deal older than her, but that does not mean it could not have been a match.'

'The family must have known of his reputation. What father would want his child, his very young daughter – she was only eighteen, after all – to marry a man fifteen years her senior. A man with a reputation for violence?'

'A man who had put all that behind him.'

'Does any man truly put such violence behind him?' Mickey asked. 'From what we had seen of your brother, violence had become habitual. He took what he wanted, he did what he wanted, and he had no conscience.'

'And all that changed when he met Sarah.'

'I think you are deceiving yourself,' Mickey told her bluntly. 'Every sister wants to think the best of her brother, even when the evidence is all to the contrary. I do not blame you for fighting his corner, any more than we should blame this young girl for, as you say, being attracted to the wildness and the glamour, if you like, of an older man who was undoubtedly of a type completely beyond her ken. You cannot blame a young woman for having her head turned; as her aunt suggested, most do grow out of this. They mature and find that what they really want is someone gentler in aspect. Even you seem to feel that Sarah might eventually change her mind. She may well have grown to fear him, Miss Brewer, and then what?'

Elizabeth took up her knitting once more and did not meet Mickey's gaze. For all her protests, these thoughts had also crossed her mind, Henry thought. Was that the reason she would have insisted on staying on, even after her brother had married? Was she secretly afraid Brady would have hurt the love of his life, turned violent and impatient, especially when the babies came and this tiny cottage was filled with noise and inconvenience?

'So what happened? Obviously she did not leave home to go and marry her young doctor.'

'No, she did not.' The knitting was laid aside now and placed back in the basket, as though this final telling would take all of her attention. 'As I told you, her father and aunt kept her locked in her room, and she had pretended to be reconciled to their ideas, so their guard was down. Her family had arranged for her to go away for a time. They seemed to think that a break might bring her to her senses. On the night before she was due to leave, she climbed out through the window and turned up here. Well, I knew they would come here looking for her and there was nowhere to hide, but when I told her so, she became angry and said I didn't care about her either, and she went running off into the night. About half an hour later, her father turned up – you will find this all on the statement that I made to the police constable and that idiot Inspector Walker. Well, he turned my house upside down looking for his child, and finally believed me when I told him that she had run off. That she had been here but that I had no idea where she had gone. Of course, he then assumed that Brady must have fetched her away and he began talking about elopements and disgrace and all of those things that trouble men like him. The fact that his daughter was missing, on a rainy and bitter night, seemed secondary.

'I was about to go and search for her myself – her father had gone and I was worried. And then Brady came home. He'd been drinking. He'd been doing a lot of that in the days after he had been told that Sarah would be sent from home. Anyway, off he goes out – steaming drunk he was, but he understood that Sarah was missing and that perhaps . . .'

'What do you think he hoped to do?' Mickey asked, his voice gentle now.

'I told him to bring her back here. I had no doubt that her father would set the police on us, but I thought if he brought her back here, I might be able to speak sense to her. Perhaps I could send for her aunt, and two women telling her the way the world worked might just get through. As it turned out, when she'd stormed out of here, she'd gone to the Greens' farm and taken shelter with Miss Lucy.'

'I have the impression you thought it might be better for her if she did leave, if she did go and marry elsewhere.'

'I have learned to be pragmatic,' Elizabeth told them. 'I have spent a lifetime bending to circumstances. I hoped once to become a teacher; our family was not always poor, and my parents believed in education. We were never well-off, but Mother believed we should better ourselves, and I think she understood that I would probably never marry. I was never a small and pretty thing, the sort that men chase, but believe me, I have a good brain.'

'I have no doubt of that,' Mickey told her.

'And then our parents died. Mother of a winter fever and Father of the drink. While she was alive, she had managed to keep him in check, but, of course, after she was gone, he would listen to no one. It was left to me to look after the younger ones. Poor little Sally died of scarlet fever when she was only eight; after that, there was only me and Brady, and we had to survive the best we could.'

Henry shifted in his seat. He would not normally have commented, but there was, unexpectedly, something about this woman that he actually liked. 'My sister was fifteen when our father died; our mother was already gone and it was left to her to raise me.'

There was a hint of a smile on Elizabeth's face when she asked, 'Did she do a good job, Inspector?'

'She did; anything that happened after I left her care I think I am responsible for.'

She studied him thoughtfully, but he could not tell what she was thinking. She said, 'I did the best I could, but Brady was wild even when he was a boy. Some children seem to be born with the devil in them. Not that he was an evil child, or even a particularly bad child, just that he seemed not to think any rule applied to him. I would tell him, "Brady, you can't do that," and he would say, "Why can't I? Who will stop me?"

'A few days after that, the poor lamb was dead. She was found by the side of the road, not a mile from where poor Penny Soper ended up. She had been strangled and, worse still, she had been raped.'

Henry raised an eyebrow; he'd not been aware of that.

'I don't remember that being in the report,' Mickey said quietly.

'No, the family have powerful friends. But Inspector Walker knew, of course, and in his mind, it stood to reason – Brady couldn't get what he wanted legitimately and so he had taken it by force. And the girl had fought back and he had strangled her. Of course, a lot of people knew what had happened, those that found the body—'

'But there were those who thought it bad enough that a respectable young woman had been murdered. Knowing she had also been raped would further stain her name.'

She nodded. 'People closed ranks; of course they did. Sarah did not have an enemy in the world. She was a sweet girl. For that matter, so was Penny.'

'You knew the second victim.'

'Yes, of course; she grew up in this village.'

Henry realized that both he and Mickey had forgotten momentarily. 'So the mother lives . . .'

'Just beyond the church – the white painted cottage. You won't find her there just now; she and the children have gone to stay with relatives. I doubt they'll come back.'

'And the father?'

'Went off with another woman about a year ago. I have no idea where he might be now.'

'And Sarah's mother. You made no mention of her.'

'Because the poor soul died giving birth to little Sarah. Sarah's father thought about remarrying but never did. The brother is older, from a previous marriage – lives down south and only turns up here when he's summoned. Sarah's father had a heir and I believe he genuinely loved his wife and did not feel he could find any to take her place. His sister was widowed in the war and so she came to run the household.'

'And as Sarah got older, there was no tension in the household? She did not wish to run from the home herself?'

'Indeed not. As I told you, she intended to marry. To have a husband and a home of her own. The aunt's position was not under threat if that's what you mean. As far as I could tell, they all ticked along nicely.'

There did not seem to be much more to say and so they took leave of Miss Brewer.

Back at the car, Mickey interrogated their driver about where they might get some lunch, and he pointed to the pub across the road. It would, he said, still be open for another half an hour; the landlord could usually be persuaded to make sandwiches or at least produce bread and cheese and pickle. Mickey decided that would do nicely. The three of them made their way into the public bar, and a few minutes later some basic but perfectly adequate lunch was provided.

The constable had noticed an acquaintance standing by the bar and gone to join him in conversation, and Mickey and Henry found themselves alone in a corner with crusty bread, ham fresh cut from the bone, fine stilton cheese and a rather good pickle.

'The beer is not bad, either,' Mickey said.

Looking around, Henry decided that the few customers were either farmworkers or perhaps travelling salesman, judging by their cheap suits and air of world-weariness, which surprised him as this little village seemed well off the beaten track. He made a note to study the map more closely and familiarize himself with the area. And to ask the landlord if his analysis of the clientele was indeed correct.

'So, what have we learned so far?' he asked his sergeant.

Mickey spread his bread thickly with butter and pickle and topped it off with a piece of cheese before responding. 'That Miss Brewer was at great pains to tell us how perfect the poor dead girl, Sarah Downham, was,' he said. 'I know most folk count it bad luck to speak ill of the dead; even so, such a paragon, born of such a good family, with such a good and innocent heart . . . it makes me wonder how she ended up even meeting Brewer.'

Henry nodded. 'Nevertheless, we will keep to the custom of not speaking ill of the dead for a little longer,' he said. 'I suspect the relatives will be more inclined to give us the time of day while we are not maligning the young woman's honour. But I am troubled, Mickey, and, as yet, I'm not quite sure what it is that is wrong. Something is not right here.'

'Beyond the fact that two young women are dead and a man, perhaps not guilty of one of the crimes, may have been hanged?' Mickey quirked an eyebrow.

'Apart from that,' Henry agreed.

For a few minutes, they ate in silence, and then Henry said, 'What did you think of Elizabeth Brewer? I cannot imagine a woman more different from her sibling.'

'Indeed not,' Mickey agreed. 'She is an interesting woman and an intelligent one. So why did she countenance her brother's involvement with this young woman? She obviously understood that it would cause trouble for both of them that her brother was daring to look far outside his class and status, and that the girl's family would never stand for it.'

'*He* did not understand that, though. And people do marry outside of their station. Look at Cynthia. There are always those around to remind her that she was merely a secretary before her marriage.' He said this with a wry smile. Cynthia's usual rejoinder was yes, but her shorthand speeds were excellent. She also always corrected the usual assumption that she had been her husband's secretary, when in fact she had been his father's. She also probably knew more about the business than her husband did, and for that acumen the family had reason to bless her.

'In my limited experience, it is more often women who marry up,' Mickey observed.

'That's probably the case,' Henry agreed. 'Whatever the situation, women are less likely to have control of their own finances or their own means. It is unusual even to find a widow who is totally in charge of her affairs. Men do seem to have the idea that women will fall apart if they are not present to supervise, and unfortunately the law seems to support that.'

Mickey laughed. 'Clearly, they have never met the likes of your sister or my wife,' he said. 'Though Miss Brewer seems to be responsible for her own affairs, through necessity no doubt, and she never married so she never became the property of anyone.'

'I wonder how much influence her brother had. It can't have been easy living with the likes of Brady Brewer. I would guess it to have been a matter of convenience – two wages coming into a single household would certainly ease things.' He frowned. 'We did not ask her what Brewer's occupation had been. That was remiss.'

'And easily remedied – we can call back at the cottage before we leave.'

Even so, this nettled Henry. It was not the kind of thing he would usually have forgotten, or that Mickey would have forgotten for that matter. It seemed to Henry that the pair of them really were out of sorts, and he wondered if Mickey was as unsettled by the fact that the partnership would soon be broken as he was. He withdrew his notebook from his jacket pocket and noted down questions they had not asked Miss Brewer. He realized he had not confirmed where her brother worked, how he had met Sarah, how often Sarah had come to their home. Doubtless, it was all in Walker's files, but Henry was disinclined to trust those.

Mickey leaned across and read what he had jotted down. 'We should ask also if Brady Brewer had other relationships,' he said. 'I know we are not officially here to investigate the death of Sarah Downham, just Penny Soper, but we should still have the background.'

Henry wrote that down and then sat back in his chair and regarded Mickey thoughtfully.

'We are being unwontedly careless,' he said. 'I think we are influenced by the fact that we neither care nor grieve that Brady Brewer is dead and might have been hanged for something he did not do, but as you have previously reminded me, we are here to uphold the law and not allow personal prejudices to get in the way. If any of our colleagues had missed these pertinent details, we would quite rightly have reproached them. I despise the man, Mickey, dead though he might be. But that is no excuse. There is an excellent chance that whatever Brewer did or did not do, there were links between him and the two dead girls and whoever did commit the murders. My gut feeling is that the tangle of this will all wrap around Brewer, just as it wrapped around them, and so we must do a good job. Not just accuse Walker of doing a bad one.'

Mickey raised his glass to that sentiment. A few minutes later, they left the constable in the bar still chatting to his friend and went across the road again to ask the other questions of Miss Elizabeth Brewer. She was a little surprised but answered readily enough, and by the time they had recovered the driver and returned to the vehicle, Henry could feel the links beginning to build. Brewer had worked a number of different jobs according to season and the casual needs of his employers. One of these jobs was down at the Selford wharf, where the canal boats loaded and unloaded and the goods were taken by road to Northampton and Peterborough and Market Harborough, sometimes to the railways, sometimes to the small towns and businesses in between these bigger towns. So Brady had definitely known Penny Soper, and not just due to the fact that they lived in the same village. At times, he went to the warehouses in Market Harborough where Sarah Downham's father held his goods and helped with the unloading there. At times, Elizabeth Brewer had provided extra assistance at the Downham residence.

Sarah Downham had also known Penny Soper from childhood, her mother having worked for the Downham family from time to time and being related to the family cook.

Frankly, Henry could have kicked himself. He had let emotions get in the way, and that was something he despised. Perhaps not as much as Brady Brewer himself but certainly with a passion. As he had said to Mickey, he would have soundly berated any man who had not asked these questions, not sought to understand the detail of how victim and murderer – or victim and accused in this case – lived their lives.

Must do better, Henry Johnstone, he told himself. *Must do a great deal better.*

FIVE

They were a little late getting to Dr Clark's, but he seemed unconcerned by their tardiness, waving the apologies aside and saying that he knew investigations were not easy to schedule.

He led them through to a pleasant room at the rear of the house and apologized for the noise of carpenters coming from the front room. 'For too many years, that was my surgery, and my waiting room was a little parlour next door,' he explained. 'I still see the occasional patient and I'm still, as you know, on call as a police surgeon, and I help out with the post-mortems when they interest me. I expect that will cease, soon enough, when they get a permanent replacement. In the meantime, I am reclaiming my home. My wife has plans for guests and dinner parties and Lord knows what else, but she has agreed that I can have the small parlour as my study. I think she suspects I'll be sitting there with my feet up drinking whisky all day and reading scandalous novels.' He grinned at them. 'I suppose there are people who consider Thackeray to be scandalous.'

'My wife likes Thackeray,' Mickey said unexpectedly, noting Henry's surprise at that. It amused him when there were still things about Belle that Henry did not know. In fact, Belle was a voracious reader.

'Then your wife must have very good judgement.' Dr Clark smiled.

A neatly dressed housemaid brought a tall pot of coffee and another of hot milk and poured the two expertly so that the streams of liquid blended. Too late to tell her that he preferred it black, Mickey thought, watching as she retreated as silently as she'd arrived. It smelt good, though.

'I have copies of both post-mortem reports for you,' Dr Clark said and handed them over to Henry. 'The findings are very similar in both cases.'

'I understand from the reports that both young women were raped,' Henry said quietly.

Mickey watched the doctor for his reaction.

Clark frowned. 'Unfortunately, yes. We managed to keep the scandal out of the newspapers in the case of Sarah Downham. The family had suffered enough.'

'You consider the fact that the young woman was raped to be worse than the fact that she had been murdered?'

Mickey saw that the doctor shifted in his seat, looking distinctly uncomfortable, but he answered easily enough. 'No, not worse, but it would have added to their misery. Bad enough to have lost a loved one to an act of violence, but for the common public to know how much she suffered beforehand, I'm sure you'll agree, somehow makes the whole thing worse.'

Henry frowned. Mickey could see he was fighting back words, and it appeared the battle was being lost. 'So if the young woman had merely been raped, but had survived,' Henry asked, 'would you have considered that more unfortunate?'

The doctor had just raised his cup to his lips, but now he set it aside. 'Indeed, that was not what I meant,' he said sharply.

'We visited Miss Elizabeth Brewer,' Mickey put in quickly, hoping to distract the doctor.

Clark shifted his glare to Mickey. Mickey got the impression that he was annoyed at the interruption from someone he viewed as an underling. But then the doctor's face cleared, his expression smoothed, and he reached for his coffee cup.

'She seemed to believe that Brewer had a genuine affection for the young woman,' he said.

Clark considered this. 'You should know that I am a friend of the Downham family,' he said. 'Sarah was a lovely young woman, but she was not terribly bright. She could be easily led.'

'Even by the likes of Brady Brewer?' Mickey asked. 'Forgive me, Doctor Clark, but we knew the man previously, and I find it hard to believe that any young woman from a good family could be attracted to such a man. It could be, of course, that he had changed since we knew him – his sister certainly seemed to think so.' He left the thought hanging, and Clark seemed to be considering it.

'The man could seem charming, I suppose. He had a way of saying what people wanted to hear. He was, at heart, dishonest – you only had to know him for a short while to realize that. Unfortunately, poor little Sarah didn't have the wisdom or experience.'

'Did you know him? You said that you knew the Downham family, but were you also acquainted with Mr Brewer?'

'Socially, no. But I did know Miss Brewer slightly. Inevitably, I ran across the brother occasionally.'

'So how did you know Miss Brewer?'

Dr Clark looked puzzled for a moment as though he knew the woman was difficult to define. Eventually, he said, 'Miss Brewer was, like many mature women in village communities, a source of help who could be called upon in times of need. She had some nursing experience in the war, and several of the local doctors made use of her when nurses were in short supply. On occasion, I called her in to help look after mothers who had endured difficult births, and from time to time she assisted in the births themselves, helping local midwives. As I say, she had had some training, but like a lot of women after the war, she gave up her full-time work to run her home and to provide for her brother. I believe she did a year or two at the local hospital before that; Brewer did not return to the area until about 1920, I understand. And before you ask, no, I have no idea where he was in the intervening time. I have never spoken to Miss Brewer directly about this – from what I could gather, she felt that she must provide him with a home, and I think she hoped to "straighten him out", as she put it. I think she thought she had succeeded until this bad business. He certainly seemed able to hold down a job and mostly kept himself out of trouble.'

Dr Clark fell silent and helped himself to more coffee, pouring from the two vessels as expertly as the maid had done. He did not offer any to Henry or Mickey – a sign, Henry thought, that he wanted to be rid of them as quickly as possible. He wasn't sure what to make of the doctor; Henry was certain there were things he wasn't saying.

'And the young woman recently murdered – Penelope Soper. Did you know her?'

'I knew of her; that is to say, I knew who she was because

I'd seen her working in the Red Lion and the Wharf. She was a pleasant, polite young woman; that is all I knew.' He looked expectantly from Mickey to Henry as though to say, *I hope that is all*, and Henry duly rose and picked up the folders.

'We may have to speak to you again, you understand.'

'Of course,' Dr Clark assured them. He tugged on an embroidered bell pull, and when the maidservant appeared, he said, 'Dora will see you out.'

In the hallway, while they were waiting for Dora to bring their coats, Henry was aware that Dr Clark was speaking to someone. He assumed that he must be speaking on the telephone and wondered whom he had to call in such a hurry that he could not even see his guests leave the premises first.

'He may be affable enough, but I do not like the man,' Mickey remarked as they walked away from the house to the hotel where they would be staying.

Henry nodded. He wasn't sure he liked Dr Clark either, but then he did have something of a prejudice against doctors. However, Mickey's judgement was usually very sound on these matters, so he was not inclined to disagree.

SIX

Rooms had been booked for them at the Three Cranes Hotel, a Georgian building that was a step up from the places they usually stayed when out on an investigation. Mickey commented on this is as they crossed the carpeted lobby to the front desk; this was not the class of establishment that the Metropolitan Police would usually stump up for, let alone the local constabulary. The puzzle was cleared up, to some degree – though another one was posed – when the desk clerk handed Henry a letter and said, 'Sir Joseph Bright hopes you will be comfortable here, gentlemen, and hopes, sir' – this to Henry – 'that you will also join him for dinner tomorrow night. He will be sending a driver for you at seven.'

'Sir Joseph Bright?' Mickey asked as they were climbing the stairs to their rooms.

He wasn't sure from Henry's face if the man was pleased or mildly irritated. Mickey was certainly happy to be staying somewhere nice; more often than not, they ended up lodged in the spare room of a pub, or the cramped attic of a boarding house or, on more than one occasion, bedded down in police cells if that was all that could be found at short notice.

'I phoned Cynthia before we came up here and told her where we were going. She mentioned Sir Joseph – he's a pleasant enough sort, and she did suggest he might put us up, but I didn't think that would be quite . . . well, you know, appropriate. Neither, it seems, did our superiors. although they were happy enough for him to arrange and pay for our accommodation.'

Mickey raised an eyebrow. That was unusual, but he wasn't about to argue about it. Local dignitaries could, on occasion, be prevailed upon to provide accommodation for visiting investigators. 'Local landowner?'

'Yes. An acquaintance of Albert's. The families have known each other for years, but Cynthia likes him well enough and I have met him twice. You might approve of him, Mickey – he has a collection of microscopes.'

'Does he indeed?' Mickey brightened considerably. His own beloved microscope had been bought second-hand and was a little battered but still worked perfectly well. He enjoyed making slides and once or twice had made use of the microscope during cases they had both been on, examining fibres and seeds that had been found at crime scenes. It was a passion he shared with Melissa, Henry's niece. 'And is he likely to be helpful to us? Is he likely to know those involved in this case?'

'As it happens, I think he might be. The man who found the second body is in his employ, but that is not so much of a coincidence: Joseph owns a lot of the farmland around here and leases it to tenant farmers. He is also a local magistrate. He may well be useful. It seems at any rate we also have him to thank for comfortable rooms,' Henry added as he opened the door to his room.

Mickey nodded approval. 'Looks like a good bed,' he said. 'I hope the food matches up. So is the letter from this Joseph or from Cynthia? I thought I recognized the handwriting.'

Henry opened the letter and skimmed the contents and then handed it to Mickey.

'"I am being presumptuous,"' Mickey read, '"I telephoned Joseph and asked him to recommend a decent hotel, and to ensure that you are looked after! Give my best regards to him and Julia, and I hope to see you soon."'

'I do love your sister,' Mickey said with deep feeling and went off to find his own room, which proved equally comfortable and with what he guessed would be a good view of the market square beyond, had the evening dark not begun to close in.

He was a little concerned about his boss – his friend. Henry seemed out of sorts, and Mickey could guess why. His imminent promotion would separate them after almost a decade of working together, not always in partnership but moving up in tandem through the ranks until Henry stepped ahead of him and Mickey was appointed his bag man. He knew that Henry fully supported his promotion and acknowledged that it was long overdue, but it would change things irrevocably.

He put the thought aside as he got washed and changed his shirt, looking forward to what he hoped would be a decent meal. When they had come up here, Mickey had assumed that this would be a simple case, a murder with a small number of suspects, the murderer likely known to the young woman. Of course, it was much more complicated than that now, as it was also a case of reinvestigating and perhaps clearing a dead man's name. Mickey felt guilty about Brewer, although he suspected that Henry genuinely did not. While it was true that there were good reasons for disliking the man, or even hating him, Mickey was aware that he more easily found within himself the sense that justice trumped all of this. Henry, for all his good points, could be a right bugger when he set himself against someone, Mickey thought.

They had just finished dinner when a man came and stood in the entrance to the dining room, looking around as though trying to spot someone. Mickey noticed him first and recognized Inspector James Walker. He nudged Henry and indicated that he should look over to the door.

'What the hell does he want?' Henry growled.

'Whatever it is, it's business,' Mickey reproved gently. He stood up and beckoned Walker over. The waiter arrived at the same time as Walker, and Henry, evidently having got over his fit of pique, suggested that they have coffee and take it into the guest lounge where they could speak more privately.

Mickey noticed that Walker looked discomfited, but the inspector nodded and they made their way into the other room. The guest lounge bar at one end was comfortably furnished with easy chairs and small sofas, and they found themselves a private corner. Coffee was delivered and the waiter departed.

Walker was the first to speak. 'We got off to a bad start,' he said somewhat awkwardly. 'I wanted to come and straighten things out. Fact is, I'm not a bad copper and I genuinely believed that bastard . . .' He paused and looked around to see if anyone else in the room had heard him swear but no one seemed to be taking any notice. 'That Brewer was guilty. There had been complaints about him from young women who reckoned he went too far with them, or would have done. He was accused of a street attack, but I couldn't prove it. And there were rumours . . . a lot of rumours about him from the war. There were men who'd served with him, now come back, and when they talked about him, he was a man who was out for what he could get, no matter what the circumstances, and who did things that, well, even in times of war . . .'

'We served with him, briefly, towards the end of the war,' Mickey said. 'I can assure you that the rumours were true. Putting that aside, the issue here is that two young women are dead, and the man accused of killing one of them *may* have been innocent. Our task now is to find the guilty man, or men, and bring them to justice. The rest is unimportant.'

Walker looked gratefully at Mickey and then turned his attention to Henry who, after some hesitation, nodded.

'Mickey is right. We need access to your investigation, to all the notes you made, all the thoughts you might have had that you did not set down because they were too ephemeral or you considered them unimportant at the time. We need to interview everyone who knew these young women, even if you have spoken to them before. You're a local man; a stranger might ask questions that a local man might not and vice versa. I would rather work with you than against you, Walker, because to work in opposition will get us nowhere. All that matters is two dead girls.'

Walker nodded agreement. He drained his coffee. 'Tomorrow morning, then,' he said, 'I will ensure you have access to everything.'

Mickey, eyes narrowed slightly, watched as the inspector strode back across the room. 'What brought about his change of heart?' he wondered.

'Perhaps no more than that he is essentially a good man and a good police officer. You and I both know that local officers feel slighted when the Yard is fetched in. You think there is more to it?'

'I don't know,' Mickey told him. 'I have the sense that something has upset the man, over and above us being here – I mean, over and above the fact that he perhaps saw the wrong man hanged.'

'Then tomorrow we will sift through the evidence and see what he missed,' Henry said.

SEVEN

In the end, the meeting with Walker the following morning was delayed. A message came from Mr Thomas Downham asking if they would be so good as to come and speak to him before eleven a.m. as he had a business meeting after that and would be leaving by the twelve o'clock train. He expected to be absent for the next few days. At nine thirty, they were knocking on his door, having sent a message to Walker that they would be with him later in the morning. Downham joined them after a few minutes in what was obviously a study, a booklined room with a large desk taking up, in Henry's view, far too much space.

Downing himself was a smartly dressed man with greying hair and, to Henry's eyes, rather greying skin. The house was in mourning, blinds and curtains closed and even the hall mirror covered, and Henry was a little surprised that these outward expressions of mourning should have continued for so long. After all, the daughter of the house had been dead for more than two months. Downham must have seen Henry glancing at the curtains because he said, 'My sister does not feel ready to face the world yet, even figuratively speaking. To be frank, I do open the curtains to this room when I'm in here alone and she cannot see, but I would not want to hurt her feelings. She loved Sarah as though she was her own daughter – indeed, she raised her as though she was her own child. Emily is in great pain. I've no doubt you'll need to speak to her, but please be gentle.'

Henry assured Downham that he would, by which he meant that he would hand the questioning over to Mickey. 'You understand that we will be reinvestigating your daughter's death,' he said. 'The verdict that sent Brewer to the gallows has now been called into question.'

'Inspector Walker came and explained this to me. I admit I was very angry. I told him that if he had got things wrong, then he should help put things right, that he had a moral duty to do so. If he sent the wrong man to the gallows, then that means the right man has not yet been found, and the likelihood is he has also killed this other poor young woman, the Soper girl, and, if I'm not much mistaken, is likely to kill again.'

'It is possible,' Henry agreed.

'So I asked to see you this morning in the hope that you would not put my family through such a terrible ordeal as Inspector Walker was forced to do last time. Surely all questions have been asked and answered, and the only element that needs reinvestigation is that some other man killed my poor daughter and that Walker made mistakes. I see no reason why our family should be dragged through the mud yet again. I realize that you will wish to ask your own questions, so I'm asking you to do so quickly and kindly and then to leave us alone.'

'We promise to do what we can,' Henry told him, 'but investigations create their own terms and I cannot promise that you and your household will not be disturbed again.'

Downham grimaced. 'I understand you must do your job, Inspector. But please understand my position. These last months have been terrible for us, as you can see.' He paused and indicated the heavily shrouded windows. 'My sister is still in deep mourning and the household is still desperately upset, so I'm appealing to you: please leave us alone to grieve.'

'I'm sorry, I can make no promises,' Henry told him. 'As I have already said, investigations go where they go, and I cannot promise that more questions will not become necessary, that digging deeper into your daughter's life won't throw up friendships or behaviour that you might not approve of. All I am concerned with is finding the man or men who killed these two young women – nothing more, nothing less – and sadly I cannot let the very natural feelings and sensitivities of others get in the way of that.'

Downham's face had darkened. 'And so you'll continue to persecute her grieving family. We had believed that all of this was behind us, that the man who had killed my daughter had been hanged, that this episode in our life could be slowly put behind us.'

'That belief may well have been wrong,' Henry said flatly. 'I am sorry, Mr Downham, but I have a job to do and I will do it. My job inevitably causes grief to the families of the victims – there is little I can do about that, and I am sorry for it – but surely it is better to find out all that happened and who was indeed responsible than to remain in ignorance?'

Downham stood, now clearly irritated. 'I had hoped to appeal to your better nature,' he said, 'but I see that hope was in vain. You cannot imagine the damage that has already been done to this family, the pain that has been caused, the reputations sullied. And now you propose to drag all of this up again. Surely, you came here to look into the murder of Penelope Soper, not that of my daughter.'

'The circumstances of both deaths are so similar that it is very possible both were committed by the same man,' Henry told him. 'I would be very remiss if I did not connect the cases and examine this first investigation again. Inspector Walker knows that and will be working with my sergeant and me. We have a meeting with him later this morning to examine the case notes.'

If Downham had looked irritated before, he was now apoplectic, his face purple with rage, and Henry was wondering what exactly he had said to bring such an escalation of feeling. It was impressive, this transition from almost grey to deeply beetroot.

'I spoke to Walker last evening and demanded his assurance that we would be left out of this affair; then I heard that he had come to speak with you, and I had hoped that perhaps he had prevailed upon you to leave things as they stood. I had heard that you were a reasonable man, a well-connected man, a gentleman. But it seems I was ill-informed.'

'According to your definition, probably so,' Henry told him. 'And Inspector Walker had no right to make promises.'

'Then I must ask you to leave.'

'And I must ask first that we speak to your sister and the servants. Mr Downham, if you don't permit it now, we will only come back, and you cannot deny us entry – or if you do, then we must ask outside of the family for the information we need, and I'm sure you'd find that far more distasteful.'

Henry could feel Mickey's eyes upon him, but he did not look at his sergeant, unsure of whether Mickey was approving or not and at this moment not particularly caring. Downham was annoying him, was being obstructive, and Henry was asking himself why would anyone possibly want to obstruct a murder investigation when the victim was their own child? Was he afraid of something they might find that would impugn her reputation or that of her family?

'Very well,' Downham said, 'you may speak to my sister, and you may even speak to the servants for all the good it will do, but then you will leave, and I hold you responsible for further distress caused.'

Twenty minutes later, they were speaking to Mrs Emily Forsyth, Downham's widowed sister. She was dressed from head to toe in black, silk trimmed with black jet, thick lisle stockings but rather elegant shoes. Her dress was clearly expensive and in the modern style with a low waist and pleated skirt, and her hair was neatly bobbed. She was, he guessed, in her thirties but she dressed almost as though she felt the need to look older. Perhaps, he thought, she felt this gave her a sense of authority, but oddly she reminded Mickey of the late Queen Victoria when she was dressed in full mourning. That could, he thought, have been because of her stoutness, or perhaps it was the look of disapproval. The heavy black of dress and jewelry was broken only by an odd little silver whistle which she wore on a long chain. Did she have a dog? Mickey wondered.

Like Henry, he had been surprised to find old-fashioned expressions of mourning in this house; the closed drapery and veiled mirrors were something from his mother's time, although even then such expressions would have been finished with after the first week or so, when practicalities took over and people had to pick up their lives and work in order to survive. He supposed that did not apply here. The business of grief could continue alongside the business of making money.

Not so long ago, in his own streets, the death of a very elderly man had brought out a reversion among the neighbours to this older expression of mourning, and on the day of the funeral, when the hearse collected the body, all the curtains in the street had been closed in sympathy with the family. The neighbours had still come out on to their doorsteps to see him off because that was also proper; where Mickey lived, no matter if you were Protestant or Catholic or Irish or Jewish, you paid your respects to the neighbourhood dead.

'So tell me about your niece,' he asked gently.

'She was such a good child. A little wilful perhaps – I suppose we had indulged her – but a good girl.'

'And her' – he paused as though considering – 'relationship with Brewer, this was her first—'

'Relationship! That man had nothing to do with relationships. He did not have relationships – he used young women and discarded them. He had absolutely no morals whatsoever. His sister did her best, and I still believe her to be a good woman despite the fact that she failed to reform him. After all, what can a woman do when a man is so stubborn and set in his ways and those ways are so disreputable?'

'And she had no other beau?'

Emily Forsyth looked as though she was about to explode again, but she did not. Instead, she shook her head and said, 'There was a young man that we had chosen for her and hoped she would marry. They knew each other well; they had grown up together and had been firm friends ever since babyhood. Philip is three years older than poor Sarah and is away at medical school. When he qualified, of course, Sarah's father would have helped him set up in general practice and would have sent patients his way. My brother is a man of great influence in the community.'

'I'm sure he is,' Mickey agreed. 'We will need this young man's name and present address.'

'And why on earth would you need that? Philip had nothing to do with this.'

'Because it is possible that Sarah had contacted him. It would be natural if they were close friends. He might have some light to shed on what happened.'

'If Philip knew anything, he would have told us. It's a ridiculous suggestion.'

'Nevertheless, we will need those details,' Mickey insisted.

'According to Miss Brewer, you allowed the relationship with her brother to continue because you believed that it was a girlish crush that would run its course and be forgotten.'

Emily Forsyth looked a little put-out, but she nodded reluctantly. 'Young girls can be foolish. And . . .' She hesitated as though unsure how to proceed. Mickey cocked his head to one side and regarded her patiently. Finally, she sighed and said, 'I suppose I had better tell you. If you interview the servants, someone is bound to let it slip. Sarah had a small history of such silliness. When she was perhaps twelve or thirteen years old, she had a ridiculous pash on the young boy who delivered groceries; he was not much older than her and, with her encouragement, he did become overfamiliar. We had to tell the greengrocer that the boy must be dismissed or he would lose our custom. Of course, we ensured that he had another job elsewhere; we would not have seen the young man in dire straits because of Sarah's foolishness. Cook assured me he had done nothing to encourage it, and when I told Sarah what had happened and that the young man had now lost his job, she was mortified. I made it plain to her that nothing is without consequences, and we had no further trouble – not until Brewer came on the scene and turned her head. Frankly, I would have expected her to have had more sense and more self-respect. We had decided to send her away – out of harm's way, you understand. In fact, we had decided she would be better safely married off, and Philip had agreed to bring their wedding forward. Of course, we would have supported them both, so he could continue with his studies, but at least Sarah would have been with the young man that we had chosen. She cared about him and would have grown to love him properly; I have no doubt of that.'

'But she didn't want that.'

'Young girls don't always know what is good for them or what they actually want. And I should know, Sergeant Hitchens; I was a foolish young woman once. I fell in love with my husband when I was just seventeen. My parents made me wait, of course, and we finally married two years later. I was headstrong; the whole thing was a dreadful mistake. My parents told me that he was not the man I thought he was and so it proved. Within six months, I was back home with them again, disgraced and mortified. I was fortunate that they didn't simply tell me that I had made my bed and would have to lie in it, but they were kind enough to forgive. I did not want that for Sarah.'

So she was only in her mid-thirties, Mickey thought. Why make herself look older and staid? 'And then you were widowed.' Mickey's tone was gentle, but the question was pointed.

'My father gave him money if he would join the army. This was the start of the war, and so join the army he did. We did not know the war would be so bloody or take so many lives. I would not have had it end that way. I bore him no real malice; I just realized that what I thought was love was . . . Well, that is my business and not yours, and it has no bearing on the current conversation, except to prove that I do know how young girls' hearts betray them.'

She sighed, and Mickey thought there was no doubt the hurt in her eyes was genuine. She felt she had done her best, but, despite that, things had gone badly wrong and she had let her niece down. 'Did you have any doubt about Brady Brewer being guilty?'

The look she gave him told him that the question was ridiculous. 'Not for a moment,' she said. 'The man was evil incarnate; I should have rectified this situation long since, and if I had done so, then Sarah would still be alive.'

'Miss Brewer is quite convinced that her brother loved your niece.' It was the first time Henry had spoken, and the gaze that Emily Forsyth turned on him was filled with fury.

'Then she was thoroughly mistaken and more stupid than I thought her to be.'

'And you don't doubt now that Brady Brewer killed your niece?' Henry asked.

'Of course not. Brewer paid the price for what he did, but that doesn't bring Sarah back. And now it seems to me that someone else must've killed this Penelope Soper girl, no doubt to muddy the waters.'

'That seems extreme,' Mickey observed.

'Why does it? Who knows what riffraff that man associated with?'

'If someone wanted to throw doubt on Brewer's conviction,

would it not have made more sense to have murdered another girl while he was still in prison, but before he was hanged?' Henry asked.

'How should I know how people like that think?' She dabbed at her eyes with a lace handkerchief, the sudden flash of white linen seeming stark against the full mourning. Mickey had no doubt that the tears would have become a flood, had she not been in company. 'Now, gentlemen, if that is all. You may interview the staff in the kitchen, but please don't take too much time; they have other duties, you know.'

She didn't wait for them to dismiss her; she sailed off like a very large galleon, trailing silk and sparkling faux jet, her back unnaturally straight and her heels clicking on the parquet floor.

'Well, that's us told,' Henry said.

Mickey smiled at him. 'She *is* grieving,' he said, 'for all the things she couldn't do or couldn't change. Reading between the lines, I suspect Sarah Downham was more of a handful than her aunt would like people to think.'

'That would not surprise me at all,' Henry agreed.

The maid who had brought in coffee now returned to take the tray and then led them down the back stairs to the kitchen. She was, Mickey thought, probably around twenty years old, and he wondered how long she had been in service. It had been quite typical for girls to start as a scullery maid at around fourteen or fifteen, but the Great War had changed the social landscape even in this respect, and young women now more often chose shops or offices or factories as their place of employment. The wages and conditions were often better, as were the freedoms afforded. He had often overheard women at Cynthia's home complaining that it was so hard to get good staff these days, and he had also often heard Henry's sister quietly suggesting to them that times had changed and young women expected a little more accommodation to their needs these days, and perhaps they should offer better wages and more than half a day off a month.

The kitchen occupied most of the basement area of the house, the rest being taken up by storerooms, broom cupboards and the like. Mickey caught a quick glimpse of the kitchen itself through the wide-open door, but the girl took them into a side room.

'Mrs Forsyth said you wanted to talk to the staff,' she said, 'so Mrs Evans, the housekeeper, suggested you use her room, where she does the accounts and the ordering and such. There's a list on the table of all the staff. Cook asked if she could be first, because she's got lunch to get up.'

Mickey glanced at Henry, who nodded, and Mickey assured the girl that they were quite happy to see the cook first. Whatever she was preparing for lunch smelt good. The scent of fresh bread and cooking meats drifted through to them, and it crossed Mickey's mind to wonder who on earth they were cooking for. The master of the house was now away, and Mrs Forsyth was the only inhabitant above stairs.

The girl might've been reading his mind because she said, 'Mrs Forsyth has guests coming tonight; they will be staying for a few days, and so when lunch is out of the way, Cook has to prepare.'

'We promise not to delay her longer than necessary,' Mickey told her.

She nodded, and then, curiosity obviously getting the better of her, she leaned towards Mickey and asked, 'Is it true what they're saying in town, that the man who hanged for killing Miss Sarah might not have done it? We thought we could breathe easy with him out of the way, but now there's another maniac on the loose.'

'Now, now, Edie,' said a voice coming from the doorway. 'Stop your gossiping and get back into that kitchen. I'm sure these gentlemen would like some tea, and I expect there is a bit of cake going, so you can bring that in, too. But go and see what Mrs Forsyth wants first. I heard her whistle a moment ago.'

The woman now filling the doorway introduced herself as Mrs Everett and was apparently the cook. Edie disappeared rapidly, and Mrs Everett took her seat on the opposite side of the table to the police officers. She set her clasped hands on the table and looked at Mickey and then at Henry expectantly, finally focusing her attention on Henry. She had obviously identified him as the senior officer.

'Whistle?' Mickey queried. He had heard a faint blast just before the woman had come in but thought little of it.

'The mistress swears we ignore the bell. So if we take too long she gives a blast or two just to wake us up.'

So that explained the pretty silver bauble hanging round her neck, Mickey thought.

'What do you want to know?' Mrs Everett said. 'And I'd be obliged if you make it quick; I haven't got all day and I doubt there's anything I can tell you that I didn't tell Inspector Walker before, unless you think you've got different questions to ask, of course.'

As Mrs Everett seemed to have directed her observations to Henry, Mickey sat back and allowed his boss to take the lead.

'Did Miss Sarah Downham meet Brady Brewer here?'

'No, she did not.' Mrs Everett was indignant. 'And if that's the level of question you have to ask, then I suggest you go and read the case notes first and not waste my time.'

Mickey's mouth twitched into a grin, and he watched with amusement as Henry's eyebrows raised and his pale eyes hardened. But then his boss nodded, and he too sat back in the chair, regarding Mrs Everett thoughtfully.

'You're right, of course; we have not yet had time to speak properly with Inspector Walker or to fully acquaint ourselves with the case notes, so perhaps I should ask you: is there anything you have thought of since that might be pertinent to this case?'

Mrs Everett seemed mollified. 'I doubt it,' she said. 'The sister, Miss Brewer, used to come in and help out from time to time when we needed extra staff. She was always a capable pair of hands, and I must admit I will be missing her. She won't be able to set foot in this house again, nor in most in the neighbourhood. She'll no doubt be struggling for work, thanks to that damned brother of hers.' She paused, a thought striking her. 'Though I doubt this house will be seeing parties ever again – there's too much grief. A house can be killed by grief.'

'I have a question to ask about previous friendships,' Henry said. 'Mrs Forsyth mentioned that Sarah had what she called a "pash" on a young boy about her own age – she would have been twelve or thirteen at the time.'

Mrs Everett laughed, clearly a little bemused but seemingly glad to be back on more cheerful ground. 'Young Harry Aitken,' she said. 'Nice boy, used to work for the greengrocer until he got too friendly with Miss Sarah and her aunt put a stop to it. There was nothing to it. Miss Sarah was lonely – she didn't have many friends of her own age, and her aunt didn't want her to go to school until she was older. It would have meant going away, and her aunt didn't want that for her. She wouldn't let her go to the local schools, said she didn't want her mixing with the wrong kind of people, so . . . I suppose Miss Sarah spent too much time below stairs. She would sneak down and spend time in the kitchen when she was a little thing. She loved to make cakes and help with the bread. She had a light hand, did Miss Sarah. But then, when she got older, Miss Forsyth didn't think that was appropriate either.' She shook her head and Mickey got the impression that she had felt sorry for the girl.

'So she did not approve of the local schools,' he put in. 'Why was that, do you think?'

'I think people get fixed ideas in their heads,' she said. 'Mrs Forsyth is a *lady*; she married well, and I think she feels she has standards to keep. In this house, when we serve the family, we serve them like gentry – we don't stack.'

Mickey was bemused by that but noticed that Henry seemed to understand, and so saved it up with the intention of asking later. Mrs Everett didn't seem to have much more to add and they let her get back to her cooking. As she was leaving, Henry asked, 'And so who is visiting tonight?'

'Mr Philip's family. Mr Philip Maddison's parents. The young man himself will be joining them at the weekend, I believe, and the master will be back by then, too. It's a dreadful business. Mr Philip and Miss Sarah were so close when they were little; it got even lonelier for her when he went away. They sent him off to school, as the gentry usually do. She would get so excited when he came home for the holidays. Even after his family moved away, he would come and stay with us often.' She wiped her hands on her apron as though wiping off the dirt of her contact with policemen and then added, 'It's a bad business all round, a very bad business.'

The rest of the staff filed in, one after the other, and questions were put to them, even though it seemed they had more of their own to ask than answers to give. The death of two young women had unsettled everyone, especially as it had been assumed the murderer of the first had paid the price and that had been an end to the matter. And now this other girl was dead. There was a sense that the killer might strike again, which Henry articulated to Mickey.

'And so he might,' Mickey said as they left, finally heading to their meeting with Inspector Walker.

'I would like to speak to this young man, the grocer's boy,' Henry said.

'You think young Sarah kept in touch with him, after all?'

'It seems she was lonely, and I also suspect that the young are very loyal to their friends, even if their parents disapprove. I was thinking what Melissa would have done in similar circumstances, not that Cynthia would have been as overbearing, but if Melissa made a friend and if that friend was from a different class or station in life, she would still want to keep in contact with them. And I think it must be harder for young girls to make friends; boys can go away to school and forge their own friendship groups. Melissa has young female friends who come and share her tutor, but as they get older, unlike the girls from working backgrounds, protective barriers are thrown up around girls from this class, and I think they must find that confining.'

Mickey nodded; he knew that Cynthia herself had had no such protection, but yes, he had noticed that even she was more concerned about keeping Melissa safe and was inclined to be a little overprotective. He had thought that this was more to do with the kidnapping than with any particular class protocol. He said this to Henry, who nodded and agreed that certainly did not help. The fact that she had nearly lost her daughter, that both Melissa and Henry could have been killed, was bound to make Cynthia more defensive.

'Oh, yes,' he said, suddenly remembering what Mrs Everett had said. 'What is meant by the gentry and not stacking?'

Henry laughed. 'Oh, you see, the gentle class must have their plates taken away two at a time, not stacked on top of one another. I suspect this is both to protect their fine china and also to demonstrate that they have sufficient servants to remove plates two at a time. I'm told it was quite usual for new servants to enquire if their employers were gentry or if they stacked.'

'Well, you learn something new every day,' Mickey said. 'I wonder if any potential cook or serving maid or footman turned the job down if their prospective employers stacked. Professional pride, you know. I don't know that I've ever owned enough plates that it would take more than Belle and me to clear a table, and that's without stacking. Maybe that makes us gentry!'

Before he left to catch his train, Mr Downham had made a telephone call to Sir Joseph Bright. The two were known to one another, both being members of the local hunt and on various committees around town, and with Sir Joseph also being a magistrate, Downham felt he was the right man to complain to.

'The man is rude and inconsiderate,' he said. 'I see no reason for these further enquiries. The man who killed my daughter was caught and hanged, and he has no business mud-raking.'

'He's here to look into the death of the Soper girl,' Sir Joseph soothed. 'It's only because there are similarities in the cases that he's re-examining poor Sarah's death. He must be seen to be dotting the i's and crossing the t's.'

'And that I could understand, but I spoke to Walker just last night and he assured me that my family would be left alone. Then, this morning, that man comes to my house and tells me that Sarah's murder is still being investigated and that he must talk to family and servants and even disturb her friends.'

'Inspector Walker was in no position to make any promises. He'll be lucky if he gets through this with his reputation intact.'

'I don't give a damn for his reputation. Brewer killed my daughter. He hanged for it, and it will take more than an upstart policeman from London to convince me otherwise. I made time for the blasted man this morning and what do I get for my trouble? Outrageous bad manners and a poor attitude. Just who does he think he's dealing with?' Downham glanced at his watch and tutted in exasperation. 'I must go,' he said. 'I have a train to catch. Speak to him, will you? There's a good fellow. Before he upsets everyone again.'

After he had hung up, Sir Joseph Bright sat at his desk and stared at the phone in a state of mild irritation. He had heard that Chief Inspector Johnstone was not just an efficient officer but rather brilliant at his job. He knew also, from previous encounters with Henry, that the man could be a little cold and perhaps even spiky in his manner. He had hoped that having Henry come up to handle the case meant he could in some way make use of their brief acquaintance; that it would be to his advantage to have someone he knew in charge of the investigation. Now, he began to second-guess himself and also feel inordinately irritated. Of course Johnstone would be intent on doing a good job, and of course he wouldn't care whose toes he stamped upon in order to achieve that. How could he have thought otherwise? A fine detective he might be, but, like his sister, very likeable women though she was, he had not been born into a class that understood the bigger picture.

Or was that right? Sir Joseph had to ask himself if Henry's attitude arose from understanding the bigger picture all too well.

Oh well, he thought, the chief inspector was going to be his dinner guest that evening. It was his duty to entertain and be courteous to a man who, given other circumstances, he would genuinely have wanted to welcome into his house. As it was, this evening would be about assessing what the inspector knew and how he might be steered away from facts it would do Sir Joseph and his friends no good at all to be revealed.

EIGHT

The sky was grey and heavy, and a fine drizzle had Henry and his sergeant damp and chilled before they reached the police station in East Harborough, the Downham household being on the edge of town and the police station facing on to the cobbled market square. Walker awaited them in his little office, crates of paperwork and evidence stacked around, and it was clear that he had already been working through this in preparation for their arrival.

'So you've spoken with the family?' he said. 'I hope it fits with your plans, but I have arranged for us to go and see Penelope's mother, Mrs Soper, this afternoon. She's staying with her sister, but it's only a few miles up the road. I also sent a message ahead that we would like the keys to her house. I thought you might like to see Miss Soper's room in case she's left anything behind. She shared a room with her younger sister and the baby, apparently. There are also two boys,' he added. 'Penny Soper's wages were helping to keep the family afloat. Lord alone knows what they'll be doing now.'

Henry decided that he liked Walker more for this concern; he decided that he was disposed to give the inspector another chance. 'I had hoped to view both crime scenes this afternoon,' he said.

'And so we can. The first on the way there and the second on the way back. I'll instruct the driver to loop around the back roads. That will also give you some idea of the lie of the land. It can be confusing; not all the roads are named or even sign-posted. The locals know their way around and there are few people that come here without cause. If they do, they stay in town or go out to view the battlefield, such as it is. Or they are coming to and from the wharf and more likely to be travelling the main road.'

'The main occupation round here is agriculture?' Henry enquired.

'By and large. Once upon a time, it was all sheep. From here to Lincolnshire, the keeping of sheep occupied whole villages, and some rather fine churches were built on the wool trade. When that died down, a switch was made to mixed farming. The land is good but not that easy to plough. Sheep didn't mind steep valleys, but horses and tractors can find it hard going. The best tenant farms are on the uplands or right down in the valleys, so you'll still find a fair few sheep on the slopes, though they're mostly bred for mutton.'

'You're from farming stock?' Henry guessed.

'For generations. My older brother tried to make a go of it when our father passed away, but it's hard to make it pay. We came back after the war, and although our mother had done her best, it was more than a single person could manage. She died a few years later and we sold up. It didn't seem right to do so when she was still alive, but' – he shrugged – 'Jim had a family to provide for, and it was plain the farm wasn't going to cut it. Sir Joseph offered us a decent price and we took it. He owns a good proportion of the land around here, and our little farm connected two of his fields.' He paused. 'The Brewers were tenants of his, before the parents died. The father worked in the stables and the mother ran a market garden.'

'Sir Joseph and my sister are acquainted,' Henry said. 'And so you became a police officer. Have you dealt with many murders during your career?'

Walker bristled at the inference, but he held his temper. 'Some,' he said. 'Most were domestic in nature.'

'Most are,' Mickey said.

Henry glanced at his sergeant and took the hint. 'True enough,' he said. 'And any with this level of seriousness or complication?'

'I consider all murder to be serious, no matter who the victim. And all are complicated. Murder or manslaughter may well be the result of a moment's anger, but there is always a history to it and that history is never simple.'

Henry studied the man, aware that he was being provocative and that the inspector was trying not to rise to it. He nodded, reappraising the man and liking him a little better. 'That too is the truth,' he said. 'So let's see what three heads, bent to the same task, can achieve.'

He and Mickey had taken their places opposite Walker and now began to sort methodically through the paperwork. 'So, Mr Soper, the father, left some time ago?' Mickey enquired.

'Went off with a barmaid, around three months before the last baby was born. You can imagine what a state this has left them in. The sister and her husband are taking care of the family for the time being, but obviously they can't keep that up; they'll be on parish care before long, such as it is.'

Henry nodded soberly. 'Such as it is,' he echoed. 'Well, we must focus on what we *can* change, and that is finding out who killed the girl. I understand that you spoke to Mr Downham last evening, before you came to see us at the Three Cranes.'

'I did indeed, and I must admit the man riled me, which is why I thought I would come to make peace. I was *not*, as he implied, careless in my investigation; I was as assiduous as the lack of manpower allowed me to be. I believed Brewer to be guilty and, if I'm honest, I still do. From what I saw of the man, a girl like young Sarah Downham, whatever faults of her own she might have had, could not help but be the victim. How could she . . . How could anything in life, *her* life, have prepared her for a man like that?'

'Whatever faults?' Henry said.

Walker shrugged. 'Like some young girls, she was a little wild – she perhaps formed friendships that her family would not have approved of. I investigated these friendships and they seemed innocent enough, but they were not young people of her class, and I suspect it is through them that she met Brewer. The sister says she did not introduce them.'

'And was one of those friends Harry Aitken?' Henry asked.

Walker looked surprised. 'Indeed it was. He's a good enough lad, hardworking and never in any trouble, apart from that one time, which you clearly know about, when Mrs Forsyth lost him his job.'

'And did he bear her any malice for that?'

'You can imagine he wasn't pleased, but Sarah's father must

have believed that the situation had been exaggerated and he pulled strings and ensured that the lad got an apprenticeship. He's now working for a local carpenter and by all accounts is good at his job. He is about to marry the man's daughter at any rate; I suppose a good apprentice is hard to keep, so best to bring him into the family.'

'And were there other friends,' Henry pursued, 'that her family knew nothing about?'

'Harry's sister, and a few others in the same social group. The family was familiar with some but not all. They did nothing more than go to the pictures together, and yes, they did drink occasionally in the local public houses, and Sarah accompanied the girls to the odd Saturday dance. As I say, I have an inkling this is how they met Brewer, though nobody seems to know for certain – or if they do, they're not saying. It could have been simple coincidence, being in the same place at the same time, and it's quite likely that Miss Downham had glimpsed the man when he was with his sister and so could claim a passing acquaintance.'

Henry nodded. All of that seemed likely. 'We will need to speak to them,' he said.

'Not that we doubt you have done a thorough job,' Mickey placated, his glance at his boss making Henry aware that his tone had been a little sharp. 'You won't have asked them if they knew Penelope Soper because, at that time, no one knew she was going to be killed. It is possible that there is a link via this group of young people.'

Walker nodded, accepting that, although he continued to look uneasy, and Henry could see that he still resented their presence, even if he had decided that he must now cooperate with them.

As per Henry's earlier request, evidence from the Sarah Downham murder had been brought out of storage and two crates with exhibits taken from the scene and otherwise relating to the case had been placed on the side table. Henry went over to them now and began to examine the contents. 'Are these the clothes Sarah Downham was wearing the day she died?' he asked.

'They are, apart from the glove – the man's glove. That was

identified as belonging to Brewer. It was one of the key pieces of evidence, found at the scene under her body.'

'Pretty damning,' Mickey observed.

'Indeed,' Walker agreed. 'When he was arrested, he still had the second in his possession and didn't seem to have realized he had lost one.'

Henry thought back to the notes he had just read. 'And you sent officers to find Brewer very shortly after the body had been found. You already suspected him?'

'The family had already complained about him – said that he was harassing her, hanging around. Of course, she said that she welcomed his company, and when I investigated the complaints, I discovered that they had been seeing one another on a regular basis. I went to speak to Miss Brewer, and she confirmed it. Of course, when we found the body, Brewer with his record came immediately to mind. The constables went to bring him in, and I showed him the glove; he looked surprised, and produced its mate from his pocket. He never denied that it was his. He said he didn't know he had lost it.'

'The weather was cold – surely he would have needed his gloves,' Henry observed.

'He claimed to have had them the day before when he came back from work. That day, he'd been at the wharf, helping to unload a barge, and then took to drinking at the bar with a group of cronies. There's no doubt he was there that evening, and several people attest to him donning his gloves before leaving.'

Henry examined the glove from the evidence box. It was knitted from grey wool but with a distinctive band of fancy work – something like Fair Isle, he thought – around the cuff and a second just below the fingers. 'This was knitted for him?'

'By the sister. She earns money from knitting socks, gloves, baby blankets and sometimes complete layettes. I've seen her work. She's very skilled. She also does some fine embroidery. I doubt there's a prominent family in the neighbourhood that doesn't own some of her table linen.'

Henry tried to imagine the robust Miss Brewer, with her almost mannish hands, creating such delicate work. He thought back to what the cook at the Downham house had said. It was doubtful her services would be required again, at least for the foreseeable future. Did a woman like that have money put aside for an extremity of this sort? But then, who could foresee this kind of extremity? Cynthia would have helped her, he thought. That was the kind of thing Cynthia did, but Cynthia was miles away and knew nothing about Elizabeth Brewer and her problems. Irritated by the realization that he had actually liked Miss Brewer, he pulled his thoughts back to what Walker was telling him.

'So Brewer had the gloves the night before. And the following day?'

'His sister testifies to her brother wearing them when he left for work that morning. Brewer owned an old pair of leather workman's gloves that he sometimes wore for heavy work. He had left those at the wharf, knowing he'd be returning the following day. The barge they had unloaded had contained a load of stone and lime mortar for building work at the pub. The canal isn't in such frequent use as it was, but for heavy loads, it still serves its turn, especially for short-haul destinations to nearby farms and villages. There are still some around here send their grain to market that way and bring heavy loads in. Brewer returned in the early morning, laboured for the mason for the day and departed just after seven, after another round at the bar.'

Mickey had been reading through the notes. 'By all accounts, he was in good spirits,' he said. And then to Henry, 'And several of his drinking companions attest that he was off to meet a woman.'

'And did he mention Sarah Downham by name?'

'He did not,' Walker said. 'But the circumstantial evidence is compelling.'

Henry nodded. On the face of it, certainly. 'And how far from the wharf to where the body was found?' he asked.

'A little under two miles. His home another mile further on. Sarah Downham's residence is some five miles away from the wharf, in the opposite direction. If you take the path that runs across the top of the battlefield, then the Downhams' house is a couple of miles from where she was found. Maybe a mile further round by road.'

'And what was the state of her footwear?' Henry asked. 'Did her shoes show evidence of walking across the battlefield? It would have been muddy and hard going, I would have thought.' He looked back into the box. 'Where are her shoes?'

'They were nowhere to be found,' Walker said.

Henry looked across at Mickey who was once more tracing the notes.

'It says here that her stockings were torn and her feet muddied and cut as though she'd run in stocking feet,' he said.

Henry frowned. 'And the Soper girl?'

'Still had her boots on.'

'Curious,' Henry said. 'And the Downham girl's footwear – you say that's not been found?'

'Not been reported as found,' Walker said.

'So it's possible someone found her shoes, not knowing the connection, and thought it was their lucky day,' Mickey observed. 'I imagine the footwear would have been of good quality.'

Henry nodded thoughtfully. 'So how far had she run?' he wondered. 'Are there any barns or outbuildings that the couple could have been using for their meetings? Is it possible that he pushed her too far and she ran from him?'

'We checked all possible locations but there was no sign of them being used, by Brewer or anyone else. Which in itself means little, and it poured with rain that night – the body was soaked when it was found – so any footprints left would have been washed away.'

'But the ground beneath the body was dry.'

'Previous days had been frosty and dry.'

'So it's unlikely a woman running in her stocking feet would have left any trace anyway.'

'True,' Walker conceded.

'And the second young woman, Penelope Soper, she worked at the Wharf?'

'As a maid of all work, yes. Sometimes she helped out behind the bar, though it took me a while to get the landlord to admit that. The girl was not yet twenty-one and so too young to be dealing with alcohol sales.'

Walker glanced at the clock on his office wall and then

compared it to his pocket watch and made some small adjustment to the latter. 'We should go,' he said, 'if you want to see the first scene before we get to the Sopers'. I promised the family we would be with them around three this afternoon. I'll fetch torches so you can see where the second body was found. It's likely to be dusk when we get there.' He paused. 'Unless you'd prefer to wait until morning.'

Henry shook his head. 'We've delayed too long already,' he said. 'Delayed in being called in and now delayed in visiting the scene. I'd like a first look today and then, if you'll arrange for a car, I'd like to return to both scenes tomorrow, preferably with someone familiar with the area so that we can walk it thoroughly.'

Walker shrugged. 'As you wish,' he said.

He still resents our presence, Henry thought, *despite what he's said. He is still painfully aware that he got things wrong and he's mortally afraid that we might put it right. And I'll bet my own that there's more than reputation at stake.*

NINE

By the time they had been driving for ten minutes, Mickey understood what Walker had meant when he spoke of the countryside being confusing. Give him busy streets with signs and traffic and directions, Mickey thought, and he could get from anywhere to anywhere, but one hedge looked pretty much like another, and the road seemed to have been surveyed by a drunkard. In places, it was, he felt, only wide enough to comfortably accommodate a horse or a bicycle. Twice they met cars coming the other way, and each time both vehicles crept warily on to the grass verge and skimmed by one another with only inches to spare. Through the gaps in the hedges or glimpses afforded by farm gates, Mickey observed a rather beautiful landscape full of trees, sheep, deep valleys and ploughed fields. He wondered where they were in relation to the battlefield. Then he wondered how on earth anyone would have found a battlefield if the hedges had been as high in Charles I's day. Presumably, things had changed since then.

They skirted the village of Naseby, turning away along an even narrower lane and then the police driver pulled off on to the verge and they all got out.

'She was found here,' Walker said, 'close to the farm gate. If you look across, you can see there is a well-trodden path at the field edge – we reckon that's the way she came.' Two men and a dog were walking towards them along the path that Walker had indicated, and from their dress Mickey took them for local farmers. As they came closer, he noticed that the tweeds they wore were of solidly woven cloth, ageing but still obviously of some quality, and that the dog was very large. The older man carried a stick and seemed to be waving it around and indicating things to the younger man rather than using it as support. He greeted Walker in a familiar manner, and it turned out that the Greens, as they were introduced, were the owners of the adjacent land. Mickey recalled Elizabeth Brewer having mentioned a Lucy Green in relation to Sarah Downham. That they had been friends.

They, spent a few minutes commiserating with one another about Sarah's murder, and about the second murder, and then with Walker for having got the wrong man, and then with Mickey and Henry for having had to take on the case. It had been one of their farmworkers that had found Sarah Downham's body and apparently the man was still very shaken, even after all these weeks.

'Too young to have seen the trenches,' the older Green asserted. 'Soon get over your squeamishness if you spent a few years in the army. I was in the Boer Wars, you know. Forced march to Ladysmith. My son just missed the last lot.' He sounded deeply regretful.

Mickey looked at the son and guessed he was in his mid-twenties. He hadn't had much to say for himself, and Mickey supposed that he could probably get away with being the strong, silent type with so voluble a father. Not that he looked either strong or particularly inclined to silence; the wry amusement in his eyes and twitching at the corner of his mouth spoke volumes. He was a slender, almost frail man with a delicate face and a mass of strawberry-blonde curls Mickey guessed many a woman would kill for.

Noting that the father seemed most intent on speaking to Walker and Henry, obviously the senior officers so more in keeping with his rank, whatever that might have been, Mickey drew aside and addressed the young man.

'Do you know exactly where the body was found, what the position of it was? No one thought to take photographs of the body at the scene.'

Linus Green cast an uneasy glance at his father, but Green senior seemed fully occupied. He then led Mickey to a point closer to the gate. 'Jeb Mortimer – he's only a young lad. He came upon her when he was on his way to work. You see that smoke rising over there, down in the dip – that's where the farm lies. Jeb lives on the other side of Naseby, so along the footpath is his quickest route. Just past the farm, the footpath splits; the locals use it all the time to get to East Harborough or the other way to Husbands Bosworth. Anyway,

Jeb found her, then ran down to the farm. We called the constable from the farm. Father was away, so I came back with him.'

He paused as though recollecting the scene. 'It had rained all night and her clothes were sticking to her because the fabric was so sodden, and do you know the first thing I noticed?'

Mickey shook his head.

'Well, it was the strangest thing. I noticed that she had nothing on her feet and that her stockings were worn through. It just seemed so' – he paused, searching for the word – 'pathetic . . . sad. It made it worse somehow.'

Mickey nodded encouragingly. 'And the position of the body?'

'Sarah . . . She was lying with her head over here' – he indicated a point close to the gatepost – 'her body at a diagonal, with her feet pointing towards the road.'

'And the state of the body? What were your impressions?'

Linus Green looked at Mickey as though at that moment he hated him.

'I'm assuming you knew her, seeing as you called her Sarah, and I am sorry to have to ask this, but all observations are useful. One person might miss something another sees, and someone who knew the young lady will notice different things to someone that didn't.'

Linus Green took a deep breath. 'I didn't know her well, but I did like her. She was sweet. She knew Lucy better – that's my sister. When we were all little things, we attended the same school for a while. I'm not sure where they met up again – at a dance, I think. Sometimes I'd go along with Lucy, more as an escort than anything, though – I'm not much of a dancer. Lucy says I've got two left feet.' He smiled and Mickey sensed that he had a real affection for his sibling.

'And that was the strange thing.' Linus glanced again at his father as though not wanting to draw attention, but Green senior was still in full spate and had barely noticed that his son had left his side. The dog, a large mastiff crossed with who knew what else, had lain down, clearly realizing that once his owner got started, he wouldn't shut up in any great hurry.

'What was strange?' Mickey asked.

'My father says that I'm imagining things – how would I

know about the way women dress? – but Lucy thinks I'm right. The dress she was wearing – it was a going-out dress, not the kind of thing to wear when trekking across the field, even if she had been visiting friends.'

'Can you describe the dress?' Mickey knew that it would be detailed in the records and ought to be in the evidence box, but it would be useful, he felt, to get this young man's impression.

'Yellow, with a drop waist and a pleated skirt, and some kind of fancy fabric overlaying the top of the pleats. I can't explain it . . . kind of like a sash. I'd seen her wearing it once before when we all went to a dance at the Temperance Hall in East Harborough. That was only a few weeks before she died, and I know she'd not long bought it. Lucy admired it. As I say, it was a going-out dress. But her stockings were all wrong.' He looked embarrassed now, and Mickey prompted him gently.

'All wrong?'

'They were thick – you know, everyday stockings. When girls go out and dress up, they like to wear their fancy stuff. I know Lucy saves her silks for best and wears cotton or wool the rest of the time, and I asked her if this seemed right. She reckoned that must have meant that Sarah was wearing her boots, that maybe she planned to change into shoes when she got to wherever she was going. Apparently wearing fine stockings with boots can cause them to run.'

He was definitely embarrassed; his cheeks flushed. Mickey thanked him and then gave the young man time to recover, wandering over to where the others were speaking. He looked pointedly at his watch.

Henry took the hint. 'We are meant to be somewhere at three,' he said. 'You must forgive us, but we have an appointment to keep.'

Green was cut off in mid-flow and he grumbled a bit, huffing and clearly put out, but Henry was heading for the car and the others fell into line behind him, Mickey nodding gratefully to the young man who now seemed to have recovered himself.

'Green seems distinctly miffed that someone should get murdered on his land,' Henry said when they were all seated in the car.

'Strictly speaking, she wasn't,' Walker said. 'His boundary

ends at the gate. The road beyond belongs to the council,' he added dryly.

'Green junior had some interesting things to say,' Mickey told them and recounted what the son had speculated.

'He's an odd sort of boy,' Walker commented, 'very close to his twin, Lucy. She's a nice girl and was one of those friends of Sarah Downham's that I told you about. And yes, that yellow dress was the dress she was wearing. You must have seen it in the evidence box this morning,' he added.

Henry was looking at him in an odd way, and Mickey wondered what was wrong. 'The only dress in that box is a blue wool twill, somewhat torn and water-stained,' he said. 'There was definitely no yellow dress.'

Walker looked shocked – genuinely so, Mickey thought. 'Who has access to the evidence?' he asked.

Walker frowned. 'Evidence is kept in the storeroom two doors down from my office. The door is locked, but the keys are accessible to anyone who knows where they are, I suppose. They're kept in a key cupboard behind the reception area, so it's not beyond the realms of possibility that anyone who works in or is familiar with the police station might gain access. Why change one dress for another?'

It was a good question, Mickey thought. 'What if there had been some damage to the dress that might've indicated another's involvement? And how long ago was the exchange made? That is another factor.'

'Why would that matter?' Walker asked.

'It would have been assumed, after the hanging, that the guilty man had been caught and the case was closed, and yet we come along and reopen it. If the exchange had been made while your investigation was proceeding and before Brewer was hanged, that would be one scenario. If someone feared what we might find after we decided to review the investigation, that is another scenario entirely. One that makes me wonder if something to do with that dress might link both of the dead girls.'

'Because when I investigated the case, there had been only one murder.' Walker nodded.

'I think we need to speak to Lucy Green. We know she admired the dress, and she might be able to tell us where

Sarah Downham purchased it. In the meantime, we'll examine the blue dress very minutely to see what that can also tell us,' Henry said.

'If somebody wanted to substitute one for the other, why not put another yellow dress in the evidence box?' Walker wondered.

'Presumably, they used what they had to hand,' Henry said. 'And perhaps they used what they could spare, and that might tell us a great deal about the source of the garment.'

The car pulled to a halt; they had reached the house of Penelope Soper's aunt. Another grieving family, Mickey thought. He had lost count over his career of the number of distraught parents, bereft spouses and orphaned children caught up in the aftermath of murder. He tried hard not to call their faces to mind, but sometimes they came to him in his dreams, even though he was not given to vivid dreams, unlike Henry.

Henry Johnstone studied the cottage thoughtfully. It was small, no more than two up two down, whitewashed and with a low fence in front, behind which little grew at this time of year, but which had been dug over and the ground prepared ready, he imagined, for the planting of vegetables. A few tall stalks of kale remained and a patch of winter cabbages and spring greens. The door opened and a woman stood on the threshold. She was blonde and he guessed about thirty years of age, in a fawn-coloured dress and a floral crossover pinny. Absently, he noted that she was wearing dark stockings and carpet slippers. She stood aside to welcome them into her home.

'This is my sister, Nora,' she said. 'I'm Ruby. Nora was Penny's mother. I'm sure you'd all like some tea. And I'll take a cup to your driver; he'll be chilled out there.'

Henry thanked her and, after a moment's hesitation, took the hint and went back to the door and beckoned the driver to come inside and get warm. Ruby nodded at him with a 'that's more like it' expression on her face as she went to make the tea. She reminded him immediately of Cynthia, and the thought made him smile – an expression he immediately wiped, realizing that it was totally inappropriate in the face of such grief. When he had met Sarah Downham's family that morning, he had been struck by how controlled they were, or the father had been, at any rate. Clearly getting over their grief and now more annoyed that what they had believed had already been resolved was being questioned, rather than because they were anguished. He wondered if they had ever been as devastated as Nora obviously was. There was no colour in her face, not in her cheeks, not in her lips, and even her eyes looked faded, dark-ringed and of the palest blue. Her sister's eyes were like forget-me-nots, but Nora Soper gave the impression that even that much colour had been drained from her.

She had a baby in her lap, perhaps eight or nine months old, Henry guessed, and two young children stood protectively on either side of the chair, the girl perhaps ten and a boy a little older. He had a hand on his mother's shoulder and was glaring at Henry, daring him to upset his mother further.

'We are sorry to bring you more grief,' he said quietly. 'The last thing you must want is to go over all of this again.'

'You can't take anything else from me,' she said. 'Like a second mother to her brothers and sister she was; I don't know what I'm going to do without her.' There had been, Henry thought, quite an age gap between Penny and her younger siblings, and he wondered if she had been a child from an earlier relationship. He found himself reaching the conclusion that Nora must have been very young when her elder daughter was born.

Ruby waved him to a chair, and Henry was suddenly aware of how crowded this room, both kitchen and living area, was with the family, three police officers and now also the police driver who was standing by the door and looking awkward. Ruby busied herself giving them all hot drinks; Henry noticed the driver seemed especially grateful and he chided himself for not taking better care of the man's welfare. Sitting in the car, waiting for things to happen, was a cold and boring task.

He was acutely aware that both Nora and his sergeant were now watching him to see how well he would handle this situation, and Henry felt a moment of irritation. Did they think he could not be sensitive? But looking into the face of this bereaved mother, he found himself wishing that he had handed over the interview to Mickey, who undoubtedly did have a gentler manner. He knew exactly how Mickey would begin this inter-view and he took the same tack almost automatically. 'Tell me about Penny,' he said.

Nora looked at him as though she didn't understand the question, and then she said, 'I don't know where to begin.'

'She looked after us when Mother was sick.' It was the younger sister who had replied to him. 'After our daddy left.'

Henry was conscious of Mickey coming over to the fire and crouching down so that he could look straight into the face of this little girl. 'Maybe you'd like to tell me all about that,' he said. 'We should go and sit over there, you and me and your brother, and you can tell me all about when your daddy left and about your big sister and how she helped. Can you do that for me?'

The child looked to her mother for permission; having received it, she and her brother went with Mickey. Ruby, the aunt, positioned herself, Henry noted, so that she could intervene should either police officer overstep the mark. Walker, looking ill at ease, now stood beside the driver at the door, drinking his tea.

Henry could hear Mickey's quiet voice and the children's slightly hesitant responses. He turned his attention back to the mother. 'So she was your right arm, your daughter?'

'She worked so hard, all hours they could give her at the Wharf, and any spare hours she had she charred for people in the village and sometimes at the big house when they needed extra staff.'

'The big house?'

'Sir Joseph Bright's place. They employ the local girls from time to time, when they have extra guests and need the staff. They offered to set her on full-time but that would mean she'd only get two Sundays off a month, and although the money would have been good and she would have had her own bed and board sorted out, she knew I couldn't manage everything without her at home.' She hesitated. 'I've not been well since this one was born.' Nora indicated the child in her lap. 'Doctor warned me I shouldn't have another, but what can you do when your husband . . .? And in the end, he left anyway; left me when I was expecting this one.'

'And you've not seen him since?'

She shook her head.

'Do you know where your husband is?'

Again, the shake of the head. She looked utterly defeated, although he guessed that she had been utterly defeated long before the death of her eldest child.

'So what friends did she have? When she had a little free time, how did she like to spend it?'

For the first time, Nora Soper smiled. 'She had good friends, but she couldn't go out with them as often as she would have liked. I made certain she could go to the Saturday dance – every two weeks they are, at the Temperance Hall in East Harborough. She looked forward to it so much. It was the one proper break she had, and I always made sure she kept a little bit of money back, so she could pay for the ticket. And every now and then, she bought a few yards of fabric and made herself something nice to wear. Old Alice Cotter from a few doors down, when she died, she left Penny her sewing machine. She was a seamstress, you see, Alice was, and she taught Penny when she was little, so she's been able to make things from being a tiny mite.'

'Did she ever sew for anyone else?'

'Oh yes, the girls would buy her the fabric and she would make things up for them. They would take pictures out of the magazines and bring her pictures of what they wanted, and she would make copies for them. They paid her what they could.'

'She sounds like a very talented young woman. Perhaps you could compile a list of these friends for me? I'll need to talk to them.'

Nora Soper nodded and then dissolved into tears. 'We'll have to sell it, the sewing machine; we'll all be on the parish, I know it.'

Ruby hurried over to her sister's side and put an arm around her shoulders. 'Now then,' she said briskly, 'that's enough talk like that. You'll be back on your feet in no time, and we'll find a place for you to live close by. And we'll all pitch in, you know that, and I'll have the sewing machine here – I'll keep it for you.' She scowled at Henry, as though daring him to challenge her on that. The implication, he knew, was that she would claim it to be hers so that the parish inspectors could not force the sale. He nodded approval and wished he could do more.

'Was that useful?' Walker asked when they returned to the car. He sounded gruff and ill at ease, and Henry felt that he could sympathize.

'The dressmaking – that could be important. It might have brought her into contact with people her mother did not know. I have a list of her friends, and it is likely that they overlap with those of Sarah Downham. It seems they both attended the same dances.'

'There are very few forms of entertainment in the area,' Walker observed. 'Most of the young people will attend at least some of the dances at the Temperance Hall and also those at the church hall on Henbury Street. Next to St Matthew's. I would be surprised if their paths had not crossed.'

Henry took the point. 'And did the children have anything much to say?' he asked Mickey.

'That their big sister was like a mother to them, that she was always very kind, that she made her younger sister a rag doll for Christmas . . . I could go on. More importantly, though, it seems that the father has been in touch. They were out with Penny one Saturday, shopping in the local market, when he approached them and tried to convince the young children to go away with him.'

'Did he indeed?'

'Penelope apparently sent him on his way. As you might have guessed, she is the half-sister to the younger ones; they didn't seem to know anything about her father, although the boy thinks he might have been killed in the war. Apparently Penny threatened to set the local constables on the father if he didn't clear off. The children were naturally upset.'

'Did you get the impression they would have liked to have gone with their father?'

Mickey grimaced. 'It seems he was promising them all sorts of luxuries if they decided to go with him. He had sweets with him, promised them that their new mummy would be able to play with them and wouldn't be sick or sad. But I think he misjudged them. Toby, the brother, told me that when their father was at home, he was often angry and sometimes hit their mother, even while she was pregnant with their little brother. He and his sister have witnessed this, so I don't think they really believed the father's blandishments. Had they been younger, he might have succeeded, but I think they are old enough to understand how the marriage worked.'

'And how long ago was this?' Walker asked.

'They aren't sure, but Ruby was listening to the conversation, and she remembers the children and Penny complaining about this and thinks it was about three weeks ago.'

'A reason to bring him in for questioning at any rate,' Walker said.

'Reason enough, but can we believe that this man would have raped and murdered his own child?'

'She was not his own child, though,' Walker reminded Henry.

'But he was still in loco parentis; he was married to the girl's mother.' Henry frowned. It was a possibility, of course; he had seen men do worse. 'But yes, we must bring him in. Do we know where he might be found?'

'Patrick Soper apparently has several haunts and plenty of drinking companions. Someone will know where he is,' Walker said, and Mickey nodded in agreement.

'But I'm interested in knowing why he came back for the children,' Mickey said. 'I don't for one minute believe that it had anything to do with their welfare.'

'Well, you can ask him when we find him,' Henry said.

'Would you still like to visit the second scene?' Walker asked. 'I told the driver to take a route back that way.'

'Yes, though viewing it by torchlight is not the most satisfactory method,' Henry said. They had been more than an hour at the sister's house, and dusk was now starting to creep across the fields and between the high hedges that bordered the road. The driver had the headlights on and the artificial light seemed to emphasize the twists and turns in the road, illuminating hedges on the opposite side, making the road seem even narrower.

A few minutes later, they pulled up at the roadside and Walker handed out the torches. It was interesting and probably significant, Henry thought, just how similar this was to the first location. The farm gate, and the footpath that Walker indicated, disappearing into the darkness beyond the hedge. The location of the body.

'Laid with her head next to the gate, feet towards the road. Her dress rucked up and her coat open; the man who found her admits to having tried to pull it back over the body. He knows that was wrong, but he felt sorry for the poor lass, lying there exposed for all the world to see.'

Henry nodded. 'We'll need to come back in daylight,' he conceded after trying and failing to work out where the path went and the size of the adjacent field. Darkness was falling rapidly now, and the high hedges and tall trees seemed to magnify the shadows and increase the gloom. 'And maps, OS maps for reference of the footpaths and the locale. I need to get the lie of the land. And, Mickey, tomorrow I want you to interview those who found the bodies and any other witnesses that were present on those days, while I come back and walk the scenes. You'll have noticed the similarities in the two locations?' This last to Walker.

'Of course, but frankly you could say the same for half a dozen sites hereabouts. It's a rural area. Winding roads, farm gates, footpaths.'

'While I'm sure that's true, it's still worth remarking upon. You'll agree that someone would need to know their way around in order to take full advantage of the landscape.'

'I would agree with that. You or your sergeant would be lost in no time. You wish me to come with you tomorrow?'

'No, a constable will do – the driver if he knows the area. I would like you to track down Mr Soper and also the addresses of her daughter's friends that Mrs Soper listed. She knew only two or three. Finding the others will take local knowledge.'

He glanced at his watch and decided they should return to the hotel if he was to be in time for his dinner appointment with Sir Joseph Bright. He hoped the man might have some decent maps in his possession and also another kind of local knowledge, that of a landowner about the land he owned and the more usual miscreants, poachers and itinerants that might make use of it.

TEN

I t was after six when they returned to the hotel with just enough time to wash and change before the car arrived to take Henry to Sir Joseph Bright's 'big house'.

Some of the original witness statements in the case had been sent over, so that Mickey could look them over after he had eaten dinner. Henry planned to check in with him later when he had spoken to Sir Joseph.

'Don't work too hard,' Henry instructed. 'And I will see you when I return, provided it is not too late.'

'I thought I might take a walk,' Mickey told him. 'I can borrow an umbrella from the front desk.'

'You'll need it; it's turning into a foul night.' Henry knew that Mickey liked to walk when he was thinking; he said it helped his mind to unravel the investigative conundrums. More often than not, back in London, he walked home from work in order to give himself some thinking time.

Henry went to his room, washed and changed his shirt and tidied himself up, aware that he would be underdressed for such an evening but also aware there wasn't much he could do about it. He was down in the reception area when the driver arrived to pick him up. Once in the car, he was glad he had brought his big overcoat with him; even with the heater on in the car, there was a feeling of damp that ate into the bones. The warm coat had been a present from his sister a few years before; much abused and often muddied from trekking across fields or kneeling at crime scenes, he was glad that he had remembered to brush it down and was now very grateful for its warmth across his knees. Henry was not good with the cold, not since the war. It had ruined his physical health for a time, and he was conscious that it had damaged his mental health for even longer.

Mickey had seen him in all his moments of weakness, and it crossed Henry's mind now that he would have to either allow another into that space or learn to hide it better than he currently did. There was no hiding anything from his sergeant.

The journey was about half an hour in length, and Henry wondered if the torrential rain was adding to the time, noticing that, despite powerful headlights, the driver had to lean forward to see the way ahead. It was indeed a filthy night, and he wondered if Mickey would go for a walk after all. Henry decided he probably would.

The car took a sharp right. Ahead of them, Henry could see the lights of their destination. The car stopped in front of the house and a man came running forward with an umbrella and escorted Henry inside. A staircase and four doors led off the square, tiled lobby, and Sir Joseph Bright stuck his head around one of the doors, a broad smile on his face.

'Chief Inspector. Henry. Come along inside. What a night, eh.'

The manservant took his coat and hat, and Henry crossed to where Sir Joseph now stood with his hand extended, ready to shake. 'I think I'm a little late,' he said.

'Not a bit of it. The roads around here leave a lot to be desired. We saw the rain and knew Bates would have to take it slowly. Better a little late than in a ditch, what!'

Henry had only met Sir Joseph a couple of times, on both occasions at Cynthia's house. He was a man in late middle age, affable and well-scrubbed, with a polished red face that spoke of outdoor pursuits and thinning grey hair. Cynthia's husband had known him all his life, Joseph being a friend of his father's, and it seemed Sir Joseph was one of that rare group of the landed gentry that did not disdain new money.

There were four others already at the table, and Henry felt embarrassed at his tardiness even though no one else seemed concerned. Sir Joseph's wife, Julia, who was also known to him, and one of their married daughters, Olivia, who was visiting for a few days. There was also one Mr Gibbs, who, as Sir Joseph put it, 'Manages this place for us. Right-hand man, what!'

Although the ladies had dressed for dinner, the men were in lounge suits, and Henry guessed that this had been proposed so that he would not feel too out of place. He was grateful for the consideration.

He found himself seated opposite the daughter and next to Mr Gibbs, and food was served immediately, wine poured, and the shutters at the window closed. It was obvious that Sir Joseph had been keeping an eye open for his arrival, and now the house could be properly shut up for the night. Henry found that he was not looking forward to the journey back.

Lady Bright – 'call me Julia' – watched as the maidservant closed the shutters and said, 'If the weather gets worse, then you will, of course, stay the night and we will get Bates to drive you back first thing in the morning. Rather that than risk the two of you in this storm.'

Henry was about to protest, even though he saw the sense in that, but Sir Joseph was nodding agreement. 'In fact, best decide that now,' he said. 'Millie' – this to the maid – 'send word to Bates that he can pack up for the night, put the car away and retire to his room. Our guest will be staying with us, and Bates should make himself available just after breakfast. And telephone the Three Cranes Hotel and inform them that Inspector Johnstone will be staying the night with us. There, that's decided,' he said, smiling across at Henry who felt that it would be better to give in to the inevitable and thanked him for the courtesy.

The meal proceeded with several courses, all of which were excellent and with the kind of small talk that even Henry could handle. Julia asked about his sister, and her daughter talked about her children who, it turned out, were at school with Cynthia's two boys.

'And a right barrel of monkeys they are when they get together,' Sir Joseph pronounced. 'Boys will be boys, but there's no harm in any of them.' He smiled affectionately at his daughter, and Henry was drawn to the feeling that this was a similar household to his sister's – warm and friendly and not standing on ceremony.

When the meal was over, the two women withdrew. As Henry watched them cross the lobby, arm in arm and chattering happily, it crossed his mind not for the first time how nice it would have been for Cynthia to have had a mother with whom she could chat and share confidences. Melissa would be more fortunate.

He and Sir Joseph and Mr Gibbs, whose first name was Ishmael, withdrew to Sir Joseph's library and brandy was poured, cigars offered.

'I asked Ishmael here tonight and I brought you into the library because I thought you might need some help. You've probably already found out just how awkward the lie of the land is hereabouts – it's all holes and corners, hills and hollows – and the state of the roads – well, let's just say they leave a lot to be desired. I've been making improvements on the estate, but one can't do everything or be everywhere.'

'I would be very grateful for any advice you could offer and even more grateful if you happen to have some decent maps,' Henry told him.

'Maps we have plenty of, and what is on the maps Ishmael will know about or I will, so we can interpret for you.'

Sir Joseph pulled a large table away from the wall and drew out the leaves so that it extended into a dining table that would have seated half a dozen people easily. Ishmael was already extracting maps from a set of drawers on the opposite side of the room, some modern Ordnance Survey, some rolled and obviously older. It was clear that he was very familiar with the library, and that these two men were completely at ease with one another. Ishmael was obviously as much friend as estate manager.

Sir Joseph found the map he wanted and laid it out on the table, weighting it down with two glass paperweights and a couple of spare whisky glasses. 'Now,' he said, 'as you can see, East Harborough is that top corner there – it goes off the map but you can discern enough of it to get your bearings. Here' – he jabbed a finger – 'is where that poor girl, Sarah Downham, was found. And here is where that poor little scrap, Penny Soper, was laid out. I expect you want to speak to the man who found her? One of mine, Ronan Kerr, works over at Glebe Farm.' He pointed out the farm and then to a nearby symbol for a church. 'It was once associated with this church here, St Luke's. It's semi-derelict now, unfortunately. It must've been a fine building in its day, but at some point, long before my time, the steeple fell and the rest was carried away by locals for building stone. A bit of the nave is still standing.'

'It seems to be in the middle of nowhere. There's no associated village,' Henry observed.

'It's thought that there was a village there, in medieval times, and the Black Death took the inhabitants. There are other rumours that the village was abandoned in the time of Henry VIII, after he went about dissolving all things monastic, although, as far as I know, there was no monastery thereabouts. I keep meaning to get some of the archaeological bods over, from the local university; one of them approached me a few years ago about doing a summer dig, but we never quite got around to setting it up.'

Ishmael was pointing now to an area outlined in blue and with the symbol for a battlefield set in the centre of it. 'This, of course, is the battlefield – Civil War, you know. It's mostly under the plough now, so not the easiest to walk, but there is a footpath here, at this northern edge, which takes you back to East Harborough.'

'Where is the Greens' farm?' Henry asked.

'Ah, you've run across old Green, have you? The farm's down here in that hollow. You can see how the path branches – one branch goes to the farm and then beyond and comes out near Husbands Bosworth. Actually, there's a break in the path there; I've no doubt that once upon a time it used to cross at the edge of this field, but now it just emerges on to the main road, near to the school building. And this branch, of course, goes to East Harborough. The theory, as I understand it, is that Sarah Downham walked to East Harborough along this way, and met her death beside this road.'

For a few moments, the three men fell silent as they thought about that. Henry leaned over the map and traced the route Sarah must have taken. It was straightforward enough and, he estimated from the scale, some three miles long; it would have been rough going, the sort of path where boots would definitely have been preferable to stockinged feet.

'And the other girl, Penelope Soper, was found here. And there's another footpath?'

'Not so clear or well-marked,' Ishmael told him. 'This crosses Sir Joseph's land, and while we maintain access to the footpath from here to here, the line has not been properly established from where this section joins to this, and up until recently that land belonged to another family and access was not always properly maintained. You'll find many landowners hereabouts do not like others tramping across their land, not even where the historic right has been well maintained.'

'You take a different view?' Henry asked.

'I take a pragmatic view,' Sir Joseph told him. 'Where so many people believe that they have inalienable rights, established by their ancestors and our ancestors to take a particular route, it's often best just to give in and allow it to happen. At least if a footpath is maintained, then they will follow that particular route and we can control both their numbers and their route. Otherwise, they might trample crops or decide that their preferred direction is straight across the middle of a field.' He laughed shortly. 'And it does make sense to maintain these byways so that local people are able to get about more quickly. Especially as everyone and his dog around here works on the land, and we need our labourers to be able to access their place of work; otherwise, we'd just be storing up trouble for ourselves. The same families have worked for my family for generations, and that goes for many of the landowners hereabouts. In the last few years, it's been hard enough to keep them on the land, and to keep young girls in service. They used to follow their mothers and their aunts into employment, but understandably, I suppose, they don't want to do that any more. Three generations of some families we had working in the house and the gardens or on the farms, but times are changing, and if we don't change with them, well, I think we will soon be in trouble.'

Henry studied the map carefully and traced the paths with his finger, looking at the relationship between where the girls lived and where they ended up. 'And the wharf, where Penny Soper worked?'

'Right at the bottom of the map, you can see the section of canal. You need the adjacent map to see the rest of it. Brady Brewer worked there from time to time as well,' he observed.

'True, but we know he didn't kill Penelope Soper.'

'You'll find a fair few people around here believe he came back from the dead to do exactly that,' Ishmael told him sourly. 'The man had something of a reputation, I can tell you that.'

'There does not seem to have been much doubt about his guilt at the time of his execution,' Henry said, 'despite his sister giving him an alibi for the night in question.'

'Can a sister's alibi be trusted?' Sir Joseph sounded doubtful. 'What sister would not seek to protect her brother? And as I understand it, the circumstantial evidence was overwhelming.'

'It did seem to be. But the sister has a good reputation within her community; I would have thought her reputation alone would cast some doubt on his guilt.'

He was aware of Ishmael and Sir Joseph glancing at one another before Ishmael said uncomfortably, 'I suspect most people who had had any dealings with Brady Brewer were just glad that he was out of the way.'

'And frankly, most will be very disappointed that you are reopening the case and casting any doubts now,' said Sir Joseph. 'Brewer was an appalling human being. You may know that I'm a local magistrate; I put him in prison twice and believe him to have been deserving of prison on more than those occasions.'

'What crimes did you convict him of?'

'The man had a temper. On the first occasion I met with him, he had beaten a fellow bloody over some imagined slight. It had taken four strong men to pull him off, and they practically had to sit on Brewer to get him to stop fighting. Once the man lost his rag, that was it: there was no stopping him. He was unpredictable, and he was violent. Had it been in my power, I would have put him inside for longer than the two years I did.'

'And the second time?'

'A similar offence, less serious only because the constables arrived and beat Brewer to the ground. He claimed a man owed him money and attacked him in the street, put him down with a single blow and then proceeded to kick him where he lay. He seemed unconcerned that there were witnesses, on both occasions. The constables on the second occasion applied their truncheons and gave Brewer a taste of his own medicine. The fact that the victim agreed that he owed money and that he had been extremely tardy in repaying Brewer, and that witnesses attested to the fact that he had goaded Brewer about the debt, lessened the sentence somewhat. I had to accept that there had been mitigation.'

'And then there were the young women who brought complaints about him,' Ishmael said. 'Brewer was not inclined to take no for an answer when he set his cap at someone. None of these incidents came to court; it would have done the young women no good for that to have happened – you know how people gossip and a woman's reputation, once sullied, is very difficult to clean. I understand that brothers and fathers dealt with these complaints on their behalf.'

'And you both approve of that?' Henry asked mildly.

'It didn't come to court, and I wasn't asked to intervene or to hold an opinion and so I did not. In my view, it's best not to interfere unless interference is asked for.'

Henry made no comment. Instead, he said, 'I presume you know the Greens?'

'Of course. In fact, cousins of yours, aren't they?' This to Ishmael.

'Second cousins on Mrs Green's side. Milly is related to my mother's family.'

'And they have just the two children? Linus and Lucy?'

'That's right, yes. Why do you ask?'

Henry studied the man. There was a certain wariness in his tone now. 'Linus Green mentioned that Penelope Soper and Sarah Downham were both known to him and his sister. That they attended some of the same social events. We're just trying to put a picture together – who these young women socialized with, who would have been familiar with their movements and habits. It's standard procedure in an investigation of this nature.'

'I see, but you can't think that either of the young Greens could be involved. Lucy is a sweet girl and Linus is . . .' He paused as though trying to find a word to describe his distant relative.

'A gentle soul,' Sir Joseph said. 'Not a man to do harm to anyone.'

Henry again noted the tone. 'I got the impression he was not the sort of gung-ho son his father had hoped for,' he said carefully. 'Not inclined towards military matters.'

Sir Joseph rewarded him with a wry smile. 'No,' he said. 'I imagine not. But he's a knowledgeable farmer and a good stockman, and his father understands that this is what really counts. Like the rest of us, he is a pragmatic and practical man.'

'And Linus is engaged to be married next year,' Ishmael said. 'To a young woman from a neighbouring farm. She has no brothers, so the hope is that the two properties will be combined in time. He'll do his duty and provide heirs, I've no doubt.'

'And what of Lucy? Will she remain at the farm?'

Sir Joseph laughed and the tension was broken. 'Lucy has other things on her mind. She plans to go to art college of all things. But don't misunderstand: she will do well. She has been awarded a scholarship at Ruskin College and leaves in the autumn. Her parents may not fully understand why she wants to do such an outlandish thing, but they have supported her. Better for her to forge a life of her own than to expect her brother to keep her. There are not enough young men hereabouts that her father would approve of, so that might have turned out to be a problem. Better for her to make her own way.'

It seemed like a long answer to a simple question, Henry thought. He wondered what the full story was but decided now was not the time to ask. 'Good for her,' he said. 'And were either of you acquainted with Penelope Soper?'

'Only as a girl who worked at the Wharf. By all accounts, she was a good worker. We both used to pop in there from time to time – if you look at the map, you'll see that it is on the boundary of my property on the southern side. In fact, if an ancestor of mine had not been so averse to change, the canal might have run through our land – as it turned out, it had to take a little curve away.' He laughed, seeming to find this very amusing for some reason that Henry could not quite fathom. 'Let me refresh your glass.'

Henry had barely touched his brandy, but he allowed Sir Joseph to add another splash of spirit. Ishmael seemed to have recovered from his unease and was now showing a different map, illustrating the way that the land boundaries had pretty much remained the same since the Middle Ages and talking about the route that the king would have taken to get to Naseby, 'To give battle with that bounder, Cromwell.'

For a while, Henry allowed himself to be distracted; the conversation was discursive and interesting, and it was clear that both his host and the land manager had a genuine love for the area in which they lived, its history and even its wildlife – as long as it wasn't something they could hunt on horseback.

As they prepared to say goodnight, Henry said, 'One thing does puzzle me about Brady Brewer. He was a man of such a bad reputation and yet he seems to have had no problem finding employment. He worked at the wharf, held down jobs at various farms, from what I gather, and brought in a regular income. I would have thought . . .'

'People around here don't discriminate as much as you might imagine. Labour is in short supply, and provided a man is willing to work, they will employ him. I must admit, somewhat to my shame, I did speak up in Brewer's favour on the odd occasion when I was called upon to give a reference for him. When the man was sober, he worked as hard as any. It was only when the drink was in him that he showed his bad side – and, believe me, on those occasions he was not fit company for any.'

Henry nodded and thanked his host. He wondered what it was that held him back from admitting to knowing Brewer. He had told Walker easily enough, had not thought twice about it, but there was something about the present company that made him uneasy, for all that he was inclined to like Sir Joseph and Ishmael Gibbs. His sister's communication with Sir Joseph aside, a communication that might have guaranteed them a decent place to stay, he had the feeling that the man had wanted to meet him properly, not as the brother of a friend but as a policeman. As an investigator. Sir Joseph wanted to know what he had found out, and what he thought, and what he felt about the situation. Henry felt in turn that he was not yet ready to put his cards on Sir Joseph's table.

While Henry was being entertained at the big house, his sergeant had eaten a substantial dinner of his own and then taken himself out for the promised walk, the desk clerk being surprised at the request for an umbrella but providing one all the same. 'I could call you a cab, sir; it's not a fit night for walking.'

Mickey had assured him that his boots were waterproof – he oiled and polished the leather daily when at home – and that he liked to walk in all weathers because it helped him think. He could see that the clerk was puzzled, but then Mickey Hitchens puzzled a lot of people, so this experience was not new. Thanking the man for the loan of the umbrella, he took himself off to explore the delights of East Harborough.

The hotel faced the market square, a substantial space with the main road, imaginatively called Main Street, entering from one end and leaving the other. The road was tarmac, but the square itself was cobbled and some of the shops facing the hotel looked as though they might have been medieval. At one end there was a church, set to the left of the main road as it entered the square. As Mickey passed it, he learned that it was dedicated to St Luke. That rang a bell, and he immediately looked to see where the church hall might be – one of the places where young people met for Saturday dances. He should have asked where the Temperance Hall was, he thought, but he didn't have to wonder for long because it was just down the road, on the same side as the church on Main Street. It was a substantial building, late Victorian to judge by the architecture, brick-built and very self-assured, its position somewhat elevated above the pavement and reached by a dozen steps. A noticeboard outside advertised a Saturday dance and promised live music. A closer look at the noticeboard indicated that on other occasions music would be provided by a Mr Grosvenor and his gramophone; patrons were invited to bring their own recordings – in good condition – and that contributions of gramophone needles would be much appreciated.

Entertainment at the Temperance Hall was clearly something of an ad hoc affair, Mickey thought, but that would not have made it of any less value to the young people out to have a good time.

He walked on, approaching the edge of town, and the side road of more substantial houses on which was set the Downham residence. Curiosity took him that way, and as he passed the house, he was interested to see that it was well lit up, the curtains not completely closed, the deep mourning they had observed when he and Henry had visited seemingly alleviated. Perhaps in honour of their guests, he wondered. He stood in the shadows opposite the house for a few moments and watched, caught glimpses of servants passing windows where drapes were not quite closed. Observed the second motor vehicle parked on the paved area in front of the house and thought he heard laughter issuing from a downstairs room. Then he walked on.

This rather fancy road ended abruptly about a hundred yards further on. Streetlamps ceased and countryside impinged. There was a bus stop, he noted, but beyond that a strange and almost vertiginous feeling that the world ended, the heavy rain and the darkness of mid-evening conspiring to block his view of anything beyond that final garden hedge. Mickey took a few steps into the dark and found what he'd been looking for. Beyond the garden hedge was a field hedge and beyond that again and to the side of a gate was a stile. This, he guessed, must be the start of the footpath that eventually led across the top of the battlefield and to another farm gate, where poor Sarah Downham had met her end.

Satisfied that his imagined map matched reality, Mickey turned. He stood for a moment in the dark, looking back into the brightly lit street, afflicted by a sense of dislocation as though he was staring into another world. There would be absolutely no light on that path, Mickey thought, and she would have been walking it at dusk and then after dark. Would she have taken a torch with her or, on nights when there was a moon, would her eyes have grown accustomed to the darkness on what must have been a familiar route? And if she was visiting friends in Naseby, why would she have not asked to be driven there and arranged to be collected? That second question was easy enough to answer: she had arranged to meet Brewer in all probability. But would her family have approved of her walking out at night, in pitch-dark, on a lonely route? The answer to that was also simple: they hadn't known.

He walked slowly down the street, past the Downham house, pausing only briefly to glance up at what had been Sarah's room. It was possible she might have climbed out of the window; there was a convenient tree, branches reaching almost to the window, which might have made that possible. More likely, Mickey thought, imagining the layout of the house, she had slipped down the servants' stairs and gone out through the back door. She had the sympathy of the cook and serving maids, and they were used to her coming into the kitchen and making it clear that she liked their company. She could easily have gone out that way, and it was unlikely she had even been seen or, if she had, that any notice was taken of her.

'Strikes me neither your aunt nor your father had any control over what you did,' Mickey said softly. 'Strikes me they had given up trying and now they feel guilty for that.' So she was something of a wild child, Mickey thought, but perhaps only in the way that many young people liked to run a bit before life caught up with them. She certainly hadn't done anything deserving of the death she had endured.

He turned his steps towards the market square and the hotel. The rain was getting heavier, and even Mickey's tolerance for walking in wet weather was wearing a little thin. Worse, the wind was gusting now, and he was having trouble keeping the umbrella turned right side out. Time to go back and get on with looking through some of those statements.

Reaching the hotel, he was told at reception that Inspector Johnstone would not be returning that evening after all but would be driven back after breakfast in the morning. Thinking of the route they had taken earlier that day, Mickey was not surprised. It was probably a sensible decision for Henry to remain at Sir Joseph's place, but he still found himself feeling a little put-out. Then, having asked if he might have some coffee sent up to his room, he went off to get himself dried out and, after the coffee had been delivered, took the bold step of getting into his pyjamas and dressing gown, so that he might sit and read in comfort.

Mickey was not the only person involved in the enquiry who was walking the streets that night. Elizabeth Brewer had endured a cold and wet trek, first walking from her home into East Harborough itself and then through the centre of the town where, a few streets back from the market square, there were several rows of terraced streets. Many of these had been converted into cheap boarding houses, and it was one such that was her destination.

The lights were on in the front parlour, but Elizabeth did not knock at the front door; instead, she slipped down a shared entryway and into the backyard. She knew from experience that the rear door would be unlocked, and she let herself in quietly and stood listening in the scullery for a few minutes before satisfying herself that she could go inside without being heard. The wireless was on in the parlour, the faint sound of music reaching her, but there was no conversation and, as she crept into the hall, the distinctive sound of a woman snoring could also be discerned. Clearly, the landlady was asleep.

Elizabeth knew that there were three boarders, and the one she wanted kept the room at the rear of the house. She knew that she was taking a major risk, but she could not see any other way out of her dilemma. She climbed the stairs as quietly as she could and stood listening on the landing, thinking what excuse she could make if anyone discovered her. Then she made her way down the hall to the back room and knocked very softly on the door. When the man answered, she pushed her way inside, holding a finger to her lips and relying on the fact that he would not want it known that a woman had come to his room. The landlady would have had him out on his ear.

'What do you want?'

'I know what you did that night. I know my brother was with you.' She wasn't sure, but she had certainly wondered, and that wondering had nagged at her until she had to find out for certain, however much it might hurt. She hadn't intended to lie to the police, hadn't wanted to believe that her brother had lied to *her*. 'You and Brady were up to something. I want to know what it was,' she declared with as much conviction as she could muster. 'He hanged for what happened to Sarah. It seems to me that you should have hanged with him. Maybe you will for Penny's murder. I want the truth.'

'The truth, is it?' He was laughing at her now. 'Then I'll give you the truth.'

Abruptly, he leaned forward and pinioned her arms. Then he whispered something to her that left her reeling.

'I don't believe you.'

'Don't you? Think on it, woman. See if you really believe I'm lying.' He released her then. 'Now go,' he said.

Elizabeth Brewer did not think she had much choice. Yes, she could raise merry hell in getting chucked out of his room, cause a scene that would embarrass them both. Yes, she could go to the police and tell them what she knew, but why would they believe her? She was not usually a foolish woman, but she accused herself now. She had thought this would be easier – after all, she had spent a lifetime dealing with difficult men, her brother foremost among them. But she could see from his eyes – this man, this killer – that she had never challenged anyone of his ilk before, and suddenly she was genuinely afraid.

Elizabeth Brewer squared her shoulders, pulled her coat tight and turned on her heel. She opened the door and trod softly along the hall and down the stairs. The landlady still snored, the music still sounded, and outside the rain fell. Nothing had changed, but Elizabeth knew that she had played her hand too boldly and without sufficient thought, and that might well cost her dearly.

Would he come after her? She hurried away, listening for footsteps, wondering if he knew where she lived, knowing it would not take much effort to find out. But she did not think he would risk coming out tonight, not on such a filthy night; he preferred a bright moon and clear skies if the previous deaths were anything to go by, and she had heard reports of other women being frightened by a man approaching them prior to this.

A man who began as a random, predatory pest could on occasion, she thought, quickly become someone who would resort to violence to get what he wanted. She had so little proof; that was the problem. What had she hoped? That he would confess? She cursed herself for her own stupidity. She had been no wiser than young Sarah had been.

A few streets further on, she stopped off at a tall house and knocked on a kitchen door. When the woman she wished to speak to came down, she stayed long enough to exchange a few words before disappearing into the night once again. She set off on the long walk home, knowing that she had certainly made things no better and could perhaps have made them worse.

ELEVEN

By morning, the storm had cleared and Mickey was still at breakfast when Henry arrived back at the hotel. He joined his sergeant for another cup of tea and, to Mickey's eyes, seemed relieved to be back.

'How was your evening?' Mickey asked. 'Hobnobbing with the gentry.'

Henry laughed. 'It was generally useful and reasonably pleasant. I have a clearer picture in my head of the lie of the land, and of local politics, I think. I also asked Sir Joseph at breakfast this morning what itinerants, gypsies and the like he had to deal with. It seems that most itinerant workers and travelling folk move through the county and up into Lincolnshire for the picking season, and it is, of course, the wrong time of year for anyone to be on the road.'

Mickey nodded. 'Most will still be in winter quarters. Besides, any strangers to the area would stick out like a sore thumb, especially if they can be labelled as gypsies or tinkers.'

'Sir Joseph is a magistrate – he reckons he has to deal with the odd poacher, but it's a line of enquiry I think we can rule out both in terms of poachers and travelling folk. It wasn't something that troubled me greatly, anyway; I just wanted it squared out of the way. It will be expected that we ask and that the questions and answers go in our report. More interesting, though, Sir Joseph, in his role as magistrate, was on the panel that had twice jailed Brady Brewer, both times for violence. But then we knew he was something of a brawler. I will ask Walker to look at the records just so we understand the background more fully. Did you go for your walk?'

'I did indeed. I now know the location of the Temperance Hall, and I walked past the Downham residence. The town runs out of steam just a little further down the road and comes to a sudden stop. Beyond the end of the street, it's all just countryside and dark as Hades. The footpath that Sarah Downham must have taken across the field begins at the end of that road; I thought it must do, and confirming that was part of the purpose of my walk. It would have been a lonely route, right from the beginning, and a dark one, too. I checked: there was a gibbous moon the night she was killed, and it was clear early on, though we know it rained after nine. Same for Penelope Soper. The night was clear, rain began in the early hours of the morning, but the moon was just after full.'

'So they could see their way but it would still have been a lonely and perhaps frightening walk, however familiar. Sir Joseph loaned me some maps; we can examine them more closely later.'

They were interrupted by one of the hotel staff bringing a stack of newspapers over to the table. 'I rustled up what I could, Inspector, but we're not in the habit of keeping newspapers past the day they were issued. I managed to rescue these from the staffroom, and from the housekeeper before they were used as kindling.'

Henry thanked him, and the stack was laid on a nearby chair. Mickey eyed them speculatively. '*The Harborough Clarion*,' he said. 'So a local rag.'

'I spotted an A-frame in front of the newsagent's when I arrived back. Advertising the fact that Scotland Yard had sent its finest up to investigate.'

Mickey laughed. 'Its finest – well, there's a compliment, I suppose. I can't see Inspector Walker being impressed.'

'Indeed not. But I wanted to see how the local newspapers had covered the case. We will have to go to the newspaper office to find out what was said about Sarah Downham, but the Soper murder is likely still to be figuring heavily in the daily newspapers as it's only been a little over a week since it happened. I'm interested in seeing what angle the press is taking, and who is writing about the investigation. Local knowledge is always useful.'

'Indeed. So where do we begin today? I know you want to return to the scene, and one of us should examine the Soper house. You still want me to interview the witnesses who found the bodies?'

'I do, which means that we will both be needing transport.

I suggest I go and view the scene this morning, and you continue your perusal of Walker's files. I'd like you also to discover who assisted him in the investigation and to—'

'Chat to them on an informal basis, sergeant to sergeant, or sergeant to constable,' Mickey finished. 'Walker is to go and track down Penelope Soper's friends – should I not go with him?'

'No, let him do the legwork. You can reinterview them later if the need arises. I'd also like you to examine the newspaper reports – who was covering the killings and how – and perhaps make contact with the journalist or journalists involved.'

Mickey raised an eyebrow. 'Any particular reason?'

'I'm sure there is,' Henry said. 'I'm just not certain what it is yet.' He frowned, thinking. 'It was something I noticed at Elizabeth Brewer's cottage. She had a stack of newspapers by the fire, common enough for use as kindling, but there were certain articles carefully folded and placed on the sideboard. It wasn't something I particularly registered at the time, beyond the observation, and it could be that she simply kept them as morbid souvenirs, but . . .'

'Something is nagging at the back of that brain of yours,' Mickey commented. 'Well, when something nags, it's best to pay attention to it. You'll return around lunchtime, then?'

'I will, and then you can make use of the police driver and go and do the interviews. You can also make yourself agreeable to the driver; he seems like a decent sort, and drivers are like servants – they often see and overhear what others don't.'

Half an hour later, Henry was on his way, the car having come to collect him at the hotel, and twenty minutes after that, he was standing where Sarah Downham had been found.

On all sides, the view was restricted by high hedges and the curve of the road as it swept away from the scene. They were, Henry estimated, approximately halfway up quite a steep hill. The footpath followed a ridge in the land, alongside a stand of trees ascending the hill on the one side and a field which fell off quite deeply on the other. There were sheep in the field, and the trees looked like half-grown forestry rather than natural woodland. There was a more natural and ancient-looking copse topping the hill, just visible above the hedges.

Henry told the driver to wait with the car and hopped over the stile into the field. He walked a few hundred yards, examining the ground. It was rutted and muddied, but the path was clear and obviously well used. On the field side was a scrubby hedge, somewhat lower than those lining the road but not as well maintained, which surprised him. The hedges on the main road were plashed and laid, and had obviously been recently renovated, new growth just showing from where the branches had been half cut and bent over, woven together to block the inevitable gaps that opened up at the base of the growing structure. There was evidence also that the ditches had been recently cleared out after the winter rains, piles of mud and leaves and an overgrowth of weeds dumped on the verge.

Close up, it was obvious that the trees were forestry, and a sturdy fence of post and wire ran along the perimeter and presumably would have kept any sheep at bay if they happened to get through the unkempt barrier on the field side.

The difference, Henry mused, between Sarah Downham's murder and that of Penelope Soper was that the Downham girl must have made her way along this path, probably running from her killer who, it seemed, had caught her at the farm gate. Penelope Soper had been walking home up the road. Her killer had presumably been lying in wait by that other gate – but had he arrived there by coming along that other footpath? Henry recalled from the maps he had studied that it mostly led past farmhouses on Sir Joseph Bright's estate. Coincidentally – or was it coincidence? – it also led across land that had once, a generation before, been tenanted by the Brewers.

He walked a little further on, so he could see the house and outbuildings that belonged to the Greens. And he asked himself the question that had occurred the previous day. If Sarah Downham was in trouble, why did she take off along the path towards an almost certainly empty road instead of running to the farm?

The answer, he decided, was a simple one. Her assailant was blocking her way. He was between her and the farmhouse. The forestry was fenced, and even had she climbed the fence, she would have had to run uphill through the trees. The scrubby hedge, though it might well let a sheep or two squeeze through, was still too much of a barrier for a person to bypass. So, her choices diminished, she was left to run towards the road. Without her footwear. And wearing her going-out dress.

If Linus Green was correct – and Henry sensed instinctively that he was – then the girl would have left home in boots and an ordinary dress. An early telephone call made that morning to the friends she had visited confirmed that she had been dressed in a plain brown skirt, a linen blouse and a hand-knitted cardigan – and boots. It had revealed something more. That her friends had believed she had a lift home. That her father had arranged for her to be collected. Henry intended to clarify this when he had finished at the scene.

So she had changed her clothes and put on the yellow dress. But where? Walker and his team of constables had searched the surrounding area for possible trysting spots, and Henry was conscious that these would have to be inside, due to the coldness of the weather. Had the death occurred in summer or even late spring, then the idea of the couple meeting outside would have been far more plausible.

No, she had changed somewhere and then she had gone to meet her killer, or she had gone to meet *someone* and been intercepted by her killer. If Elizabeth Brewer was telling the truth, and Brady had been with her all evening, than Sarah Downham's assignation couldn't have been with Brady Brewer.

Henry paused, gazed out across the landscape and allowed his brain to mull things over. It was a beautiful spot; he estimated that he must be able to see for ten miles from here, and the contrast with the enclosed roadways was quite startling. He glanced again towards the farm and then back the way he had come. Sarah Downham's killer had intercepted her somewhere between the field gate and the Greens' farm. She then turned and ran back towards the road. With nothing on her feet.

That, Henry realized, was what didn't make sense to him. He tried to analyse why and then it came to him. What was the likelihood that Sarah Downham had changed her clothes, or at least her dress before she had entered the field or set foot on the path? What if there was some location between her friends' house and this, which she had used to change her clothes?

What about her stockings and shoes? Was it possible that she had changed into the yellow dress but, knowing she still had a good walk ahead of her, had left on her thicker stockings and her walking boots, intending to make that last transition just before she met . . . who?

Henry turned again to look at the farm. There was a variety of outbuildings surrounding the main house, and he assumed they too would have been searched, but looking for what? Presumably, looking for boots. No one seemed to have considered at that point that she might have changed her clothes; they were just looking for her footwear. It was only Linus Green, as far as Henry knew, who had commented on the way she was dressed, and Walker, in the original investigation, had not asked the friends how she had been dressed when she visited them. He'd had no reason to imagine she might have changed her clothes.

He began to walk back towards the police car, knowing that he had set himself even more conundrums now. If he was right, she'd changed her dress somewhere. That spot needed to be located. She had taken off her boots here on the path, intending to switch out for lighter shoes and lighter stockings, which implied she must be close to her destination. Was that the farm? Had she planned to meet someone in one of the outbuildings or even in the house itself? Were the Greens not so innocent? Had Walker even considered they might be implicated? From what Henry had seen, he was clearly on good terms with them.

The killer could have taken her boots away. Most likely, he had surprised her in the act of removing her footwear.

He arrived back at the car, and the driver, who had been sitting reading a newspaper, made ready to set off. He seemed surprised when Henry climbed into the passenger seat beside him. 'I've been having a thought,' Henry said. 'And I need your help. I'm assuming you're local to the area.'

'Born and bred not two miles from here.' He was regarding Henry with interest and obviously hoping that the day might turn into something more exciting than just driving the car around.

'I want you to drive me to Naseby to visit the Simpsons, those friends that Sarah Downham was visiting the night she was killed. On the way there, I want you to point out to me any place you think might be suitable for a young woman to change her dress. Some shelter, some abandoned building, anywhere that ensures privacy and is dry enough in which to change clothes.'

The driver, Constable Cronin, looked at him in shock. His brow furrowed and then he said, 'You think she changed her clothes before she got here, not after. Oh.'

'I think it's possible. I take it that was not considered at the time?'

'I wouldn't know, sir.'

'And can you think of any location that might suit? All that's required is that it's private and dry enough for a young woman to change out of one dress and put another on.'

Constable Cronin thought about it and then nodded his head. 'I can think of two or three places, all on the route she would have taken, but how will we know if any of these is the right one?'

'We won't know anything until we look,' Henry told him.

They took the drive slowly, keeping a weather eye open for any additional location the driver did not know about. Henry spotted the remnants of a field shelter, the roof partly caved in and probably intended originally for horses. A quick investigation of this one proved it unsuitable. It was wet and muddy, and although, in extremis, he guessed it would have done, he thought it unlikely Sarah Downham had made use of it.

Of the three locations the driver had mentioned, one was in a much worse state than he remembered: an outbuilding for what had once been a farm, the house itself demolished a year since and the stone reused elsewhere. Since the driver had last had reason to notice it, one of the walls had fallen down and it was now exposed to the elements.

The second and third stood quite close together and looked more promising. One was another field shelter, but this one much better maintained, and the horses in the field looked askance at Henry as he ducked inside. He sent the driver to look at the brick shed and the Dutch barn that could be glimpsed through the hedge in the next field. It didn't take long for Henry to realize that the field shelter was unlikely to have housed anything apart from a cantankerous horse or two in bad weather. It was weatherproof, and a halter and other pieces of rope tack had been hung on nails just inside, but it was also muddied and fouled with horseshit, so again it would do, but . . .

Henry was beginning to wonder if his ideas had gone astray when an excited shout from Cronin had him hurrying through to the next field. There, he found a brick outbuilding and the large Dutch-style barn he had caught sight of over the hedge.

The small brick shed next to the barn had a broken lock on the door, but was crammed with old tools, sacks and a random assortment of abandoned gear.

The barn had been curtained with tarpaulins; they flapped in the wind but kept the rain off the timber that had been stored inside. At first, Henry could not see the driver but heard him calling from somewhere in the middle of the barn. It was dimly lit, tarpaulins blocking much of the light from outside, and Cronin popped up suddenly from what Henry had taken simply to be a stack of timber.

Between the stacks was a space, and in that space was a sack that looked like one of those Henry had noticed in the shed.

'I didn't touch anything, sir,' Cronin said excitedly, 'but there's definitely something in it, something brown and it looks like it's knitted.'

'She was wearing a brown skirt, brown cardigan and a white linen blouse when she left her friends,' Henry said. Cronin stood aside so that he could kneel beside the hessian sack. It hadn't been placed on the floor; instead, it was laid out on top of a piece of timber that formed a rough shelf. As Henry looked more closely, he saw that a stub of candle, melted wax securing it in place, had been attached to another plank, presumably so the girl could see what she was doing.

'It looks as though she intended to come back and collect this,' he said quietly. He opened the sack just enough that he and Cronin could see the skirt and cardigan and blouse inside. 'Now all we've got to do is locate her boots and her shoes and the yellow dress,' Henry said.

TWELVE

Mrs Simpson and her daughter, Ingrid, were at home. The father and brother were out at work. It turned out that Mr Simpson was a solicitor, and his son was training to be a solicitor's clerk. The house was redbrick, solid, square and detached, sitting in a little parcel of its own land, with identical flowerbeds in front and what looked like an orchard behind. Henry glimpsed this beyond the garage that stood beside the house.

Mother and daughter had been half expecting a visit. 'Seeing as the investigation appears to have been reopened.' Mrs Simpson did not sound approving. Her daughter, Ingrid, was seventeen and so a little younger than Sarah Downham. The son, Simon, was older and had been a friend of Philip Maddison before he went off to university, and the families, she said, had been good friends forever.

Mrs Simpson regarded Henry and the sack he carried in his hand with the utmost suspicion. She offered them coffee, and Henry, who had brought the driver in with him, accepted on their behalf. Cronin perched nervously on the edge of a chintz-covered chair, and Henry could see that he was trying not to allow his hands to shake as he held the delicate china cup and saucer.

'And now, what more can I tell you?' Mrs Simpson asked.

Henry addressed the daughter and said, 'Miss Simpson, as I understand it, Miss Downham came to visit on the night she died. Could you describe the events of that evening?'

'Chief Inspector, we have already told Inspector Walker what went on,' Mrs Simpson said. He could hear that she was annoyed both at having to repeat herself and the fact that he was addressing her daughter.

Imperiously, Henry held up a hand signalling that she should be quiet, and she seemed too astonished at first to be anything but. 'Miss Simpson? When did Sarah Downham arrive and what happened while she was here?'

Ingrid Simpson looked anxiously at her mother and then back at the police officer and said, 'She arrived a little after seven and Mother let us use the parlour so we could play records on the gramophone. We drank tea and chatted, and then Simon, my brother, arrived and stayed for a bit. Then, at about a quarter to nine, she said she must go. I was surprised – usually, she stayed for longer, and then my father would take her home in the car. But she said no, she was getting a lift from someone else. That a friend was picking her up at the end of the road. I asked why her friend wasn't coming to the house, and who it was, and she said it was someone her father knew, and he didn't know the village very well, so she had told him she'd meet him at the crossroads.'

'Close to the church?' Henry asked. 'Where there's a triangular green and the roads go off in three directions?'

She nodded. 'I told all this to Inspector Walker.'

'Did you tell Inspector Walker that she was meeting someone, that someone was coming to collect her?'

'Yes, but Inspector Walker decided that she'd been lying to me. That she just intended to walk home but didn't want to tell me that. She knew Mummy and Daddy wouldn't approve, and her father would be really angry with her, and her aunt.'

'And she had walked here?'

'She must have done; she was wearing her boots when she arrived.'

Mrs Simpson looked suddenly outraged. 'You never told me that.'

'I didn't think about it. Inspector Walker seemed to think that she had walked here, so I didn't think about it after that.'

'You assumed someone had driven her here?' Henry asked Mrs Simpson.

'Well, yes. It was dark and cold, and it's a lonely path; it's all very well walking it in the daylight, but at night? That is just such a stupid risk.'

'And she was definitely wearing her boots when she arrived.'

Ingrid nodded. 'She took them off in the porch and tucked them under the bench – they were muddy. Then she put on her shoes and she came inside. I answered the door to her; I was expecting her, so I was watching out of the window for her to arrive.'

'And the boots are definitely gone?'

Again, Ingrid nodded, and Henry got the impression that something had just dawned on her. 'She changed out of her shoes and into her boots,' Ingrid said, as though this was a sudden revelation. 'Why would she do that if all she was doing was walking to the car, even if it was at the end of the road?'

'Why indeed?' Henry said.

He had put the sack beside his feet and now he placed his coffee cup on a small table set beside his chair and removed the garments from the sack. The brown pleated skirt, the cardigan, the white blouse. 'Are these the clothes she was wearing?'

'Wherever did you find them?' Mrs Simpson asked. She leaned forward for a closer look and then nodded. 'I believe Sarah's aunt knitted the cardigan for her – see how fine the stitches are and how complicated the pattern; I don't have the patience to do something like that. Where did you find them?' she asked again.

Henry looked at Ingrid for confirmation, and the girl nodded. 'We found the clothes in a Dutch barn used to store timber, about a mile from here,' he said. 'We have Constable Cronin's local knowledge to thank for the discovery.' *And my conclusion that she must have changed en route*, he added to himself.

He turned back to Ingrid. 'Did she have a bag with her?'

'Yes, I told Inspector Walker she had a bag with her shoes in it. I didn't realize there was anything else. So she got changed somewhere. Into other clothes. Why would she do that?'

'Judging by what she was wearing,' Henry said carefully, 'perhaps because she wanted to look her best for someone. She was wearing a yellow dress with a pleated skirt and a sash in some finer stuff.' He repeated the details Linus Green had given him.

Ingrid looked shocked. 'That was her new dress,' she said. 'Sarah had only had it for a few weeks. I think she had it made for the New Year party. You remember?' She turned to her mother.

'A very pretty dress,' her mother said, frowning a little. 'We attended the party at the Downhams' house. Her aunt, I remember, was not best pleased by it; I do recall that. Sarah waited until the guests were present and then made her entrance. She looked beautiful, but her aunt was thunderstruck. There was nothing wrong with the dress, you understand. The neckline was a little lower and it left her arms bare, but it was simply fashionable, not outrageous.' She sighed, shook her head gently. 'Mrs Forsyth liked Sarah to be modest, I suppose. This was nothing like any dress her aunt would have chosen for her.'

'A going-out dress.' Henry realized he had unconsciously echoed Linus's description again. 'The sort of dress a young woman might wear if she wanted to make an impression on someone?'

Mrs Simpson pursed her lips and nodded, and Ingrid looked expectantly at first her mother and then Henry.

'Why would she do that?'

'This man who was supposed to be collecting her. Did she say his name, or tell you anything about him?'

'Only that he knew her father. I didn't really think about it. I was just disappointed that she was going so early. I suppose she said that she was leaving, and I didn't think much about it after that – to be truthful, I was a bit miffed.' She looked suddenly very troubled and added, 'I think I was a bit sharp with her. I'm so sorry for that now. I was disappointed because she said she was coming for the evening, and usually she would have stayed until about ten. I don't have many friends close by, so . . .'

Henry nodded his understanding.

Mrs Simpson was frowning. 'She had left before I realized or I would have questioned her further; you may be certain of that.'

Henry nodded. He had no doubt she would. That might well have saved Sarah Downham's life. He wondered if Mrs Simpson had realized that yet and if the guilt would hit her hard. He hoped not; the fault was not hers.

'You can't really believe that dreadful Brady Brewer was innocent,' Mrs Simpson said. 'He was a terrible man.' She broke off suddenly and looked at her daughter as though wishing she hadn't said anything. Ingrid was looking eagerly at her, clearly hungry for any detail.

At seventeen, Henry thought, her mother still viewed her as a child and would no doubt have protected her from the worst of the rumours and the most dreadful of the details. Would she be able to continue to do that now? Ingrid was almost bound to hear the inevitable gossip.

He thanked them both for their time, and he and Cronin took their leave.

THIRTEEN

While Henry was tramping around the countryside, Mickey was sitting behind a desk examining paperwork. When they were working from the Central Office at Scotland Yard, it was commonplace for the two of them to share this task, frequently sitting on opposite sides of the desk so that they could compare notes. It was a companionable thing and an efficient division of labour, and Mickey found that he was missing his inspector.

On the face of it, Walker had carried out a reasonable investigation, but Mickey could see that he had from the first assumed Brewer's guilt – and who could blame him for that, Mickey thought, given the man's character and the evidence against him? But it did mean avenues of investigation that perhaps should have been examined had been sidelined and ignored. The police had their man, the community concurred that this was a good thing and the general consensus seemed to be that the world would be better without Brady Brewer in it. It was interesting, though, Mickey thought, that the man had continued to protest his innocence right up to the time of his execution, and that his story never changed – not one iota. He had spent the evening with his sister, at home, and had been nowhere near Sarah Downham on the night she died. If a man had wanted to produce an alibi, Mickey thought, there might have been better ways to have gone about it.

He got up and went to look at the evidence boxes again, at the blue dress that, it now turned out, was completely out of place. He spread it out on the table and examined it carefully, taking a magnifying glass from his murder bag. The first thing that was obvious was the lack of blood, and the second the lack of any tearing or damage. There were traces of mud here and there, but nothing that would have resulted from a young woman being pushed to the ground and struggling with her assailant. There were no bloodstains from that young woman when she had been violently raped. He paused for a moment and then wondered if there was, in truth, any rape other than the violent kind. But there was no tearing, no damage at all beyond the understandable crumpling from the garment having been packed anyhow into a box. He picked the dress up and sniffed at it. The scent of damp and mildew and some faint women's perfume greeted his nostrils. The smell could simply mean that it was packed into the box while damp or had been stored in less than adequate surroundings, and from what he'd seen of the evidence cupboard, it was a dank and miserable place full of boxes packed higgledy-piggledy on to the shelves.

The trace of perfume was floral, but too faint for him to be able to decide what it was. There was something rosy about it, and a faint undertone of violet. The dress had quite a high neckline, and when he examined it, there were traces of face powder on the inside, perhaps from where it had brushed against a woman's chin. If that was the case, then the violet could be the scent of orris root, which he knew was added to many loose or pressed powders of the kind most women had in their compacts.

He looked at the style of the dress and the fabric and at the way it had been made. The seams had been sewn on a machine, but there were little bits of mending and repair that spoke of everyday wear and tear but also that the dress had been valued. It was not the latest fashion; the style was quite basic, with the top section of sleeve grown on to the bodice and with a little turn-back cuff at the wrist, and it took him a moment or so to place it because he knew it was familiar. Eventually, he remembered that it was a version of something called the one-hour dress, a simple pattern that could be readily bought and made up quickly by the home dressmaker. The next-door-but-one neighbour, back at home, often took in sewing and she had made a couple of such garments for Belle. If he remembered right, there were variations on a basic theme, all cut from the minimum of fabric and with as few seams as possible. On this one, the front hung flat and there were small gathers at the hips on both sides and long, straight sleeves. The lower, tubular section of sleeve had been sewn on to the upper, the construction obviously created to save on fabric: when he looked closely, this section was made in several pieces all carefully matched. He remembered that Penelope Soper made dresses for the local women and that she was apparently a good seamstress. Could she have made it? Or was that too much of a stretch? Many women of his acquaintance either fashioned their own clothes or knew a woman who did it for them. He glanced at the neckline and the side seams, in case there were shop labels there, but he didn't expect to find any. This was a home-made, well-made, well-loved dress, and its provenance might be important. Of more pressing concern was how it had made its way into the evidence box and where the yellow dress had gone.

He was reminded of a recent case he and Henry had worked on, where a young woman's body had been found on a beach. A young woman wearing a dress and shoes that did not belong to her. He knew from discussions with his wife, and by observing Cynthia and her friends, just how important wearing the right clothes could be. How much symbolism was carried by the specific fabric and the correct cut, and how much care was taken in suiting an item of clothing to a particular location or event. Such things, Mickey noted, mattered to women. Wearing the right dress, Belle would say, is like donning a suit of armour.

Men had it easy, he thought. It was either work clothes or a lounge suit or evening dress. Not that Mickey often had occasion to wear formal dress, and when he did, he hired it by the hour.

He took another look into the box, just to see if there was anything that had been missed. Brady Brewer's glove – the one that, truth be told, probably got him hanged – caught his attention. It was rather beautifully made, the Fair Isle pattern running across the back distinctive and complex. And it was clean. No mud, no blood, no tearing. He looked back at the records and satisfied himself that the hand that strangled Sarah Downham had been a man's left. This was a left-hand glove, so presumably it had been removed before Brewer strangled the poor young woman. If indeed he had, of course. Reluctantly, Mickey was coming round to the idea that he may have been innocent after all. But just assuming for a moment that it had been Brewer, and that he had removed his glove in order to get a better grip on the girl's neck, how likely would it have been that the glove then fell beneath the girl's body? He remembered suddenly that Penny Soper had been strangled by someone placing both hands on her throat. It struck Mickey that that was a significant difference.

Mickey thought about it and fervently wished there had been photographs taken at the crime scene, as had become normal practice both in the Metropolitan Police and many provincial forces throughout the land. Looking through the reports, there had been little recourse to any forensic examination. As far as Mickey could tell, there had not even been the taking of fingerprints.

Mickey frowned and told himself he was probably being too harsh. What fingerprints would likely have been left at the scene anyway? He assumed they had tested the size of Brady's hand against the size of the bruises, but he could find no record of that having happened either.

Now, he conceded that Walker had done a reasonable job in as much as he had drawn the evidence together and interviewed his man; although he had never gained a confession, the evidence had been strong enough for the case to go before the court. The jury had found Brewer guilty, and Mickey wasn't sure he could blame them. It was simply that he was now looking for faults, examining the evidence with a critical eye and finding it wanting that made him doubt Brewer's guilt. He fully knew the man to be capable of acts of extreme violence. Did it really matter that he had been hanged for this rather than for his other crimes?

'Only because there is another killer out there,' Mickey said quietly to himself. 'Brewer's conviction left him free to act again, to kill again, and he will kill others if we don't get to him first.'

Henry arrived back in the early afternoon, and by coincidence Walker came in just after. Mickey announced he was hungry enough that his stomach thought his throat had been cut, and it was decided they would go and find themselves some food and exchange intelligence.

Walker knew of a local pub that would still be open for

the next half an hour and which made decent sandwiches, and so they adjourned to the Griffin, a small and rather dark establishment close to the police station. It was quiet, most of the lunchtime drinkers having gone back to work, but sandwiches were provided, together with a very welcome pint of beer.

Between bites of his sandwich, Walker explained that he had tracked down four of the young people on the list of Penny Soper's friends and, thanks to them, had addresses for another two.

'And were Penny Soper and Sarah Downham known to one another?' Henry asked. 'We had presumed they must be, but—'

'Indeed they were. They had friends in common, Lucy Green being one of them, and the young woman that Sarah was visiting on the night she was killed, Ingrid Simpson, is also a friend of the Green girl. I asked them if they knew how Sarah Downham got to know Brady Brewer, and it seems that they assumed it was through Elizabeth Brewer. The sister had a number of jobs, mostly domestic, which often entailed her working late. She also made and mended for various households, including the Downhams.

'Ironically, it seems that Brewer sometimes came and collected her from her late-night jobs and walked her home. It's possible that on some such occasion he met Sarah Downham, and although no one knows for certain how that friendship developed and deepened, we have a decent explanation for how it began.'

'When you questioned Brewer about knowing Sarah Downham, which I presume you must have done, how did he say they had met?'

Mickey saw Walker frown as though he felt this question was unnecessary. 'He also said they had met by chance through his sister. I must confess I did not ask for particulars; it was enough to know that the young woman had got herself involved with a very unsuitable man and that this, as I truly believed, had led to her death. You can't blame me for thinking so.'

'I can't blame you for being suspicious of him, no,' Henry said. 'But he did have an alibi. Presumably, you tried to check that.'

'As you well know, he was alibied by his sister. An alibi from a sister is as unreliable as an alibi from a wife. Don't tell me you don't also treat them with suspicion.'

'It rather depends on the circumstances,' Mickey said. 'I examined your notes this morning, and although the investigation seemed thorough, it was very obvious that you looked no further than Brewer, and you never even thought about suspecting anyone else.'

He was not surprised when Walker turned an angry glare on him. He knew that in addressing a superior officer in this way he was probably speaking out of turn. Walker clearly thought so. 'Is that so, *Sergeant*?' he said. No one could have missed the emphasis placed on Mickey's rank.

'If my sergeant believes this to be true, then I will accept his word.' Henry's response was chilly. 'Sergeant Hitchens' experience in all probability far outweighs your own.'

'And yet he is still a sergeant.'

'A situation about to change and not before time.' Henry's tone was now hot and acerbic.

Mickey felt he should step in. 'Inspectors, I am not the subject of this debate.' He kept his voice quiet but did not trouble to hide his annoyance. 'We should not be losing sight of the subject, and that is the death of two young women. My issue is not with the investigation,' he continued, turning to Walker, 'my issue is that because of the focus on Brewer, chances might have been missed, another suspect might have been in the frame, and Penelope Soper might still be alive. Was there anyone else, however scantily implicated, that might give us another direction?'

'Was there any hint that Sarah Downham was seeing anyone other than Brewer?' Henry added. Mickey noted that his tone was still somewhat acerbic but that, as he so often did, he had taken his lead from his sergeant and was attempting to put his annoyance aside.

'Why do you ask that?' Walker wanted to know.

Mickey was ahead of him. 'Because she was going to meet someone the night she was killed, and it is certainly possible that it wasn't Brewer. The evidence that convicted him might have been envisioned to do just that. It is possible that someone intended him to be implicated and intended him to hang. The glove was a key piece of evidence against him. What if someone else left it under Sarah's body? We have to examine Brewer's enemies as well.'

'A long list.'

'And no doubt deserved, but for once in his life, Brady Brewer might have been speaking the truth. It seems to me that if he planned to kill Sarah Downham surely he would have taken care to give himself a better alibi than the one he did. Oh, make no mistake, we both know him to have been capable of murder; in your shoes, we would probably have looked in the same direction.'

'Nice of you to say so.' Walker's tone was dry.

'I'm not intending offence,' Mickey told him. 'What's done is done and can't be set right; what matters now is finding who killed Penelope Soper, and probably who also killed Sarah Downham, before he does it again.'

For a moment there was silence at the table and Mickey took the opportunity to finish his food. And then Walker nodded. 'Don't think I don't regret all of this,' he said.

'Of course you do,' Mickey told him. 'So except for Sarah's interest in Brewer, or vice versa, was there anything to suggest that either young woman was seeing anyone?' he asked.

'No,' Walker admitted. 'But it wasn't a question I was specifically asking, and I doubt the friends of either girl would want to put them in a bad light, so they'd be unlikely to volunteer that information. I expect it seemed to all that it was bad enough for Sarah Downham to be associating herself with Brewer.'

'Then it's a question that needs asking next,' Henry said.

'One thing that does puzzle me,' Mickey said as they headed back to the police station, 'is why the father and the aunt tolerated Brewer's attentions to the girl at all. It's all well and good the aunt talking about girlish silliness and citing herself as an example, but would they really have just allowed this relationship to continue? From what I've heard, they controlled every aspect of the girl's life. Refusing to allow her to go to an ordinary school or even to send her away to school, in case she fell among an unsuitable crowd—'

'Or at least according to what the cook told us.'

Mickey took that on board. 'But long-term household staff often know more about the family than they know themselves,' he argued.

'True, and I agree it was inconsistent. They also allowed her to attend dances and meet her friends.'

'At the Temperance Hall,' Walker pointed out. 'A more respectable venue you'd be hard-pressed to find. The young people are always chaperoned, and any who infringe the rules are instantly barred.'

'So presumably Brewer never attended.'

Walker laughed. 'I would think not.'

'Did Sarah actually go to the dances when she said she did? We know she was not above lying about where she was going and how she was going to get there. She told the Simpsons that she had been given a lift to their home and was expecting one back to her own.'

'The sort of lies many young people tell their guardians,' Walker commented.

'I'm not blaming either of these young women for what happened to them, whatever their actions.' Henry's tone was harsh. 'Young people have always chafed against what they see as unnecessary constraints and usually feel that their elders have forgotten what it was like to be young. But we do need to have a clear picture of Sarah Downham's life and indeed that of Penny Soper. And it does seem to me that we keep missing the second young woman out of our discussion, that we have focused so much on the first and not yet paid enough attention to Penny Soper's life and death.'

They had arrived back at the police station. Mickey could see Henry's particular frown and knew that it presaged some change of plan. He was not surprised when Henry said, 'I think I will come with you this afternoon to interview the two witnesses who found the bodies. And we can also go to the Soper house and take a look around, see what our second young woman might have left behind. Walker, I'd like you to do the same with the Downham residence. Go and examine the victim's room with a view to there being evidence of another relationship. Speak to the cook; she seems to be the fount of all knowledge in that house, and find out when Philip Maddison will arrive. I'd like to talk to that young man.'

'When I walked past last night, it seemed the guests had arrived,' Mickey told them. 'The curtains were open and the lights were on; the house seemed no longer in the deep mourning we observed when we were there. If I remember correctly, Mr Downham is still away on business, and only the sister, Sarah Downham's aunt, is present to receive their guests. Perhaps the Maddisons have brought about a change of heart, told her that perhaps she should open the windows and let in the fresh air.'

He caught Henry's glance in his direction and knew that his inspector had caught the somewhat sardonic tone. Walker seemed oblivious to it.

'If you are both heading out in that direction, so that you can examine the Soper house as well as speak to the witnesses, then have the driver take you down by the Wharf so you can talk to the landlord,' Walker suggested. 'It can all be accomplished if Cronin does a largish circle; he knows the area so will know the best route to take. That way, the most use can be made of the afternoon. I'll go and speak to the aunt and the cook and take a good look at Miss Sarah Downham's room – see what I can turn up.'

Mickey was slightly surprised by his tone; he seemed suddenly happier as though now content to have a new track to follow.

'While I'm over in that side of town, I can check on the other two friends on Penelope Soper's list. Now that I have addresses for them.'

'A good thought. It's likely to be quite late by the time we all finish,' Henry said. 'Perhaps you could join us for dinner tonight and we can share the results of the afternoon.'

Mickey saw Walker's expression change to one of some reticence and realized that Henry must have caught it, too. The Three Cranes was not cheap; it would not be the kind of place they would normally patronize, particularly Mickey on a sergeant's wage. He knew also that London inspectors were paid at a higher rate than those in the provinces.

'Sir Joseph Bright will be picking up the bill,' Henry said

airily, and Mickey hid his smile. 'It seemed he would have put us up at his house, but that was considered inappropriate – it was suggested to him that it might look as though he was interfering in the case. But your superiors apparently considered it quite acceptable for him to pay our hotel bill while we are here.'

It was, Mickey thought, the first time since they had met the man that he had heard Walker laugh properly.

FOURTEEN

They called first that afternoon at the Greens' farm to speak to Jeb Mortimer who had found Sarah Downham's body. They were told that the family was absent, but they were directed to one of the barns close beside the farmhouse where Jeb would be working. They found an older man and a young boy, by Henry's estimation no more than mid-teens and probably younger. He wondered if the boy should still be in school or if he was simply small and skinny for fourteen. He was indeed, Henry thought, small and skinny, and rather scared-looking when he realized it was a policeman he would be talking to. The older man, who introduced himself as Ted Arnold, put down his rake and stood to one side with his arms folded, making it plain that he was not going to leave young Jeb to the mercy of these foreign officers. Henry ignored him, but he noticed Mickey give a slight nod as though in approval.

They perched themselves on hay bales, and Henry said as gently as he could, 'I know this must be hard on you, especially as you must have thought that all of this business was over and done with, but I have to ask you to tell me about that morning when you found Miss Downham's body. Did you know the young lady?'

The boy looked awkwardly at Henry and said, 'I knew who she was; she visited here, but I never spoke to her. I recognized her straight off, though, just lying there, staring up at the sky.'

'And you immediately knew she was dead? You didn't think she might just be hurt?'

Jeb nodded. 'I could see she was dead. I've seen dead sheep and dead cattle, and my grandpa when he died. Dead looks like dead.'

Henry nodded. 'It does,' he agreed. He saw the look of relief on Jeb's face that this stranger understood what he meant. 'Can you describe that moment to me, the way she was lying, what you thought? Any small thing that you observed.'

'I told this to Inspector Walker.' Jeb looked worried again. 'I'm not in trouble, am I? Did I say something wrong?'

'No, you did nothing wrong, and I've read Inspector Walker's reports, but we policeman sometimes like to ask our own questions. So humour me.'

The boy took a deep breath and glanced across at Ted. The big man shifted from foot to foot impatiently, as though he could not see the purpose of the damn fool policeman coming in and asking the same thing over and over again and upsetting the boy. Henry felt a twinge of sympathy.

Finally, Jeb said, 'She was lying on her back, her eyes open, like she was looking up at the sky. Her body looked untidy, as though she'd fallen back. Her skirt was all rucked up.' He blushed furiously. 'I remember thinking the lady wouldn't like that, not her skirts all rucked up. I touched her hand, that was all I did – I knew she was dead, but I touched her hand. She had a hand kind of stretched out on the ground and she looked so lost and sad. I know it sounds daft but I wanted to . . .'

'Comfort her? Like you might comfort a sister?'

The boy nodded. 'And then I ran to the farm and fetched Mr Linus, and Miss Lucy phoned for the police and the doctor, and Mr Linus went with me up to the gate. Miss Lucy said to take a blanket to cover her with and we took one from the stables. Mr Linus said we should cover her up, and then he said maybe not until the doctor had been there. He said something about disturbing the evidence.' Jeb looked proud of having remembered that.

'Did Mr Linus speculate on what evidence might be disturbed?' Henry asked.

The boy looked blankly at him as though he did not understand the phrase 'speculate on'. Henry let it go.

'Did you notice anything near the body – perhaps an item that had been dropped?'

He shook his head. 'I didn't notice. There were my footprints in the mud when we went back; it had rained and there were puddles near their field gate, and it was muddy on the road. They'd been ditching, fishing out mud and silt and weeds, and some of it had got on the road.'

Henry was suddenly interested. 'And did you notice any other footprints, apart from yours?'

Jeb thought about this. 'I pointed out to Mr Linus that somebody had been walking. Someone in boots. Mr Linus noticed too and then the doctor came, and he said yes, she was dead and he wrote it in his book, and that it was all right to cover her up and the police would be arriving and they would want to know what I had seen. I told him I hadn't seen anything except the young lady. But he said the police would want to know everything I had seen or heard. Inspector Walker arrived and I told him what I'd seen, and Mr Linus waited with me and told the inspector that what I said was right and that he'd come up to look at the body as soon as I told him about it.' He shrugged. 'Then I came back to the farm and got on with my work.'

'Did either of you know Brewer, the man accused of Sarah Downham's murder?'

Jeb shook his head.

Ted replied, 'I would run into the man odd times in the pub. It was hard not to know who he was – he was a loudmouth, liked to start a fight. My wife knows his sister, though, and she's a decent lady. Can't always tell, can you? Both from the same family. One turns out sound, the other turns out good for nothing.'

'And if you drank in the same places, did you ever hear rumours about Brewer and Miss Downham?'

Ted scowled. 'She was a fine young lady, visited here often enough. Ask anyone and they'd tell you she was a decent girl.'

'I don't doubt it, but even decent girls can make mistakes or have rumours spread about them.'

Ted did not look much mollified, but he said, 'From time to time, when Brewer boasted about his women, Miss Downham's name came up, but no one took any notice. She was way above him. A girl like that would never look his way. We all knew he just liked to boast. I mentioned it to Mr Linus, told him that a man like Brewer had no right to talk about a young lady from a good family like he did. Even when a story isn't true, it's like they say, mud sticks, and that ain't right. I don't like that kind of talk. I told Brewer so.'

'And how did he respond to that?'

'Same way he responded to everything else. With a loud mouth and an invitation to take the argument outside.'

'And did you?'

Ted hesitated. 'Not over that. No.'

'But over other incidents? Other talk?'

Ted looked impatient. 'Water under the bridge,' he said. 'He was mouthing off about Miss Lucy. I know for a fact Miss Lucy didn't even know the man and she'd certainly never . . . well, you know.'

Henry nodded. 'So on that occasion?'

'I gave him a bloody nose and a bruised jaw. He'd have got more if the landlord hadn't come out and told him to be on his way.'

'And this was at the Wharf?'

'The Wharf? No. I don't drink there. This was the Griffin, back in East Harborough.'

Where they'd just had lunch, Henry thought. 'It's close to the police station,' he said. 'Wasn't he afraid of the constables being called?'

'Brewer didn't give a damn about that. But the landlord didn't want that sort of trouble on his front step. Having the constables come running can give a man a bad name and that matters, especially when you have to renew your licence.' Ted frowned, 'Damn near barred me as well,' he said.

'So he barred Brewer.'

Ted nodded.

'And did you tell Linus Green about what Brewer had said?'

'I told him. Thought he had the right to know what was being said about his sister, even though there was never any truth in it.'

He pushed himself off the wall and made it clear he'd said all he was going to say. Then he unfolded his arms and picked up his fork. 'The man deserved all he got. Now, we've the beasts to muck out,' he said, 'so if you've done with the lad, we'll get on.'

Henry acknowledged that they had.

Back in the car, on their way to Glebe Farm where Ronan Kerr was employed, Mickey commented, 'He's just a boy. The sight of the dead girl is going to stay with him for a long time.'

Henry nodded. 'It is interesting that he noticed footprints. But interesting too that he talked about the ditches having recently been cleared.'

'Oh?' Mickey thought about it for a moment and then nodded. 'If the ditches had been cleaned out back in late January or early February, then what would be the need to do them again so soon? When we were viewing the scene yesterday, it was noticeable that there were piles of muck and weeds, freshly dug and dumped on the verge. Now, I'm no farmer – maybe there was a good reason. I don't know, unusually heavy rains or something, or maybe the job wasn't completed earlier.' He looked at his boss and added, 'Or maybe we are looking for clues where there are none and where we have no reason to be looking.'

'Maybe so. But . . .' Henry leaned forward and spoke to the driver, asking Cronin to head back to where Sarah Downham's body had been discovered. They had gone to the Greens' farm by another route which had taken them directly to the farm complex itself and not to the end of the footpath.

'Just to satisfy my curiosity,' Henry said.

'You're thinking it would be a good place to have thrown her boots and shoes,' Mickey speculated. 'And now someone decided they might go and fish them out?'

'Maybe. I'd just like to settle my curiosity. You know how these things nag.'

Mickey smiled. He did indeed. 'But that raises yet another question,' he said. 'If it's occurred to someone else that the killer might have thrown those items into a ditch, and it might well have done, why go looking for them now? Why not retrieve them just after the girl was killed? Or if the killer has suddenly become worried about what we might find, then the same question might apply. Anyone who had dumped Sarah Downham's footwear or who suspected another might have done so has had weeks in which to act. Why wait?'

'Why, indeed,' Henry agreed. 'And I may be chasing shadows

here, Mickey. It was just a passing thought. But if it does turn out to be a detail that bears fruit, then I can only think that someone has suddenly got worried in case the policemen from London are more thorough than the local constabulary and might look where they did not.'

'But Walker insisted that his men searched the locale thoroughly.'

'And maybe they reported that they had. But human nature being what it is—'

'And the weather being cold and wet, who'd want to go digging about in a ditch full of water or the piles of mud and foul-smelling vegetation?' Mickey added. 'Especially when everyone was certain Walker already had his man.'

They arrived back at the crime scene about ten minutes later and Henry spent some time poking around with a large stick he had found in the piles of mud on the bank. It yielded nothing and neither did his rather dangerous digging in the ditch. Henry, his sergeant thought, was leaning over much too far, and he would not have been surprised to see his boss sliding down the bank and having to be fished out. He was quite relieved when Henry gave it up and came back to the car.

'If you think it relevant, we can get some men with grappling hooks and rakes,' Mickey said.

'Perhaps. And perhaps, as we said, I'm grasping at clues that don't exist. But her boots and her shoes are somewhere.'

'And that somewhere could be anywhere. They could have been thrown into the plantation and there must be forty acres of trees to search. They could have been taken away by the killer and dumped somewhere completely different. They could have been sold on and now be on someone's feet. I'm more interested in who owned the blue dress and why they chose to take the yellow one away. What did they think it could tell us?'

Henry nodded and pulled his coat tightly around his body. 'That is a mystery to solve,' he agreed.

He's cold, Mickey thought. But then Henry rarely seemed warm; he wore a long, dark, broadcloth coat even in the summer. Even under the heat of the sun, he looked like a storm crow.

Cronin drove them to Glebe Farm, and they were directed to yet another barn, this one larger and more solidly built. A tithe barn was how it had been described. To Mickey, it looked very old and the brick and timber construction more solid than a lot of houses he'd been in.

Ronan Kerr was at the other end of the age scale to Jeb Mortimer. He might, Mickey thought, be close to seventy or he might just have had a tough life. Probably both. Somewhere in the distance, Mickey was conscious of the sound of dogs, a lot of dogs, not barking but certainly giving voice. He turned his head, trying to discern the direction. 'Are they hunting?' he asked.

'No, just out for exercise. They'll be on the leash.' Ronan Kerr nodded towards the entrance to the great barn and said, 'If you look out that way, you'll no doubt see them come along the rise.'

Curious, Mickey went across to the massive double doors and looked up the hill. Silhouetted against the washed-out afternoon grey he saw two men, running along behind about a dozen dogs. The dogs were leashed, as Kerr had said they would be. The men gripped long leads, and the pack yowled and barked and made, Mickey thought, the most undoglike noise.

'From the look of it, that'll be Roland Clark and Eddie Bryce out with the hounds,' he said, staring up at what were obviously familiar figures. 'Those dogs belong to Sir Joseph. There are two hunts hereabouts and both run beagle packs. Sir Joseph's are all dogs; Lord Rathbun takes all the bitches. But they're both from the same bloodline. The kennels are not half a mile from here.'

'They make the most ghastly noise,' Mickey commented. 'I've got to admit I like a dog with a normal bark, but I'm not too keen on any when they're running in a pack.'

Ronan Kerr seemed to find that amusing. 'As long as you're not red and don't have a bushy tail, I imagine you'll be safe enough. The morning I found the girl, there was a fox tugging at her coat. I doubt he'd have done harm, but they are curious animals.'

'We don't get that many foxes in the East End of London,'

Mickey said. 'My colleague here, the chief inspector, he grew up a country boy, so no doubt he knows all about foxes and their habits.'

Henry shook his head. 'They were certainly not welcome in my father's garden. Did you know Penny Soper? It must have been a great shock.'

'I knew who she was. She worked at the Wharf; I must have spoken to her a dozen times but no more than ordering a drink or passing the time of day. She seemed like a nice little thing – quiet. Didn't flirt as some of them do.'

'Can you tell us about that morning?'

Mickey, watching the man closely, saw him shrug. He was not a man, Mickey guessed, who was used to standing still. His hands moved absently as though he was still involved in some task, and he looked as though he would be happier when his body was once more in motion. You didn't reckon to be still when you were at work, Mickey supposed.

'I walked down as normal – there was hedging to do. A job started the day before, so we left the tools at the back of Bridges' farm, save carrying them back and forth. Bridges' land meets Glebe Farm – boundary hedges are shared between the two, so you deal with one side, you deal with both. Truth is the job should have been done a month ago, but sometimes these jobs go astray. Anyway, I walked down the road, I saw the fox rooting at something, then I saw the girl. I went close enough to check that she was dead, and although I know I shouldn't have done, I pulled her coat across to cover her. She looked . . . cold. She looked like someone had chucked her out with the rubbish, and that was all wrong.'

Mickey nodded sympathetically.

'And you touched nothing else,' Henry persisted.

The man shook his head. 'I was closer to the village than I was to the farm, so I came back to the village. Hammered on the doctor's door, and he called the police, and then we both got in his car and went back to the place where the body was. Waited there till the police got there, and I told them what I've just told you. There was nothing else to tell.'

'Did you see any footprints?'

'Footprints?'

It was clear from his tone that he'd never been asked that before, Mickey thought.

'I'm not sure I paid any mind to what was on the ground.' Kerr's body became still as he thought about it. Eventually, he said, 'I could see pawprints from the fox and yes, there were boot prints in the mud at the side of the road. A man's, from the size of them, but I couldn't tell you more than that. Work boots, cleated and hobnailed, the sort of tracks that would be left by anyone working on the farm. Nothing strange.'

It was clear there was nothing more that the man could tell them about the location or placement of the body. 'Did you know Brady Brewer?' Mickey asked.

'Saw him at the Wharf from time to time and tended to keep out of his way.' He jerked his head back towards where the dogs still howled and barked. 'From time to time he was with Roland Clark and some of the stable lads, letting off steam come pay day, so I'd be obliged to pass the time of day with him because I couldn't ignore the lads I work with. Didn't like the man. He was a loudmouth, and he had no respect, not for anyone. How that sister of his put up with him, Lord alone knows.'

'You know Miss Brewer?'

He nodded. 'Came in to help out with my wife when she was sick – she died last winter. Boss called Doctor Clark in. I was grateful; the boss picked up the bill. Doctor Clark reckoned there was nothing he could do, but he got Miss Brewer to nurse her, and the lady did a good job. She's a nice lady, kind.'

'Nothing like her brother.'

'Nothing like.'

'No one seemed surprised when Brady Brewer was accused of the murder of Sarah Downham,' Mickey said. 'Did you think him guilty?'

'Still do. Why would there be any question?'

'Because of the second death. Penelope Soper. He certainly didn't kill her.'

Ronan Kerr shrugged. 'So somebody else did it. Doesn't mean he didn't kill poor Miss Downham.'

'Did you know Miss Downham?'

'My wife used to work for the family – had to give up when she was sick. Worked in the kitchens,' he clarified. 'Miss Sarah was a sweetheart.' He smiled at what was obviously a happy memory. 'Always had the biggest smile when she was a little thing.'

'And do you have any ideas about who might have killed Penelope Soper? Surely there is not another man around here like Brady Brewer.'

Kerr laughed as though Mickey had said something really funny. 'Men like Brewer are ten a penny,' he said. 'Only difference being you could see what Brewer was just by looking; he wasn't that clever. Others hide it better.'

'Like who?'

Ronan Kerr sighed. 'Not for me to say, is it? You gentlemen know your job.'

And you would prefer to keep yours, Mickey thought. 'This Roland Clark who works with the hounds. Is he related to the doctor?'

Ronan Kerr nodded. 'The Master of the Hunt is due to retire in a few seasons; they reckon Roland will take over. Be the youngest in the history of the hunt if he does. And yes, he's related – he's Doctor Clark's son.'

'But he didn't follow his father into the family business?'

Ronan Kerr laughed and then checked himself as though his laughter was inappropriate. 'I don't think he has the temperament for doctoring,' he said. Someone called him from across the yard and he nodded to the officers and took his leave.

So, what kind of temperament does he have? Mickey wondered.

FIFTEEN

Mrs Emily Forsyth regarded Inspector Walker with a bemused expression. His request seemed to have caused her as much confusion as if he had asked for the moon to be served to him on a plate.

'You want to see Sarah's room? Why on earth would you want to do that?'

Walker decided to take refuge in blaming Henry Johnstone; it seemed easier than trying to explain anything else to this woman. She had the most obdurate expression on her face, and it was very clear to Walker that his presence was at best unwanted and at worse considered little short of an insult.

'Chief Inspector Johnstone wishes to explore every avenue,' Walker said. 'Now that we have a second murder to investigate—'

'The implication is you did not do your job well enough the first time.'

'As I say, we are exploring all avenues.' Walker tried to keep his voice even, reminding himself this was a bereaved woman; as it was now possible that Brady Brewer might not have been guilty, she could be viewed as having reason to complain.

Her look was now one of exasperation. 'Oh, very well,' she said, 'but I spoke to the chief inspector and told him all I knew, and he interviewed the staff as well. If he wished to know more, the least he could have done was to come back himself and not send an underling.'

Again, Walker fought to keep his temper in check. 'The chief inspector is presently making investigations elsewhere,' he said. 'I'm sure if there are further enquiries, he will endeavour to come and see you himself.'

Mrs Forsyth rang the bell and a servant appeared as though by magic.

'Take the inspector up to Miss Sarah's room; he wishes to

have a look around. I trust this won't take long,' she added. 'We have guests staying with us. They have gone out for the afternoon, but they will return for tea and I would like you gone before they do.'

Walker left her to her fit of pique and followed the maid up the stairs and along the landing. She opened the second door. Walker remembered the bedroom from the day Sarah Downham had been murdered. He had taken a quick look around but not felt the need to do a thorough search. After all, it had then seemed obvious who the murderer had been.

He still couldn't get to grips with the idea that he might have been wrong. In his book, Brewer was guilty. It would take a great deal more evidence to the contrary to convince him otherwise, Penelope Soper's death notwithstanding. He stepped inside the room and then stopped dead.

'Where are her things?' he asked. The room was empty. Even the carpet had been stripped from the floor, and drop cloths and tins of paint seem to indicate the intention to redecorate.

'Mrs Forsyth found it too upsetting,' the girl said. 'Her room is next door and the thought of having Miss Sarah's bedroom left the way it was, it was just too much for her.'

She shifted uneasily under Walker's gaze as though embarrassed that the murdered girl's room had been stripped so bare, her presence eliminated. This did not fit, Walker thought, with the closed curtains and air of a thoroughgoing mourning that Henry Johnstone and his sergeant had reported when they had visited.

'And when were her belongings disposed of?' he asked sharply.

The girl flushed and quailed as though she felt to blame.

He softened his tone and asked again, 'When was this done and what happened to her things?'

She looked truly awkward now, as though this was not an easy question to answer. Finally, she said, 'It was just after the funeral. The mistress told us to throw all of Miss Sarah's belongings away, but Cook said – and Miss Harris the housekeeper agreed with her – that the mistress would regret it later. That it was just the grief speaking. So we boxed everything up and put it in the big storage room at the back of the house. Cook and Miss Harris said that was the best plan.'

'Show me,' Walker told her. He followed her down the back stairs and past the kitchen, then out into the courtyard. He could see the family garden through a gate that led out of the courtyard, but this was clearly a more utilitarian space used for drying washing, and with an outside toilet and brick buildings for storing coal and garden tools.

At the end of the row of outbuildings, next to the laundry room with its coal-fired copper for heating water, was what she called the large storeroom. Inside was a mix of trestle tables, deckchairs and other garden seats, plant pots, laundry hampers and miscellaneous goods and chattels. Stacked in the corner, on a low bench, was a neat row of boxes and next to that a steamer trunk. *What would Chief Inspector Henry Johnstone do?* Walker thought, and then, knowing full well what the answer was, he took an executive decision. 'I would like you to summon a taxi for me,' he said.

She looked shocked. 'You mean to take these things away?'

'You want to know who killed your young mistress, don't you?'

'You mean that Brewer didn't do it?'

'I mean it's possible he didn't, and now another young woman is dead, and if I don't get it right this time, there may be others – you understand that, don't you? Now, I have a chief inspector and his sergeant come up from London to help me with this investigation, and we must know all there is to know. You understand that, too?'

She nodded. 'I don't know what the mistress will say.'

'Well, I hope it will be a little while before she finds out. And then I will take full responsibility. You need know nothing about it. If she asks, you can tell her that you showed me the room, but that was it. I take it she still doesn't even know that Miss Sarah's belongings have been kept?' Reason enough for the staff to keep quiet about what he planned, Walker thought. 'So, no reason for her to ask anything, is there?'

She nodded very doubtfully and then went to ask Cook to phone for a taxi, explaining that she wasn't allowed to use the telephone.

It took fifteen minutes for the taxi to arrive. Fifteen long minutes: time for Walker to ask himself over and over again if he was doing the right thing. A quick examination of the boxes indicated that some were full of books, one contained letters and what looked like schoolwork, that the trunk contained clothes. If there was something relevant in all of this, then it could be anywhere, but if they didn't go through it all, then that small, vital thing could be missed.

The taxi driver and the kitchen boy helped load everything into the vehicle. Walker found himself glancing back over his shoulder, expecting Mrs Forsyth to be staring at him accusingly through one of the windows, but she was nowhere to be seen. As they drove away, Walker wondered if he would be accused of theft, and the thought amused him. He had the feeling now that he was emulating Henry Johnstone, and it occurred to him that it was no bad thing if he was. He had deeply resented his superiors summoning of the officers from Scotland Yard, officers from the so-called Murder Squad. But, on balance, he was glad that they were here. What if someone else was killed? It came to him that there was a strong likelihood of this happening and that at least, with the other officers on the case, he would only have to share and not fully shoulder the blame.

He wasn't sure he liked himself for even thinking that.

The house that had been occupied by Penelope Soper and her family was larger than Henry expected and spoke of previously more prosperous times. The furniture was inexpensive, but well-cared-for and, though clearly old, still sound and comfortable. The famous sewing machine occupied a corner of the front parlour, in an alcove on one side of the fireplace. The other alcove contained shelves on which was sewing equipment: fabrics, baskets of threads, little bundles of lace and braid. Other shelves displayed a few treasured items: a pretty blue vase, family photographs in wooden frames, pieces of iridescent carnival glassware. A small stack of library books sat alongside another stack of cloth-bound volumes which, when Henry looked at them, seemed mostly to have been prizes for good attendance at Sunday school; from their age, he guessed they belonged to Mrs Soper. He was particularly taken by a tiny book entitled *Bingley's Bible Quadrupeds*, illustrated with pictures of four-legged animals, alongside some quite detailed description.

He left Mickey in charge of examining the rest of the ground floor, with Cronin as his assistant, while he went upstairs to examine the bedrooms.

There were two bedrooms, neat and clean, wooden floors swept and rag rugs covering the space beside the beds. The mother's room had a cot in it, which, when Henry scrutinized it, turned out to be a converted drawer. He glanced around to find the chest it might have belonged to, but there was nothing in the room that it would fit. It had perhaps been donated by a friend or neighbour, Henry thought.

The bed was covered in a thick patchwork quilt, carefully cut squares and strips stitched together, no doubt on the machine downstairs. He turned it back and examined the backing, which seemed to comprise fabric from two rather worn curtains. The fabric had once been quite rich and, though threadbare in places, still provided a resilient backing for what he guessed would be a warm quilt. From the weight of it, there was a blanket between the two layers. He remembered that first winter after his father had died when he and Cynthia had taken refuge with their mother's brother. Their uncle was a bookseller, and Cynthia had managed to blackmail him in a very public manner, sufficient that he had given them space upstairs in one of the storerooms. He had provided a mattress and some blankets, and Cynthia had scrounged winter coats from the second-hand market – those that were too worn and scruffy even for the market's customers to want. She had cut the fabric from them and stitched it together to create a thick layer to wrap over them both in the coldest weather.

They had rarely troubled the uncle for any further assistance. *We have an address now*, Cynthia had told a very young Henry. *If you have an address, you can get a job. You are not an itinerant.* He smiled bitterly at the memory, at just how many jobs Cynthia had managed in order to keep them fed, at her insistence that Henry go to school – though, later, he too had worked before and after school, as a delivery boy and anything else that came his way. They had survived.

The room that Penelope Soper had shared with her other siblings was smaller but just as neat and clean. Again, rag rugs on the floor and quilts on the bed. Shelves with a few belongings and boxes beneath the bed, largely empty. He guessed that the siblings had taken everything they owned with them to the sister's house. They would not have spare clothes to leave behind. He wondered if any of them would come back to live here. For some reason, the fact that they had not taken the quilts made him think they might. This was still home, and although at the moment it was chill, the fire not having been lit for days, he guessed that in better times it was a cheerful house, despite the father having left. Perhaps *because* he had left. Some women, Henry thought, managed better without a man.

The box beneath one of the beds had belongings inside it, and these, he realized, must be Penelope's. It contained a few carefully folded clothes; others hung on hooks behind the bedroom door, sad reminders of the young woman who had occupied this space. He shook them out gently, checking pockets. At the bottom of the box was a small bundle of letters. Henry held his breath. He untied the ribbon and opened the first, glancing at the envelope. It was addressed to Penny Soper but care of the Wharf, her place of work. Why send it there, Henry thought, unless there was some secret involved? He unfolded the letter. The handwriting was untidy; it had the look of someone writing swiftly and impatiently. There was no doubt that this was a love letter. There was no signature, just a row of x's which he took to be kisses.

He pocketed the letters and took another look around the room but found nothing more of interest. Mickey was calling him from downstairs.

Cronin stood by the cold fireplace with something in his hands. 'It was in amongst the fabrics,' he said. 'Sergeant Hitchens and I wondered if—'

Henry took the item from Cronin's hands and smoothed it out between his own. A short length of yellow cloth, fine and silky, at odds with the remnants of cotton and calico and the precious woollens with which she had made her own clothes and those of her mother and siblings.

'From Sarah's missing dress,' Henry speculated. 'We must ask Inspector Walker and also Linus Green – they both saw the dress before it went missing. And I have found something else.' He took the letters from his pocket and handed them to Mickey. 'Penelope Soper had a lover,' he said.

Sir Joseph Bright was a familiar enough figure, striding about his estate and speaking to those he employed. He was a man who knew his land, his estate, its capabilities and problems. Where a field needed regular drainage if it was to be kept from turning into a quagmire. Which crops and livestock thrived on his land and which did not. If the boundary hedges had been maintained – and if not, why not. So it was no real surprise to see him striding across the yard at Glebe Farm. He spoke briefly to the foreman and then came into the barn where Ronan Kerr was occupied spreading straw for the cows that had come in for evening milking. Sir Joseph did not keep these beasts as a commercial proposition; these were pedigree Blue Albions, with soft, brindled blue-grey coats. Sir Joseph had taken a liking to them a decade before and was now understood to be a leading breeder.

But this, Ronan Kerr thought, was not his usual time of day for a visit.

'Kerr,' he said. 'How are you? This has been a shocking year for you so far. You've barely had time to recover from the grief of losing your wife and now finding that poor girl.'

'I'm doing all right, sir.' Kerr regarded his boss with a mix of curiosity and a little trepidation.

'That's good. Very good. I understand we had a visit from our friends in the constabulary?'

'Yes, sir, they wanted to know about the day I found poor Miss Soper.'

'But you had already told all this to Inspector Walker.'

'Yes, sir, I did, but it seems this London detective likes to ask his own questions. Not that there was more I could tell him anyway.'

'No. Quite. Asked much the same things as Inspector Walker, I suppose.'

'Much the same,' Kerr agreed. 'Though he did ask if I might

have seen any footprints near the body. Inspector Walker never asked me that.'

'Footprints, eh? Interesting. And did you?'

'I told him, sir, only what you'd expect to see in mud close by a farm gate. Work boots. Footprints from men's work boots, that was all.'

'I see. Let's hope he's making more progress than just finding out that farmworkers wear boots!' Sir Joseph laughed at his own joke. 'Well, thank you, Kerr. Carry on.'

Ronan Kerr watched him as he strode back across the yard and wondered what all of that was about.

SIXTEEN

The landlord at the Wharf grudgingly admitted that the girl had letters sent for her to pick up there. But he insisted that he did not know the sender, and she'd never spoken to him about such personal matters. All he would say was that Penelope Soper was a hard worker, that she came from a decent family, and that she did not deserve what had happened.

'Did she know Brady Brewer?' Henry asked.

'Of course she did. He drank here; she must've served him from time to time.'

'She was a little young to be working behind a bar.'

The man shrugged. 'The girl helped out wherever she was needed. All the staff do. As I said, she was a good worker.'

'And did you ever have a sense that she knew Brewer better than that, than just as a customer? Or that she might have had any trouble with him?'

'She never had trouble with anyone. I made sure of that. Besides, Brewer is dead, or haven't you heard? They hanged him for killing the Downham girl. Unless you believe his ghost came back.' He laughed as though this thought amused him.

'She must have confided in someone,' Henry said as he and Mickey got back into the car.

'In my experience, young women do,' Mickey agreed. 'We need to speak to the friends that Walker has now identified, but that's a job for another day. We must deal with what we have first, see what Walker discovered and consolidate that knowledge.'

Henry nodded. 'Constable Cronin, do you happen to know anyone who is a regular drinker at the Wharf?'

'One or two, yes, sir.'

'Then perhaps you could gather some intelligence for us – see what the opinion was of Penelope Soper, and the landlord, for that matter. Find out what friends Brewer might have had, anyone of the same ilk who might have looked for vengeance on his behalf. Any gossip there might have been about the victim and a boyfriend – perhaps someone her mother would not approve of. I think you stand more chance of getting this information than we do.'

'Yes, sir,' Cronin said with alacrity. He was clearly pleased to be involved in the investigation in an active role. No doubt, Henry thought, he would be dining out on finding Sarah Downham's clothes in the barn for a good while yet.

They arrived back at the police station to find Walker supervising the dispersal of boxes and a trunk, trying to squeeze things into corners that were already full.

'What's all this?' Henry asked. He scrutinized Walker; the man looked excited and a little uneasy.

They drank very welcome tea while Walker explained to them what he had found at the Downham house and his decision to bring Sarah Downham's worldly goods back with him to the police station. It was a decision that Henry approved.

Mickey was opening the boxes and examining their contents. 'It will take us a while to get through this lot,' he said. But Henry noticed that he too sounded impressed. It was now a little after six, and they agreed that they would take the time to change shirts, wash off the grime of the day and then meet for the promised dinner. There was, Henry thought, a lot to discuss. What was less certain was what any of it meant and how it all fitted together.

Mickey announced himself to be as hungry as a hunter, and Henry was put in mind of the dogs they had seen earlier that day, the beagle pack exercising up on the hill.

'I take it hunting is a popular pursuit around here,' he said.

Walker looked up from the menu he was studying and nodded. 'Most of the landowners and a good few of the farmers partici- pate. It has a long history hereabouts, and the bloodlines of the horses and the dogs – well, some reckon they can be traced back a couple of hundred years. I don't know; it's not something that interests me particularly. It's not something that makes much trouble for the constabulary.'

'No, I imagine not,' Henry agreed. In his experience,

activities that solely involved the rich and powerful tended to
be activities that were set apart from the purview of the average
policeman. He and Mickey had on several occasions had cause
to poke about in the affairs of the gentry and knew how unwel-
come that activity made them. Cynthia was also part of that
community now, though not connected to the old money
that was so evident around here. Her husband was in business,
an industrialist, a parvenu in the view of many who had
generations of wealth and power behind them – and even those
for whom those days of wealth and power were a distant
memory. He knew many of the so-called great names who put
on a good front but were as poor as church mice when it came
to actual cash.

'It was mentioned that Doctor Clark's son may become Master
of the Hunt when this one retires.'

Walker nodded. 'He's being groomed for the position, apparently. Sir Joseph has employed him for about eighteen months
if I remember correctly. He was never an academic sort, and
though the Clarks sent him away to a good school, it never
seemed to stick. When he came back to East Harborough, he
got into some minor scrapes. Doctor Clark and Sir Joseph have
been good friends for years. I think Sir Joseph employed Roland
as a favour to the doctor, to keep the boy out of mischief.
Anyway, this time something seems to have stuck and it appears
he's doing well.'

'You seem to know quite a bit about him?' Henry said.

'Not a great deal. He got into a fist fight, was brought into the
station on one occasion. He'd come off worse, as it happens, but
he wouldn't say who'd given him the beating. We all suspected
it was Brewer; he and his cronies had certainly been present.'

'When and where?'

'A year ago, give or take. At the Griffin, as it happens. Brewer
was barred not long after. He liked to provoke arguments and
then stand back and watch the results. Liked that just as much
as he liked to use his fists.'

'And it was after this that Sir Joseph took Clark in hand?'

'No, that was the first time I really became aware of him. A
few months after that, he got blind drunk and stole a car, wrapped
it round a lamppost after a hundred yards. Fortunately, no one

was hurt, and the owner was persuaded not to press charges if Doctor Clark paid compensation. So . . .'

'Who did the car belong to?' Henry asked.

Walker laughed. 'Well, that was the odd part, I suppose. The car belonged to young Philip Maddison. It seems they'd had a quarrel about something or other – neither party would admit to what. They said it was personal. Anyway, Clark took the car, crashed it, and the constables were called. As I say, it was all sorted out privately, but I know Doctor Clark was worried about his boy. Sir Joseph seems to have stepped in to get him back on the straight and narrow. I don't know all the details, you understand. It turned out to be hardly a police matter. I just know the gossip.'

Henry nodded. 'How do you get along with Sir Joseph Bright?' he asked.

'I get along with him fine, in as much as I've spoken to him directly twice and on both of those occasions it was no more than "good morning, nice weather we are having". I have – what would the word be? – *encountered* him in his role as a magistrate on many more occasions, but that's not quite the same thing.'

'Not all of us get invited to have dinner with the gentleman,' Mickey said. Henry looked up sharply, wondering if his sergeant had been put out by the lack of an invitation, but he was reassured to see that Mickey was grinning at him, that mischievous gleam in his eye that was so familiar.

'Purely my sister's doing,' he said.

'So if Central Office at Scotland Yard had sent some other inspector to take over this investigation, Sir Joseph would have had to find another way of ingratiating himself,' Walker commented.

Henry gave him a cautious look, then nodded. 'It had crossed my mind,' he said, 'that having me here does serve Sir Joseph rather well, should he wish to keep an eye on the investigation. Or so he might think,' he added somewhat wryly. 'He does, however, have a very good selection of maps, and deep pockets when it comes to paying for our dinners and hotel bills.'

'If you plan on upsetting him,' Mickey said, 'it might be a good idea to wait until we've gone home and the bills are paid.'

The waiter arrived to take their order, and when he had gone, Henry returned to his original question. 'So you don't know him well, but you have observed him as a magistrate. And what kind of a magistrate does he make?'

Walker considered. 'He is fairer than most. He would prefer a man to be able to work off his guilt than imprison him and have the family suffer. If some arrangement can be made with the wronged party, over petty theft or damage, or drunkenness, he will do so. At least on the first or even a second offence. But if someone is brought before him the third time, then the full weight of whatever law book he can find to throw at the man certainly comes their way. He is well liked in a general sense; I've heard nothing said against him that isn't said of any landlord. He pays average wages or a little above, and he has an arrangement with Doctor Clark to deal with his tenants and his workers. He pays the good doctor some kind of stipend, I believe.'

'Generous of him, I suppose,' Mickey said.

'Generous, or simply wise, given that he would lose more work through illness that went untreated, and a landowner who is also a magistrate and trades on his good name probably won't want to have to evict too many of his tenant workers for non-payment of their rent. Most of the farmworkers' cottages are tied to the job. A proportion of the wages he pays are given back in rent. It probably balances the books one way or another. I'm probably being harsh; from what I've seen, he's a good enough employer and not an ungenerous man.'

Henry nodded. 'And from what we saw yesterday, when we were talking to Ronan Kerr, his approach certainly engenders a degree of loyalty. Kerr was genuinely grateful that Sir Joseph had called in Doctor Clark to look after his wife. Even if he did then say there was little he could do and handed over her basic nursing to Elizabeth Brewer.'

'Kerr, the man who found Penny Soper's body?' Walker asked. 'I heard he lost his wife recently.'

The conversation paused while the food arrived and then paused a little longer as they all began to eat, each man suddenly realizing he had gone without lunch and was now ravenously hungry. Even Henry recognized that he needed to eat.

Immediate hunger assuaged, he said, 'I glanced through Penny's letters when we got back to the hotel, and they are certainly passionate. And they seem to indicate a relationship going on for a while but also one that was kept quite secret.'

'But no hint as to the writer.'

'Very little. There is a sense that he does not live locally, that he is away somewhere, working most likely, and they went weeks between seeing one another. I wondered if it might be one of the barges, seeing that she worked at the wharf. The relationship, if you can call it that, has continued for almost two years.'

'So from Miss Soper being about seventeen,' Walker said. 'She didn't start working at the wharf until autumn of last year, so it's unlikely she met him there.'

'Indeed, unless she chose to work there so she could see him more frequently, without attracting too much attention. But you are probably correct. Inspector Walker, you've already made contact with friends on the list that Mrs Soper gave us – perhaps you could go back to them tomorrow and ask a direct question about this man she was involved with. Take one of the letters with you – perhaps someone will recognize the handwriting. And a sample of the yellow cloth, but leave some with me; see if anyone can confirm that it came from a dress that Miss Soper made and if that dress was for Sarah Downham. Take Mickey with you; he's good with young women. And take the blue dress from the evidence box – see if anybody recognizes that.'

Walker nodded.

'In the morning, I'll make a start on the boxes that you brought from the Downham house; I doubt much of it is relevant, but you were right to remove them, and there might be something that throws light on Miss Downham's relationships. In the afternoon, I'd like to go out to see the Greens, take some of that fabric to show Linus and Lucy Green, and also the letters. It's possible they may recognize the handwriting. I'd also like it shown at the Downham house.'

'It's a bit of a stretch, isn't it, that either the Greens or the Downhams might recognize letters written by a secret lover of Penelope Soper?' Walker asked.

'Perhaps it is, but everybody involved seems to know

everybody else involved. This is a small community with, as you yourself pointed out, few places for young people to meet. It's worth the effort, I think.'

Walker nodded. 'And all are very shaken by what has gone on. It was noticeable when I spoke to them today that they were ensuring escorts on the journey home from work, trying not to leave one another alone for too long. They are frightened, Inspector Johnstone. Convinced that the killer will strike again.'

'They are right to be so,' Henry said soberly.

She had known that he would come – she had threatened him, so what else was he likely to do? – and she had been waiting. True, she could have gone away for a time, gone to stay with friends, but Elizabeth Brewer had never backed away from anything in her life and she wasn't about to start now.

She was dozing in her chair when she heard someone pushing against the back door. It was locked, but she had no illusions about the flimsiness of the timbers. A moment later, a hefty kick sent the door crashing back against the wall and he was there.

Elizabeth was not going to go down without a fight. As he hurtled into the room, she was ready for him, poker in hand. His momentum carried him past her, and she struck out, catching him on the shoulder. He yelped and turned, slashing at her with his knife. She saw it gleaming in the firelight and brought the poker down on his hand. He yelped again and then cried out as she suddenly changed direction with her weapon, aiming for his face but catching him again on the shoulder. With her other hand she grabbed at the scarf covering his face and pulled it free.

What she had not been prepared for was the second, taller man who had followed him inside and stood for a moment in shock, clearly not expecting a woman to fight back and to do so effectively. His companion was shouting for help now, and the second man also had a knife. A moment later, Elizabeth was down, struggling for breath as the blood poured from a wound in her side.

SEVENTEEN

Where to start? Henry wondered the following morning as he surveyed Sarah Downham's belongings.

Considering that a trunk full of clothes was the least likely to produce anything of interest, he opened this first, just to get it out of the way, and one by one laid the garments out on the desk, checking pockets and linings and anywhere that a young woman might have concealed a letter or anything else of interest. Once he was satisfied that the trunk had nothing to offer, he replaced the clothes inside and pushed it back into the corner of the cramped office.

The first box he selected was full of books. These were mostly academic but with a few classics and even the odd romantic novel. The academic books – history, mathematics, basic science – had obviously been used for study and were annotated in the margins, but there was nothing of interest from Henry's point of view. Likewise, the novels and what looked to be unread classics. Odd pages remained uncut, Henry noticed, smooth, folded edges standing out amongst the deckled ones. Inscriptions on the title page revealed that they had originally belonged to Sarah's mother, although it seemed she hadn't read them either, presumably Thackeray and Dickens not being to her taste. The *Iliad* had the look of a volume that had never even had its cover cracked.

Henry replaced them in the box and turned to the next, which revealed a selection of feminine accessories. Scarves and gloves and ribbons and handkerchiefs. He was about to discard this, too, when he noticed a man's handkerchief amongst the rest, its size and practicality distinguishing it from the little squares of linen and lace. He took it out and unfolded it. It had been monogrammed with the initials AH. *Who is AH?* Henry wondered. He replaced the rest of the frippery but set this aside, noting that it was faintly perfumed as though the young woman had scented it or perhaps carried it close to her skin so that it had picked up her own floral aroma. He had noted that her clothes smelt of rosewater and something that was perhaps vanilla.

The next box contained notebooks and loose papers, and Henry was momentarily excited until he realized that these cloth-bound volumes and two little leather-bound books had also belonged to Sarah's mother. It seemed that she had kept a journal through her teenage years and into the early years of her marriage. He flicked through them quickly, placing them in date order and was struck by the poignancy of the last one which ended on 15 September, two days after the birth of her daughter. In handling the book, he had displaced pressed flowers from the later pages, and he picked them up, intending to replace them. He flicked through idly, looking for the pages they had fallen from and paused, suddenly more interested. It looked as though Sarah had used the blank pages in her mother's journal for keeping her own notes.

These were intermittent, sometimes days apart, sometimes weeks, and a quick initial glance suggested they were completely innocuous: girlish chatter about days out with friends and thoughts about Christmas and the opportunity to go to the theatre. He set the book aside, placing it beside the handkerchief, and looked through the others to see if she had used blank pages in those as well. She had: endpapers and inside covers were filled with less childish handwriting this time. From the dates, it was evident that Sarah had written these last entries in the year before her death. Perhaps, Henry thought, she was worried about keeping a journal of her own in case her father or her aunt was curious and looked inside. They would have been far less likely to examine something that had been written by another woman, so long before.

He set these aside as well, eager to read what she had written but at the same time also keen to see if there was anything else to find in amongst these boxes.

It interested him greatly that the aunt had told the servants to destroy all of this, including what were surely precious mementoes of Mr Downham's wife. Would Sarah's aunt and, more particularly, Sarah's father not wish to keep her journals, books, memories of a life lost so tragically? Presumably, Mr

Downham had grieved for his wife when she had passed. Did he even have a say in the matter of what was kept and what was discarded? Henry wondered. Or was he in agreement with his sister, that these mementoes of past lives, his wife and now his daughter, should be cast aside?

He continued the search, finding exercise books both from school and from home, copybooks from early childhood with samples of handwriting and Sarah's name, written clumsily over and over again, slowly improving. *If I had a child*, Henry thought, *I would want to keep all of this*. Well, perhaps not all of it. Essays on the Trojan wars were perhaps not particularly interesting, and simultaneous equations could get a little boring, but certainly these early examples of a child's learning. Were they not precious to the average parent? His father would have had no sympathy with such sentimental ideas, Henry knew, but he had long ago given up thinking about his father as a typical parent, preferring Cynthia's methods of child-rearing and even her husband Albert's sometimes absent-minded but nevertheless fond attitudes towards his offspring. Albert, it had to be said, was far more interested in his children now that they could actually do things; he had confessed to Henry that he was not a big fan of the baby stage. He found it messy and smelly, and considered it impossible to work out what a crying baby might want, so he had tended to leave that to his wife and nanny, who understood these things. Now that the boys could play cricket on the beach, and he could share science experiments with Melissa, he was far more enthusiastic.

Henry paused. There were plenty of memories of Sarah's mother, but where were the mementoes from her father and her aunt, the birthday cards, inscribed books perhaps, those little markers of childhood and incipient womanhood? Had they chosen to keep those things, perhaps placing them in an album or a book of remembrance or, as Cynthia and Melissa did, a treasure box?

He continued his search, looking now for anything that might have come from Sarah's aunt or father, or indeed from her prospective fiancé before she had rejected him in favour of the older and seemingly more exciting Brady Brewer. 'No,' Henry said aloud. 'I don't think I can believe this.' The more he got to know Sarah Downham, even in this precarious fashion, the more he struggled to countenance the idea that she had been involved with this older, rougher, more dangerous man.

He had engendered an image of Sarah as a wild child, trying to break free of parental control, but what he was finding was a lonely young woman who confided her thoughts to a diary, but who, it seemed, did so in such a fashion that even these thoughts were hidden. She had seemed not to particularly want to read for pleasure, unless you counted the romances which were well thumbed, but clearly had intelligence if her exercise books were anything to go by.

He went back to the steamer trunk and looked once more at the clothing. Everything was neat and plain and conventional. He thought about the clothes she had been wearing on the night she died, or at least had been wearing when she visited her friend. The brown pleated skirt, a cardigan knitted by her aunt, a white linen blouse. Clothes as boring as a secretary might wear to work. Where were the going-out dresses? The dance dresses, the more daring outfits that a girl of nineteen would want to wear? The yellow dress that Linus Green had described sounded fun and pretty, and now that he thought about it, even the scarves and gloves and stockings he had found in the other box were items he would have expected to belong to an older woman.

While it was true, Henry considered, that a less well-off girl would be likely to wear conventional clothing, to buy for quality and what would last rather than fashion, Sarah Downham was from a family that could afford luxuries. Was her aunt trying to keep her from harm by keeping her plain? Or had she perhaps taken away the fancier clothes as punishment for real or perceived indiscretions? Or was Henry now becoming fanciful?

Logging this thought and promising himself that he would address it later, Henry continued his search.

Sergeant Mickey Hitchens and Inspector Walker were interviewing more of Penelope Soper's friends, in this instance a young woman by the name of Millicent Gay. They were visiting her at work, in a haberdashery shop, and had promised the rather formidable manageress that they would only take a few minutes of the girl's time. They had been allowed to withdraw to a back room, obviously used for excess stock, separated from the shop by a curtain. Millicent kept glancing nervously at the gap in the curtain, anxious that she should be seeing to customers. Sympathetic with her anxiety, Mickey kept things short.

The yellow fabric – yes, she remembered Penny sewing the dress, but she hadn't known who it was for until Sarah turned up one night wearing it. It was, she said, a beautiful dress, with rather a low neckline. 'Not outrageously low, just lower than she normally wore. Her aunt liked her to be turned out properly.' She glanced again at the curtain and then leaned forward towards Mickey. 'I think she got changed at a friend's house,' she confided. 'It would not be the kind of dress that Mrs Forsyth approved of. I heard that her aunt told her to get rid of it and that Sarah had told her she had. Her aunt threatened to cut it up!'

Mickey expressed his shock.

She had no idea about the letter writer and didn't remember Penny talking about any young man. 'Hilary might know – Hilary Benson. They were really close. Hilary's been absolutely devastated by Penny's murder. Her mother says she might have to get the doctor in to treat her for her nerves.'

She did not recognize the blue dress but speculated that it might be one that Penny had sewn because the stitching looked like hers.

Mickey let her get back to work, and he and Inspector Walker thanked the manageress for her invaluable assistance before they left.

'Where will we find Hilary Benson?' he asked Walker.

'Probably at home. When I spoke to her yesterday, she was indeed prostrate with anxiety and grief. Her parents told me she had been like this since Penny Soper's death. She was clearly grieving her friend, but she also seemed of a rather nervous disposition. Her mother called her a delicate girl, which in my experience usually describe someone who doesn't cope very well with life.'

'I don't know that any of us would cope very well with our friends being murdered,' Mickey observed.

Walker conceded the point.

*   *   *

Hilary Benson was a pale girl. Mickey guessed she would have been a pale girl even before this added pain, but the whiteness of her skin and blueness of her lips suggested not just excessive grief but also genuine illness. Perhaps she really was a delicate girl, Mickey thought.

Her mother hovered, offering tea and then fluttering beside the couch, as though reluctant to leave her daughter with these two men, even to fulfil the duties of hospitality. Mickey put her out of her misery by refusing on behalf of both himself and Walker. Something told him that tea served in this house would be as weak and pale as the daughter, and he hated weak tea.

He glanced at Walker who took the hint and asked the mother if he could have a quick word, privately. She retreated with him to the hall but left the door half open. Mickey began to wonder if he really did look so suspicious that he needed supervision. He smiled at Hilary and took the fragment of yellow fabric from his pocket.

'Do you recognize this? Do you remember Penny sewing this fabric into a dress?'

She took the fabric between both her hands and stroked it gently. She nodded. 'She made a dress for Sarah. Poor Sarah; they're both gone now.' She looked as though she was about to cry, and Mickey carefully took the fabric from her and tucked it back into his pocket before removing the blue dress from the brown paper bundle in which he was carrying it.

'And this,' he asked. 'Do you recognize this dress?'

Again, she nodded. 'It was Penny's. Where did you get it?'

It seemed like an odd question, Mickey thought. 'Where might I have got it from?' he asked.

'She said she lost it. It was missing.'

'Missing from where?'

'From her work.'

'At the Wharf?'

She shook her head rapidly. 'No, she doesn't get changed at the Wharf. At the Bear, they have rooms there and she cleans. Or she did . . .'

'She was a chambermaid?' This was the first Mickey had heard of it.

'On Sundays. It can be hard to get people to work on Sundays. She went after church, did her shift from two in the afternoon, came back about eight o'clock at night.'

'And where is the Bear?' he asked.

'On the London Road, heading up towards Stonesby. It's mostly used by the hunting set, those that don't stay with Sir Joseph or Lord Rathbun.'

'And Penny kept a change of clothes there?'

'No, she changed into her uniform when she got there, then she changed back into her dress. The blue dress – that was one of her church dresses. She used to say it was smart and simple. She either wore that one or the grey one. The fabric was made over from a dress that was given to her – by Mrs Forsyth, I think. She took it apart and made it to fit herself. So upset she was, when it went missing; it meant she had to come home in her uniform and that's not allowed. The landlord at the Bear is very strict.'

'I see,' Mickey said. 'Do you remember when it went missing?'

'Two or three weeks before . . . before—' She looked about to break down and Mickey quickly intervened.

'Thank you,' he said, 'that's very helpful. I'm going to ask you another question now, a rather personal one, but very important.' He produced the letter from his pocket and said, 'Have you seen this before, or do you recognize the handwriting? Do you know who it might be from? I'm told you and Penny were very close, that you were very special friends and she might have confided in you.'

The pale face flushed for a moment. She took the letter and examined it carefully, and Mickey had the distinct impression that this was not the first time she had seen it, this or one similar. He leaned closer and asked very quietly, 'Did she have a young man? Someone she wanted to keep secret?'

Hilary hesitated and then nodded just slightly. 'I don't who he is,' she whispered. 'I got the impression that he was well set-up and that.' She glanced towards the door, to where her mother and Walker stood talking in the hall, and continued, 'I got the impression he might have been married. She was really secretive about him.'

'And have you any idea where she might have become acquainted with her young man? Or any special place they might meet?'

She shook her head.

'Not even a tiny idea?' She wanted to tell; Mickey could see that. Wanted to unburden herself.

'The Railway Hotel.' This was more breath than words, as though she was fearful of being overheard. 'Not here, over in Market Harborough. No one knew her over there. She knew it was wrong, but she did love him so much.'

Henry's search through the boxes was bearing even more fruit, although he wasn't exactly certain of the significance of what he'd found. A bundle of press clippings had been folded into an envelope and this envelope stacked in the middle of other stationery so that a quick glance would not reveal its presence. He opened it up and lay the contents out on the table. About a dozen clippings, carefully folded together and all on the same subject. Attacks on young women, going back three or four years. No one had died, but the girls involved had been grabbed and assaulted, and, in the later clippings, they reported that their assailant had put his hands about their neck and squeezed. Two girls had lost consciousness; one had hit her head badly as she had fallen and required stitches.

Henry checked the dates. Three years and eight months ago to the present, the latest incident from five months ago, the couple of months before Sarah Downham had been killed. The girl had been grabbed as she had left her place of work in East Harborough. She had been late out due to a stocktake, fortunately in the company of another young woman and a supervisor. She had just had time to scream before he clamped a gloved hand across her mouth, and the other young woman had come running, swiftly followed by the supervisor. Outnumbered, the man had taken to his heels. The girl had been badly shaken and her dress torn, the heel of one shoe wrenched off as he had tried to drag her into an alleyway. It could, Henry reflected, have been so much worse. Was this an opportunistic attack? Or had the man been watching the girl and just not realized that she was in company with others?

Why, Henry wondered, had he not been told about these incidents before? Had no one made the connection?

There was a map of the local area pinned on to the wall, and Henry took the clippings over to the map and studied the locations. All had taken place within something like a ten-mile radius, he reckoned, but the actual incidents were well spread out, and when he read the details closely, there was sufficient difference that it might be possible for these to be seen as individual, one-off incidents, not a series of events. He had made the connection because he had seen all the clippings in one place, and looking at the byline for each one, he realized that someone else had made the connection, too, even though he had not explicitly expressed it. Henry wondered why that might be. The journalist who had written these reports clearly had an eye for detail; he had recorded many fragments of information about the victim, often without giving away their name, about the location of the assault, about what they and the man had been wearing, but had not suggested that one man might be responsible.

And, of course, Henry realized, at least one other person had made the connection, too. Sarah Downham. What had her interest been? Had she known any of the victims? Had this interest, perchance, led her into danger? And who else had she told? He would bet whatever cash he had in his wallet that she had confided in Penny Soper.

A quick enquiry with the desk sergeant told him where he might find the journalist. A few minutes later, Henry was in the car and on his way, Cronin driving again.

'Do you know this Percival White?'

Cronin nodded. 'He is a writer of some kind – does articles for three or maybe four of the local newspapers.'

'And what does he normally cover?'

'Anything and everything. I suppose in the big newspapers journalists might specialize; I see the same person in the nationals write about crime, or politics, or cooking. My mum reads the cooking columns. And the gossip. Round here, though, the newspapers aren't very big, so many come out weekly. The *Eastern Echo* is our local and comes out on a Friday night and has a special page listing all the upcoming social events for the next two weeks. Mr White writes about everything from the hunting to the village fetes in the summer. He covers the court cases sometimes and occasionally goes into Leicester and reports on the racing. Sometimes the editor sends him to places, I think, and sometimes he writes his own articles and tries to sell them.'

'You know quite a bit about him.'

Cronin shrugged. 'Not really. I run into him quite often at the magistrates' court; sometimes there are long gaps between anything happening, so we got chatting one day. He wanted to know why I became a policeman, and I wanted to know why he wrote stuff.'

'And his private life – is he married? How long has he lived here?'

'Not married. He lives in a boarding house, could probably afford to live in a better place, but he said he likes the landlady and she does have a reputation for being a fine cook. Her name is Mrs Rogers,' he added, 'and I think he grew up round here. Went away to London for a bit, and then I think he spent some time in Manchester. He came home when his mother was really sick. After she died, she left him a bit of cash, so he decided to concentrate on his writing, live in the boarding house and work for the newspapers.'

Henry was amused. 'You seem to have interviewed him very thoroughly in your conversation with him,' he said.

'I knew him slightly before,' Cronin said. 'My mother knew his mother and they both knew Mrs Rogers. You know how it is – this is a small place, and everyone knows everyone.'

'I'm beginning to realize that.'

They pulled up outside a tall and impressive-looking terraced house on the edge of town, and Henry realized that he probably could have walked the distance in about a quarter of an hour. The house looked clean and scrubbed, in a street of clean, scrubbed houses, doorsteps gleaming and net curtains sparkling white. 'Come in and introduce me,' Henry said, noting the alacrity with which Cronin obliged. He was obviously enjoying himself, Henry thought. He wondered what the prospects for promotion were like in a place like this and decided they were probably slim.

A neat woman opened the door, dressed in a pale-blue print with a white lace collar and her grey hair curled into a high bun. She recognized Cronin immediately. 'Why, Billy Cronin, what brings you here?'

Henry left the constable to make the introduction and to ask if Percival White might be available as the chief inspector had some questions to ask about some articles he'd written.

'The chief inspector thinks they might shed some light on the Penny Soper murder,' Cronin said, an edge of excitement in his voice.

Mrs Rogers looked impressed. 'Well, there's a thing. You go into the front parlour, gentlemen, and I will go and fetch Mr White.'

What was it about front parlours, Henry thought, that they always had that same air of formality and neglect? Even though this one was clean and polished, it still had a slightly forlorn air, as though it would like to be used more often, rather than be kept for visiting vicars and policemen. The furniture was comfortable, if a little overstuffed, the mantle clock ticked pleasantly, and there were books on the shelves in the alcoves that reminded him oddly of those he had found in Sarah Downham's boxes, the ones that had belonged to her mother but had never been read. A gas fire had replaced the open hearth. Shivering suddenly, he wished someone would light the thing.

A few minutes later, Mrs Rogers was back, a dark-haired man in tow. He looked slightly perturbed but gave Constable Cronin a warm smile and extended a hand to Henry. 'Percival White,' he said. 'Mrs Rogers said you wanted to ask about some articles I had written. I think I know the ones you are referring to.'

Henry noticed Mrs Rogers nodding approvingly, as though this was something that she was privy to and it was about time the police took notice. She bent to light the fire and then announced that she was going to make them all some coffee. Henry took the newspaper clippings from the envelope and handed them to Percival White. He glanced through them and then looked up at Henry. 'You are, of course, missing the most recent.'

'Sarah Downham was not available to collect clippings about her own death or that of her friend, Penelope Soper,' Henry said.

The journalist looked at him in surprise. 'Miss Downham collected these? What on earth for?'

'Did you know Miss Downham?'

'I knew who she was. I know her father to pass the time of day with, and her aunt, Mrs Forsyth, frequently turns up on committees that I'm reporting on. She believes in good works, does Mrs Forsyth.' It was said dryly, as though Percival White was not keen on the lady.

'And what about Penelope Soper? Did you know her?'

'No, not at all. It's a bad business, Chief Inspector, and, as you'll see from my articles, one that has been continuing for quite some time. It was inevitable, I suppose, that it would end in murder.'

'And yet you have not publicly made the connection or spoken to the police about this conclusion that all of these cases may be connected.'

Percival White laughed harshly. 'My editor, or should I say my editors, for I have three, will not publish what they call dangerous speculation or anything that is not in the public interest. It was suggested that I might just frighten the horses, or the community, or whatever.' He waved a dismissive hand, but Henry could see the tiredness in his eyes, could see that he was a man who could imagine the worst that life could serve up and then had the misfortune to be present at the full banquet. White, he guessed, was in his mid-thirties, but the lines on his face made him look older.

'And the police?'

'The attacks have taken place both here and in the neighbouring county. Three different constabularies have been involved, and six local police officers, all from different stations, have looked into the incidents. As far as I know, none of those six officers has spoken to the others about any of these incidents, and they are sufficiently diverse, geographically, for them to hold to the opinion that different men may be responsible.

Particularly as the witness statements are not always consistent. Two of the girls speak of the man as being over six feet tall. Three of them say he was not tall but very broad. One that he had a local accent and another convinced that he was from London – the girl herself never having been anywhere near London but—'

Henry nodded. 'I find witness statements are rarely reliable. People notice what most frightens them and that often in fragments. Tell me, did you ever consider that Brewer might be responsible for these other attacks?'

'Considered it, did not rule it out completely, but it seemed unlikely. For one thing, Brewer was questioned over three of them and had a sound alibi for each. On one of those occasions, he was in the Wharf, the pub that's right on the border with Northamptonshire, as you might have realized. The landlord gave him an alibi for that night, backed up by a dozen patrons. The other two incidents were on the other side of the county, and again he was alibied. On one occasion, I believe, he was doing some work for Sir Joseph Bright, under the supervision of the estate manager, and on the other occasion, the Greens made a statement that he was on their farm. That's the farm close to where Sarah Downham was found.'

Henry nodded. 'I have spoken to them,' he said.

'It was harvest-time, so everyone capable of walking and holding any kind of implement was on one farm or another. His sister was there as well, I believe. Elizabeth Brewer.'

'You know Elizabeth Brewer?'

'"Know" is too strong a word; I am acquainted with her. Doctor Clark uses her from time to time as a temporary nurse, and she nursed my mother in the last weeks of her life. I came back permanently a few days before my mother died and, yes, I did get to know Miss Brewer then. To be frank, though, she was too busy looking after my mother, and I was too busy trying to make sense of my mother's affairs to have long conversations. She seemed like a pleasant lady and anybody you talk to will tell you the same. Miss Brewer is as different from her brother as chalk is to cheese.'

The coffee arrived, and while it was being poured, Henry shuffled once more through the press clippings. Then, cradling the cup and saucer between his hands, he said, 'Mr White, I'm assuming you took notes and made observations that did not make it into the newspapers.'

Percival White nodded, his eyes suddenly less tired, his face a little less lined. 'I did, indeed,' he said, 'and, believe me, I would be more than happy to share them with someone who actually listens to me. These two murders did not come out of nowhere; I'm convinced that they are linked to these previous attacks. I'm also convinced that the killer is very familiar with this whole area, that he knows the footpaths and the shortcuts and the communities, and who is likely to be alone and when and what risks he can take. I am certain, Chief Inspector, that those two girls died because no one took my earlier claims seriously. They were busy looking for some gypsy or traveller or outsider who happened to be passing through, someone who saw a girl, attacked her and then went on his way. No one looked seriously at their own communities or those of their neighbours or looked to see if there were any connections between the young women or any similarities.'

'No one except you?'

Percival White laughed. 'I suppose I became a little obsessed with the stories,' he admitted. 'And I suppose I was in a prime position to notice the similarities. I can, if I'm honest, understand why they went unnoticed, but what I find so hard is that when I drew them to the attention of my editors, to the authorities, even to Sir Joseph Bright who, as a local magistrate, should really be more concerned, I found myself dismissed. I almost found myself out of a job. No one wanted to know, Inspector. Random attacks on young women are one thing. Unfortunate, reprehensible, but isolated. The idea that these incidents might be down to one man, who was becoming more and more violent as time went on, frankly I think that frightens people to a far greater extent. Frightens them into denial. And, of course, the longer it goes on, the more people are caught up, either as victims or investigators, and the more difficult it is for anyone to admit they might have been wrong in the first place – that had a connection been made, something could have been done at an earlier stage.'

Henry nodded. 'Did you speak to Inspector Walker about any of this?'

For the first time, White seemed to hesitate. 'I did,' he said, 'but the inspector believed he had got his man. He was interested only in seeing Brewer hang for the death of Sarah Downham and made it plain he did not want the distraction of some random, barely employed scribbler trying to steal his thunder.' He paused as though suddenly aware of how bitter he sounded, and as though reminding himself that he was speaking to another policeman. He went on, 'You know, I suppose, that Walker had a history with Brewer?'

'I know that he arrested him previously. You are referring to another kind of history?'

'Yes. An argument about a woman. A woman that was engaged to Inspector Walker. It seems she was a woman of some independent means, and Brewer somehow inveigled his way into her affections. Now Walker maintains that Brewer stole from her, but Brewer maintained that the woman gave him money of her own accord. To cut a long story short, it led to a major row between the three of them; the engagement was broken off, the woman left the area, and Brewer never stopped aggravating the inspector about his not being able to hold on to his fiancée.'

'The name of this woman? You know where she is now?'

White looked confused. 'Why the devil does that matter? It's ancient history. True, it might well have coloured Walker's attitude towards Brady Brewer, but the circumstantial evidence was so strong that anybody would have found him guilty, personal grudge or no.'

'Perhaps so. But I would still like to trace this woman.'

'Her name was Holly Machin, and I believe she is now in Liverpool. She had family there. Beyond that, I can tell you very little. She was widowed; the husband was a business associate of Mr Downham's, I believe, so they may be able to tell you more. All of this happened about five years ago. Machin was a solicitor, mostly engaged with conveyancing and property law. When he died, he left his wife the house and an annuity, and some ready cash in the bank. I don't know how much of it she had left by the time Brewer finished with her – or the nature of their relationship. Whatever it was, she and Walker broke off their engagement.'

Henry glanced at his watch. Mickey and Walker would soon be back at the police station, and he wanted to see what the morning had added to their knowledge. 'Mr White, if you would be so good as to gather all of your notes together, then perhaps my sergeant and I can call back this evening. At perhaps eight o'clock – that is, if Mrs Rogers could be prevailed upon to give us use of her front parlour again.'

'I'm sure Mrs Rogers would be delighted,' Percival White told him. 'One of the young women who was attacked, Belinda Masefield, was a great-niece of Mrs Rogers. As you can imagine, she has a vested interest in this being solved.'

EIGHTEEN

B y the time Henry returned to the police station, Walker and Mickey were already there. Walker had arranged for sandwiches to be sent in, and Mickey had set aside a plate for Henry. From the look on their faces, he guessed that they too had had a successful morning.

Over a hasty lunch, they exchanged information. Henry had not yet read the diary entries that Sarah Downham had made in her mother's journals, so that was a task for the afternoon. Other friends who had been spoken to that morning had reiterated the idea that Penelope Soper definitely had a young man, or not-so-young man, that he was likely married and probably in his thirties. This speculation had been pieced together by small things she had said, and the friends had talked about it after her death but not really known what to do with the information they had. He supposed it had been a relief to reveal their suspicions and anxieties to someone, and he was aware that it must have been in all of their minds that perhaps this man had killed their friend.

'It's interesting,' he said, 'but many people still adhere to the belief that Brady Brewer killed Sarah Downham and someone else was responsible for the copycat killing of Penelope Soper.'

'I still believe that is possible,' Walker admitted.

'Well, for now we will keep an open mind. We may be looking for one killer; we may be looking for two. I don't want to close down any avenues.' Henry paused before adding, 'It was brought to my attention this morning that you had previous dealings of a personal nature with Brady Brewer. That you were engaged to be married to a woman who became involved in some way with Brewer. Because of that, the engagement was broken.'

Henry noticed that Mickey raised an interested eyebrow and that Walker, who had been about to take a bite from his sandwich, paused and set it down on his plate.

'No doubt Percival White was the source of your information.'

'He was, but what is the truth of it?'

'You believe that my personal involvement with Brewer affected my investigation?'

'Actually, no, I don't. Circumstantial evidence was strong, and Brewer had form. I would also have called him in for questioning and probably drawn the same conclusions, at least at first. Additionally, the community supported the accusation. No one seemed in the least disturbed that Brewer stood accused – in fact, from all I've heard, it's likely that they were probably relieved. He was an unpleasant and dangerous man, and his guilt would probably not be questioned. Most people would simply consider that the world was a better place without him. If this second murder had not taken place, no doubt they would continue to believe so, and I'm not surprised that so many still hold the idea that Brewer was guilty of Sarah Downham's killing. Perhaps he was. But now we have other things stirred into the mix and we have to examine them carefully.'

'The other attacks.' Mickey nodded. 'I think Percival White's analysis is correct: the attacks would escalate and, in time, undoubtedly lead to murder, though examining the newspaper reports and comparing them to the deaths we're investigating, there does seem to have been a sudden escalation of violence. That makes me question just a little, not necessarily that whoever was responsible for these initial attacks was not responsible also for the murders, but whether there was anything in between that we don't know about.'

'Sometimes criminals do take unexpected leaps in their modus operandi. But I do take your point, and that should be examined. Perhaps White can cast light on that or at least be set the task of going back over newspaper reports. I got the impression that the man wanted to be involved, so we may as well make use of him. However,' he added, turning to Walker, 'your previous involvement with Brewer is also a consideration here.'

'I treated him fairly. I put personal matters aside, I followed the evidence.' Walker's tone was sharp.

'I'm not doubting your word, but I'm also told that Brewer goaded you after your fiancée left. That can't have been easy.

I *am* saying that you were and still are predisposed to believe him capable of almost anything, and that belief undoubtedly impinged on your judgement, however careful you believe yourself to have been. I would like to speak to the lady concerned.'

Walker's face was red, and Henry could see that his hands were trembling. Of course he was angry, Henry thought; in Walker's place, he would have been incandescent. But the questions had to be asked, the doubts had to be aired. 'I'm told she left for Liverpool,' Henry persisted. 'Do you have an address for her?'

'None of this is your concern, or hers.' Walker's tone was now one of controlled fury.

'Anything that calls your judgement into question is my concern. Mrs Machin may know something that casts light on Brewer's behaviour, which perhaps even casts light on Sarah Downham's death.'

Walker did not reply. He turned on his heel and left the office.

'You're hard on him.' Henry did not think that Mickey sounded particularly concerned.

'No one seems to have asked questions that should have been asked, or to have pursued any narrative other than Brady Brewer's guilt.'

'A guilt you were ready enough to believe in when Elizabeth Brewer first asked us for help,' Mickey observed.

Henry frowned, but then nodded. Mickey was right, of course. 'Because his guilt was so easy to believe,' he agreed. 'And I don't blame Walker for drawing the conclusion he did. As you say, I was more than prepared to accept the man's guilt at face value, given what we both know of him. But now we have a second murder to consider, quite aside from the idea that Brewer may not have committed the first. We know there is someone else out there who is attacking young women and has now, it seems, graduated from assault to rape and murder. Maybe he was copying Brewer.'

'Sarah Downham's rape was not made public,' Mickey reminded him. 'The family managed to keep that part of the offence quiet.'

'Which doesn't mean that the public didn't know – only that it wasn't discussed openly or reported in the newspapers.'

'True. So a copycat or a double murderer – either way, he needs finding.'

'It's only the geographic proximity that causes us to doubt Brewer's guilt,' Henry added. 'If the murder of Penny Soper had taken place twenty miles away, it's unlikely the connection would even have been made. It would likely be a different constabulary, another county, another community looking for the scapegoat either of a stranger come into their midst or a hated member of their own town or village.'

'That's a rather stark view of humanity, even for you,' Mickey observed.

'Maybe I'm feeling in a stark mood. That aside, we must dig deeper; we do need to have some history of Brewer's behaviour since he came back here. If Brewer was responsible for Sarah Downham's death, if his sister was lying about his alibi, it means that whoever killed Penelope Soper copied Brewer's actions closely; they knew exactly what he did, even down to the way the body was laid out. The similarities are so strong and so telling, both from the evidence of the post-mortem and from the account of witnesses, and, yes, I know that eyewitness accounts often go astray, but most of the details were corroborated.

'Alternatively, if Brewer did not kill Sarah Downham, then someone was responsible for making it look as though he did, planting his glove, acting in such a way that Brewer was implicated. Either way, we're back to the observation that everybody knows everybody else around here, which means that someone in this community knows who the killer is.'

'And why particularly do you want to talk to Mrs Machin?' Mickey added.

'Brady Brewer seems to all appearances to have convinced Sarah Downham that he cared about her. Initially at least. How did he do that? She was a young woman of good education, from a family with a social position far above Brewer's. Yes, sometimes young women are careless with their affections or make bad judgements, but there is usually a reason for that. The man involved usually offers some incentive that cannot be equalled elsewhere. What was it Brewer offered? How did he convince Sarah Downham that despite what everyone said about him, he was now a different man, one she could trust? The Brewer we knew certainly didn't possess that degree of subtlety.'

'It's a long time since we had any dealings with him. Men do change, for better or worse, though it's hard to believe someone like Brewer could shift his habits so dramatically. You're thinking that however he caught Sarah Downham, he may have used the same technique with Mrs Machin.'

'I'm thinking it possible. Again, a woman of some means, from a good background and about to make a decent marriage, though perhaps a somewhat unusual one. Going from the position of solicitor's wife to the spouse of an inspector is not exactly socially – or financially – improving, for that matter.'

'But a fine match for an inspector,' Mickey agreed. 'A woman with property and an annuity and money in the bank. It would not be unappealing.'

'And so I wonder if the quarrel was not so much about Brewer taking advantage as the lady realizing that both men essentially wanted the same thing. Walker, of course, would have been a better match; I do believe him to be a decent man. More than can be said for Brewer. But the fundamental basis for the relationship might be the same, notwithstanding any attractiveness of the lady herself.'

Henry saw Mickey nod, taking all of this on board. 'So we need to make peace with Walker, find out where the lady is and what she saw in Brady Brewer,' Mickey agreed. He drank the last of his tea and reached for his coat. 'I'd better go and find him, then.'

Henry nodded. 'You'll do a better job of it than I would,' he conceded. 'Bring him back here; in the meantime, I'll read what Sarah Downham wrote in her mother's journals, see if that sheds any further light on what the girl was up to.'

'Good idea, but I think that we might go alone to see Percival White this evening; there's nothing to be gained by rubbing Walker's nose in the past, and if White is like the other journalists we know, he won't be able to resist.'

Again, Henry agreed. Mickey left, and Henry called for more tea, then settled to finish his sandwiches and read what Sarah Downham's views on life had been.

*   *   *

It was an hour later, the reception clock just striking a quarter past three, when Mickey returned with Walker in tow. The man was still scowling but seemed slightly mollified. Henry did not wait for either of them to pass comment but instead placed the journal he had been reading on the table and pointed.

> We have gathered all of the press clippings that we could find, and there are so many I can hardly believe it. After poor Rita was attacked so horribly, and we all decided that we had to do something, it has been the most exciting thing in my very dull life. Of course, it is hard for me to get out and speak to people, as Aunt Emily watches every-thing I do. Or at least she thinks she does! If she knew how many times I have escaped of an evening, she would be appalled.
>
> But I have done my utmost to gather what intelligence I can. Intelligence is what Lucy calls it, like a spy! Imagine! Rita says that the police seem uninterested, and she was warned that by making a fuss about what happened, she is making herself a target for gossip. But Rita is braver than that.

Walker pulled up a chair and sat down, and Henry knew that he was more interested in the information than he was in pursuing his grievance. He was, Henry thought, at heart a good detective. He watched as Walker flicked through the next pages, Mickey reading over his shoulder.

'There is more on the same subject,' Henry said, 'but it tells us very little more. Most of what she says refers to the clippings or repeats what Rita Covington told her or suggests that the cook likes to gossip and to pick over the more sordid details. And that Elizabeth Brewer warned her she should leave all of this well alone. Which may or may not be signifi-cant, depending on whether or not Miss Brewer suspected her brother may be involved.'

'None of the witness statements speak of a man as heavyset as Brewer. True, I suspected him because of his history, but . . . So, this Rita Covington, she was the second girl to be attacked. This was in Selford village.'

'The November before last,' Henry confirmed. 'That is close to the Wharf, is it not?'

'Very close. A few hundred yards past the public house, there is a church set off on the right. A few hundred yards past that, on the main street, is a post office, and close to that is where the attack took place. There's a small alleyway that leads back to the next street. It's not a significant village in terms of size, a main street which is mostly larger and older houses, one of which used to be a coaching inn. That's at the other end of the village from the Wharf and it's now a private residence. When the canals were at their height, the place was prosperous, but it's gone downhill in more recent times. Alleyways and narrow roads lead off the main thoroughfare to cottages, mostly for farmworkers and some who worked on the canals. At that time of night, it's a very quiet place.'

'And where was the young lady going?' Mickey asked.

'She was going home from visiting a friend, at the other end of the village. They were both student teachers at the village school and, as you'll see from Sarah's later notes, had been engaged in setting spelling and maths tests for the children. Rita Covington left at nine; she would have walked past the post office, as I understand it, and then down the alleyway where she was attacked. Her house is just at the end of that path.

'From the look of the newspaper reports,' Walker added, 'and what Sarah Downham added in her notes, the young woman had just turned into the alleyway when she was grabbed. The man put his hand around her mouth, groped between her legs. She struggled, kicked out at him and probably made contact with his shin. She knows she made contact with something hard and bony. He then pushed her to the ground and ran away, and she started to scream.'

Henry nodded. 'Help arrived within moments, but there was no sign of the man, so where did he get to? I'd like to walk the scene, try to work out the way he might've gone, and also speak to Rita Covington. And Lucy Green. Seeing that she is the other girl mentioned as having turned detective. Out of the four of them, two are now dead. The killer of Penelope Soper is still out there – let us put aside arguments over Brady Brewer just now – and the chances are this second killer believes he can be identified by these other two women. They may not know the name, but they may know something about him that is perceived as a threat. I think it's fair to assume that the lives of both Lucy Green and Rita Covington are in danger.'

Henry glanced at his watch. 'Inspector Walker, can you make arrangements for Rita Covington to come and speak to us tomorrow, or we will go and speak to her. Lucy Green, too. Though I'd like to go across to the Greens' now and talk to that young woman. I find it very significant Penny Soper was murdered so close to the Greens' farm. And I'm sure that Lucy Green must be quite fearful. She must recognize the threat.'

'I think when we've spoken to her, we should advise her to go away for a while,' Walker said. 'And Rita Covington. And we need to know who else they might have confided in.'

'With some urgency,' Henry agreed.

'You and Inspector Walker should go to visit the Greens',' Mickey suggested. 'I'd like to take a proper look at Sarah Downham's notes in her diary, see if any of it chimes with what their friends told Inspector Walker and me this morning.'

Henry and Walker eyed one another uneasily, and then Henry nodded agreement. He knew exactly what his sergeant was doing. *Sort yourselves out*, Mickey was saying. *Bury the hatchet. This is far too important for the pair of you to be at each other's throats when there are murders to solve.*

NINETEEN

'You have an unusual relationship with your sergeant,' Walker said. They had sat for the first few minutes of the drive in uneasy silence, but he was the first to break it.

'I do,' Henry agreed. 'We met in a fox hole in no-man's land. Mickey was part of a tank crew; we had both become separated from what was left of our battalions and neither of us was exactly in good shape. The rest of Mickey's crew had perished. We made our way back to the lines, or where we thought the lines were, only to find that things had moved. Anyway, the friendship began then and has continued since.'

'You mentioned he will be promoted soon. That will be hard, on both of you.'

Henry frowned; this conversation was becoming too personal for his liking. He said, 'Mickey deserves the promotion; he'll do well enough without me.'

He knew that it was on the tip of Walker's tongue to ask, *And you – will you do well?* Henry's scowl seemed to put paid to that intention.

'This so-called investigation that Sarah Downham and her friends were involved with, was there any sense from her writings that they had done more than gather information?'

'She seems to have asked questions but is a little vague about who she put these questions to. But it seems likely that someone was threatened by what the girls were doing.'

'No doubt they just saw it as exciting,' Walker said. 'Life gets dull; it must get particularly dull for intelligent young women whose only options in life are dead-end jobs or marriage.'

Henry nodded. 'And Mrs Machin – did she want more?'

He watched as Walker sought to control his temper. Yes, this was intrusive questioning, but Henry did need to know. Finally, Walker said, 'She is definitely an intelligent woman and I

considered her to be a very attractive one. Her first husband
had been older than her, but they'd had a happy marriage, and
she was very much involved in his business affairs. He always
said that she was cleverer than he was by a country mile.'

'You knew the husband, then?'

'We were good friends, despite the difference in age. He was
a very humorous man, a raconteur and also a very fair man; he
liked to look at an argument from all sides and sometimes,
as a result, he was deliberately provocative. I liked him very
much, and I also grew very fond of his wife. After Machin
died, Holly and I became close, and out of the friendship we
already had something else began to blossom. I genuinely cared
for her, Inspector Johnstone, and I believe that she cared for
me. Then she met Brewer.'

'And what was the attraction there? It seems strange.'

'It seems absurd. I made the mistake of telling her that the
friendship was ill-advised and inappropriate, which, of course,
was a red rag. She decided that he was misunderstood, that
he was really, despite what everyone said, a sound and sensitive
man – Lord alone knows how he convinced her of that. Of
course, she knew Elizabeth Brewer and that may have swayed
her opinion.'

'In what capacity did she know Miss Brewer?' He was
unsurprised when Walker supplied that it was via Dr Clark
and that Miss Brewer had helped out in the last days of Mr
Machin's life.

'She is a woman who seems to be everywhere at once,'
Henry observed.

'She's a single woman, without commitment apart from her
brother, who needs to earn a living. She's proved herself reliable, she is a capable nurse, and this is a small community.'

Henry nodded, but even so it seemed to him that Elizabeth
Brewer was thoroughly enmeshed within that community and
that this involvement had given Brady Brewer access to individuals and opportunities he might not have had otherwise.

'You clearly respect Elizabeth Brewer and yet you did not
believe her alibi or even give her the chance to prove it correct.
Why was that?'

'Because her one fault in life was her utter devotion to her brother. I think she knew what he was, perhaps even some of what he'd done, but she had looked after him as a child, raised him when their parents died and was reluctant to believe that he might be a lost cause. In short, Inspector, she loved him, and I think she still does. She believed absolutely in his innocence, at least as far as Sarah Downham was concerned. I didn't believe the alibi because I know Elizabeth Brewer and I know how devoted she was to her only family. I think she genuinely believed that he had reformed, or at least she wanted to believe so badly that she was prepared to give him the benefit of the doubt. She wouldn't be the first or the last to have a blind spot where a loved one is concerned. And, as it happens, I did examine the alibi situation closely enough to be satisfied that no one else could corroborate it. They were alone; no one saw either of them that night, so we would only have had her word. When she contacted you, why did you do nothing about it?'

It was a fair point, Henry thought. 'Because we have known Brewer, Mickey and I both, we knew what kind of man he was. And I'm afraid I thought he might be guilty of anything, including murder. I knew he had in the past been guilty of murder and rape, but this was in the war and nothing could be proved. If I'm honest, I went through the rest of the war hoping that a bullet would find him, or that he'd be blown up and bits of him scattered across some shell hole. But good men died, and he came through relatively unscathed. He took a bullet to the shoulder late in the war, but it was little more than a flesh wound. It would have left an ugly scar but no more than that. The man walked away from death; I didn't much care that death had found him now, at the end of the noose. Somehow it seemed only fair. The only thing that saddened me was the death of a young woman, and if I'm honest, I didn't give a damn whether Brewer was guilty or not of that particular crime. Or at least it never occurred to me that he might be innocent.'

They had reached the Greens' farm and were soon ushered into the massive kitchen. Lucy Green was cooking, juggling pans on a solid and impressive-looking range, helped by a young girl who looked barely old enough to be out of school but who seemed at home with the food preparation. She was clearly surprised to see them; Linus had told her that he had met Inspector Johnstone, she said. She asked what she could do for them.

'I'd like a few minutes of your time,' Henry said. 'To ask you about the little investigation you and Sarah Downham, and Penny Soper and Rita Covington were carrying out.'

She looked shocked and nervously pushed a strand of fair hair back behind her ear. 'Jenny, can you hold the fort for a few minutes?' she asked, then led the inspectors out of the kitchen and into a small sitting room. The fire in the hearth had not long been lit; compared with the heat of the kitchen, this room felt chilly. Henry watched as Lucy sought to gain some thinking time by poking at the coals and adding more wood. Finally, she asked, 'Do you think he might come after me, whoever it was that killed Penny?'

Penny, Henry noticed. Not Penny and Sarah. Lucy's voice was carefully controlled, but her pale cheeks were suddenly flushed, and he sensed that she'd been trying hard not to think of this possibility. That his arrival with Inspector Walker had crystalized her fears.

'We are concerned about the possibility,' Walker said. 'Four of you, it seems, were involved in some scheme to uncover who had attacked your friend, Miss Covington. Other young women, too. Now two of your group are dead.'

'Brady Brewer killed Sarah.' Lucy's voice was suddenly harsh. She looked directly at Walker, and Henry noted that the baby-blue eyes were damp with unshed tears. 'You arrested him. He was hanged. He killed her.'

'We are no longer certain of that,' Henry told her.

Lucy's hand flew to her mouth. 'No! He killed her – I know he did.'

'And how do you know that?' Henry asked her. He tried to keep his voice low and sympathetic but was aware that he still sounded sharp. He tried again. 'Miss Green, what makes you so certain that Brewer took Sarah Downham's life? I know the evidence was convincing, but—'

'He threatened her!' Lucy almost shouted the words.

'You never told me that.' Walker sounded aggrieved. 'Miss Green, we spoke several times and you never told me that.'

'I didn't think there was a need. You'd charged him, then he went to court and the jury found him guilty. I didn't think . . . didn't think I needed to.'

'Was there some reason you wanted to keep the threat quiet?' Henry asked her. 'Something you didn't want made public?'

She bent to poke the fire again, stabbing angrily at the logs, her face turned away. 'Sarah wanted to end all contact with him. She said that Brady Brewer wanted things. Wanted to do things that she wasn't . . . just wasn't willing to do. He said he would spread stories about her, about the two of them, and then, when she told him she didn't care and that no one would believe his word against hers, he threatened her, said she was playing with his feelings, that she'd led him on. But she'd never do that. Never! He said he'd a right to expect what she'd promised, but I knew Sarah, and she'd never have done anything, especially not with him.' The poker slipped from her hand and rattled to the hearth.

'Had she ever been romantically involved with Brewer?'

'Romantically! No, never. Never anything like that. He said he liked her, and I think she thought it might be fun, you know, to see him, but never anything like that.'

'Miss Green, this is a delicate question, but do you think . . . do you believe that your friend, Sarah, did anything that Brewer might have misconstrued?'

Walker looked as uncomfortable asking the question as Lucy Green looked trying to answer it.

'No. I don't know,' she said. 'Mostly, they met at Miss Brewer's house. Elizabeth knew both our families. She thought it was all right if she met Brady there.'

Brady, Henry noted. Not Brewer. 'And did you all know Mr Brewer well? Because of your acquaintance with his sister?'

'I . . . I suppose so. He was just always around. We knew him from when we were children. I don't think we ever thought he would . . . well, you know.'

'See either of you in a romantic light,' Henry said.

'Romantic!' She shook her head. 'Thank you for putting it so delicately, Inspector, but I don't think he had romance on his mind. Anyway, he'd have known how my father would react if he even looked the wrong way at *me*. Look, he'd sometimes turn up to walk his sister home or he'd be working here or even for Sarah's family. He was just someone we were acquainted with. That was all.'

Henry paused, getting his thoughts in order. 'So why did Sarah Downham go out of her way to be friendly with Mr Brewer? Please, don't deny it, Miss Green; there is sufficient evidence that Miss Downham was involved with Mr Brewer – even his sister believed that she had feelings for him and that those feelings were returned.'

This might have been stretching the truth a little, Henry thought. But not so much. Both Sarah Downham's family and Elizabeth Brewer had taken what they had seen as the burgeoning relationship seriously.

What little colour remained in her face now drained. 'No,' she said. 'There was never anything. How could you even think that? Sarah just thought . . . We'd been looking into the attacks on those other girls. We'd asked all sorts of questions, but no one took us seriously. We just weren't getting anywhere, and it seemed so unfair! Rita might have been killed! Those other girls might have been killed. No one would tell us anything, and we couldn't get to the people we really wanted to talk to. People who might know something.'

'The criminal classes,' Walker said dryly. 'Miss Green, it seems to me the four of you were playing a very dangerous game. Two of you are now dead.'

'And so Sarah Downham thought she would bring Brady Brewer into your little game.'

'It wasn't a game! But yes, she thought Brady might know something or be able to find out something. I mean, I know what people said about him, but we didn't think . . . I mean, surely he couldn't . . . wouldn't like the idea of young women being attacked and, well, you know . . . interfered with.'

'But something changed your mind about that,' Henry pointed out. 'By the time of his arrest, you readily believed him capable of raping and murdering your friend.'

He was aware of Walker's slight shock and of Lucy Green's more acute one. Again, the hands flew to her mouth and this time the tears overflowed. 'He threatened her,' Lucy sobbed. 'He said she'd led him on and he'd be within his rights to take what she'd promised. But I knew Sarah, and she'd never . . . never . . . not with a man like that. Not with anyone.'

She had more or less repeated what she had said before, Henry noted. It was evidently something she had thought deeply about, something she had done her best to convince herself was true. Did that mean she recognized there might be some truth in this allegation? That Sarah Downham may have seemed willing to offer more than she actually intended? Henry waited until the young woman had regained some control and then asked, 'And who was Penelope Soper seeing? Do you know the name of her young man?'

He watched the various emotions chase across Lucy's expression. He watched her working out what she should say. 'Is he married, Miss Green?'

'Married, no.'

'But you know who he is?'

She hesitated, but the floodgates were open now and she couldn't stop herself. 'It's Philip,' she said. 'Philip Maddison. They couldn't tell anyone. Their families, especially his family, they really wouldn't approve.'

'Philip Maddison. The young man Sarah Downham's family wanted her to marry?'

'Yes. Sarah didn't want him. They'd been friends as children. He was nice then. I don't really know what Penny saw in him. We thought maybe she was flattered. I mean, a man like that, with money and prospects.'

'I can see that would be appealing for a girl of her background and class,' Henry agreed. 'Did she believe that his feelings were genuine?'

It seemed to take forever, but eventually Lucy Green nodded. 'They had been writing to one another; he had his letters sent to the Wharf so her mother wouldn't see. You don't know what it was like for Penny, everybody depending on her – she was working all the hours God sent just to try to keep their heads above water. That stepfather of hers did absolutely nothing – when things got difficult, he just walked out on them.'

'It seemed he wanted his children back,' Henry suggested. 'Apparently he approached them one day in the marketplace and confronted Miss Soper about this.'

She nodded. 'Yes, Penny told me. But they didn't want to go – why should they? He was nothing but a brute when he lived with them, far too handy with his fists, especially when he was drunk – and that was all the time.'

'And yet legally he is within his rights to claim his children back.'

'You can tell it's men that write the laws,' she said bitterly. 'Penny would have moved heaven and earth to look after her little sister and brothers – she already was.'

'And do you think that she hoped Philip Maddison would help her? After all, he is a man of means with a good career ahead of him. Do you think she hoped for marriage?'

Lucy sighed deeply, and Henry had the impression that all the energy had finally been sucked out of her. For the first time since they had entered the room, she left the fire and sank into one of the easy chairs. Henry motioned to Walker to do the same, and they seated themselves on the sofa opposite. 'Do you think she hoped for marriage?'

'I think Penny knew better than that,' she said. 'His family would never have stood for it, would they? She wasn't the kind of girl they could have introduced into his kind of society. No, I don't believe she thought that, but I believe she would have given a great deal just for some financial security, just until the children were grown enough to take care of themselves, and I think she thought that Philip might provide that. After all, it's not unknown, is it, for a man to—'

'Keep a mistress,' Henry finished for her.

'It sounds so cheap when you put it like that. Look, there is only so much money that one girl can earn, even working as many hours as she did. Her mother wasn't capable; her aunt tried to help, but she isn't much better off. I think if she could have trusted her stepfather with the children, then she would have persuaded her mother at least to let the older ones go; that would have taken a little of the strain off her. As it was, I think she felt there weren't many options left.'

'Let's leave Miss Soper aside for a moment. The night Sarah died, you know she changed her clothes? When she visited her friends in Naseby, she was wearing a brown pleated skirt, a cardigan and a white blouse. But when her body was found, she was wearing—'

'Her yellow dress – yes, I know. Penny made it for her. Linus told me what she was wearing. It took ages to save for the fabric because her aunt kept track of every bit of money Sarah had. She's a mean-minded woman; she claimed she wanted to try to keep Sarah safe, but she gave her no freedom, the tiniest of allowances, and then made her account for every penny she spent.'

'And yet she was wandering at night, unaccompanied and in the loneliest of places.'

'Her family believed she would be given a lift home, because she always was. I think she lied to everybody about that. She must've got changed somewhere between Naseby and where she was killed.'

'And you also know where she was going?' Henry was guessing here, but Lucy nodded.

'I don't know all of it. She said that she was going away. That she had persuaded Philip to give her some money. It was only a few months before she would come into her mother's legacy, when she turned twenty. If she had lived another three months, she would have been independent. Her father tried to get it changed; he didn't believe that any girl was responsible at twenty, and he tried to get the lawyers to change it to twenty-five. Sarah was desperately scared that he would succeed, but it turned out that her mother had a very good lawyer draw up her will.' Lucy smiled, as though at a sweet memory. 'She was so excited.'

'And Philip Maddison had agreed to help?'

'Her family wanted the marriage brought forward; they were absolutely insistent that the pair of them would get married, but neither of them wanted it. Sarah wanted to live a little before she was tied down, and I suspect that Philip felt the same. I don't think Penny was the only one, if you see what I mean. Philip likes female company, always has. I hoped Penny would come to her senses before she committed too much to him. But I knew she was desperate. And to give Philip his due, I believe he felt as much for Penny as he was capable of feeling for anyone, and I think he would have treated her fairly. Anyway, Sarah and Philip had stayed friends, and there weren't many people she could ask.'

'And yet you told me none of this.' Walker was positively accusatory now.

'What good would it have done? She was scared of Brewer, afraid of what he would tell her family and afraid of what he might make her do. She wanted to get away from him, so she confessed to Philip, told him what we had all been doing, and why, and although he told us we were stupid and irresponsible, he sympathized. He had agreed to help her.'

'And where was he planning to meet her? Is that why she changed into the yellow dress? She was meeting Philip? From the description I've had of it, it was not a travelling dress.'

'No, it wasn't, and I don't know why she changed into it. It seems such a strange thing to do. I know she'd packed a bag and she'd left it in a barn somewhere near Naseby. She planned on collecting the bag and walking back along the footpath to East Harborough and then catching a train. That's all I know.'

'So late at night?'

'There is a train from East Harborough into Leicester at eleven p.m. She planned to book into a hotel there for the night and then go on the following morning. I don't know much more. I just remember thinking that she would be far away, and then the news came about her body being found.'

'And did Philip Maddison get in touch with you?'

'The following day, he telephoned the house, and I spoke to him. He was shocked and devastated, the same as we all were. *He'd* been able to get away and would be able to carve out a life for himself, but Sarah never would, not now.'

'You say that her aunt kept Sarah on a tight rein, and yet she went to dances, and she went wandering at night on her own.'

'What harm can anyone come to at a dance at the Temperance Hall, a five-minute walk from home? And as for wandering at night, Sarah had become an expert at getting out of the house unseen. Her aunt locked her door at night, but the window latch was broken and could be lifted, and she was always good at climbing.'

'And when she went to Miss Brewer's home?'

'The Downhams trusted Elizabeth, and at first they didn't take any account of Brady Brewer. He was so far beneath them that they didn't even seem to notice his existence, except when they needed something lifting or carrying. By the time they had to take notice of him, it was far too late. No one will trust Elizabeth now, of course, and her name is mud in every house in the area; I imagine she's lost work right, left and centre. Even Doctor Clark wouldn't employ her, not after it came out about Brady Brewer. Elizabeth is blameless. Or maybe not entirely blameless – maybe she genuinely believed that her brother had changed and Sarah might be good for him. I don't know. People delude themselves about those they love, don't they? Anyway, most of the time, her family didn't know Sarah had gone to Elizabeth's house. The family assumed she was here. Our father is away a lot, and even when he is here, if it isn't a horse or a dog, he doesn't take much notice of it. If they'd asked him if Sarah had come here on a particular night, he wouldn't have known. He would have just told her aunt and her father to ask me.'

She sounded scathing, Henry noted, and he remembered the day when he had seen the older Mr Green and his son Linus walking together at the crime scene. Linus's tolerant disregard of his father's conversation, his mind clearly elsewhere, even while he made stock answers to the older man. The impression Henry had then was that Mr Green needed neither encouragement to make conversation nor much in the way of response. He was a man who just assumed everyone must be listening to him.

He changed tack slightly and asked, 'And how far had your investigation proceeded?'

She looked embarrassed. 'In truth, not very far. We had gathered as much information as we could from newspaper reports and village gossip. We knew that perhaps eight or ten other girls had been attacked in the last two years. Rita probably found out the most – after all, she had been a victim, so people were inclined to tell her things that had happened to others, and all the rumours that had been spread about who might be responsible. She was also the victim of gossip – women, in the main, asking what on earth a girl was doing out at that time on her own. Women can be mean to other women. Fortunately, the family is well thought of, and her parents put paid to that kind of talk. But there was a moment when she thought she might lose her job.'

'It is a harsh judgement when the victim is suspected of having brought misfortune on herself,' Henry agreed.

Lucy nodded and then said, 'With Sarah, I did wonder about the dress. I wondered if it might be just a celebration for her, that she changed because she was about to get her freedom. The yellow dress was special. But I was also worried, when Linus told me, that people would judge her. It was bad enough when Rita was attacked, all the gossiping and the snide remarks behind her back, that somehow she was to blame. I couldn't bear that happening to Sarah; none of us could.'

'So did you do something about it?' Walker asked.

'Not me, but Penny did. Sarah's aunt had given Penny an old dress, of good blue wool, and Penny had made it into something for herself. Sarah's aunt is stouter than Penny was, so there was plenty of fabric. If you remember, Inspector Walker, we all came to the police station at different points, to give statements and tell you what we knew.'

'It seems that you came to give statements but told me very little,' Walker objected.

'I'm really sorry.'

'Go on,' Henry told her.

'Well, it was easy to see where the evidence was kept, as the door marked *Evidence Room* is close to your office. So we knew where the yellow dress would be. And we knew where the keys would be kept, because we'd noticed that, too – they're all on a rack behind the desk with labels. It wasn't that hard to distract the desk sergeant with a question, and then Penny slipped in and changed the dress. She put the blue one in its place, so that if her aunt or her father should happen to see it, they wouldn't . . . well, they wouldn't think badly. Or at least not worse than they already were. That was a few days after Sarah was found. She told me she waited until the desk sergeant was distracted and then slipped by him. Then she made a big fuss about her dress going missing because she knew her mother would wonder what had happened when she didn't wear it for church. Penny didn't have enough clothes that its loss wouldn't be noticed at home.'

She paused and then added, 'I have never seen anyone as angry as Mr Downham was, not even my father when someone shot one of his dogs. And believe me, he was so furious and overheated that day he could have started a fire. The day after Sarah's body was found, her father and her aunt came here and demanded to know what had been going on behind their backs. Linus and I told them that nothing had, that Sarah had done nothing wrong. And even if she had, she was dead, wasn't she?'

'And raped. But that was not made part of the public record,' Henry added.

The flush was back again, her cheeks reddening, but she nodded. 'They seem to think she deserved it, that she must've done something. Brewer had been spreading rumours, and they had heard them and believed them, and that was when her aunt started locking Sarah's door. The night she went across to Naseby, it was the first time she'd been allowed out in two weeks, and it was only because the families were close, they were considered respectable, and Mr Downham knew that they would make sure she got home safely. Or that was what everybody thought.'

'And they let her walk?'

'Actually, she walked with me. I'd been visiting that day. We walked to the farm together and then she went on.' She looked suddenly embarrassed. 'I'd brought a carpet bag with me. Sarah had packed a few things into it. When we left, I carried the bag. Everyone would have thought it was mine. Not that anyone took any notice of us. She should have been long gone from here by morning. She took the bag with her when we parted at the farm. Naseby village is only a ten-minute walk from here.'

Henry nodded but a question was forming in his mind. It was Walker who asked it.

'But why go to such elaborate lengths? The family wanted her to marry Philip Maddison. She had presumably agreed, even if that agreement was under duress. If Maddison had promised to help her, then surely she could simply have visited him, with the blessing of her family, and just not gone through with the marriage.'

'It was too late for that,' Lucy said. 'They had arranged a

special licence. The two families had agreed, and both Sarah and Philip had to pretend to go along with their plans so as not to arouse suspicion. The marriage was to have taken place three days after Sarah was murdered. They were going to escort her there and see her married. No church ceremony, no friends, no dress . . . They told her just two days before she died. Had she refused, they threatened to cast her out, and then what would she do? Everyone would have believed the rumours about her. You see, Inspector, they'd pushed her into a corner, and Sarah didn't know how else to solve her problem. She felt she had no choice, and she fought her way out the only way she could.'

'Was there no one who could have given her shelter?' Henry asked pointedly.

Lucy shrugged helplessly. 'This is my father's house, Inspector. I allowed Philip to send money for her here. He wrote to Linus as we felt that would seem less suspicious. But beyond that . . . My family agreed that I can go away to study. That fight was hard enough. It was only Linus hinting that he would not want me to be a future burden that made my father change his mind. The land matters to him. He married late, and when he dies and after Linus is married, my brother will certainly have to take responsibility for our mother. To have the keeping of a sister as well would be unreasonable.'

Henry had the sense that he was hearing the argument as they had rehearsed it. He found himself hoping that Miss Green would find the success and independence she clearly hoped for. 'And there was no one else?'

It was more statement than question. It was clear that none of Sarah's friends was in a position to offer her sanctuary. All young, most not as financially well-off as Sarah Downham, and if she had come to them with the rumours and threats represented by Brady Brewer piled on her shoulders, that would touch them as well. In a city, she might have found a place in a women's hotel or hostel, decent places which gave a young woman a secure address – as Cynthia had always maintained, once you had an address you could get a decent job and climb through life from there.

'And so she tried to leave—'

'And someone killed her, and I still believe it was Brady Brewer. The things he said about her . . . no wonder she needed to get away.'

Henry paused, glanced at Walker and wondered how he should phrase the next question. He decided he should be direct. 'Miss Green, did you have any sense that Miss Downham had feelings for anyone? Not for Philip Maddison, obviously, but for someone within your circle?'

She frowned. 'Why would you think that?'

'I've had reason to look through her belongings, as you know. That is how I found out about your . . . investigation. I also found reference to a young man she seemed fond of—'

'You examined her personal things?'

He could see that she was genuinely shocked. 'Murder removes all claim on privacy,' he said as gently as he could, aware that his tone still sounded cold. 'There was mention of someone with the initials AH.'

She looked puzzled. Shook her head. 'I can't think of anyone. Except, except maybe . . . but he wasn't a friend of Sarah's; he was someone Philip and Linus used to know, someone their age. And that's Aiden Hughes. But I don't think they've seen him in ages; he was just a school friend.'

'And you can think of no one else? Nothing she might have said that did not make sense at the time?'

Again, she shook her head. 'Poor Sarah,' she said softly. 'Inspector, I think I've had my fill of men. It seems to me that they are far more trouble than they are worth.'

'I suppose that is one mystery solved,' Walker said as they left. He was clearly still deeply annoyed.

'One of many. If I remember right, Philip Maddison was due at the Downham house this Saturday, so tomorrow. I think we will pay them all a visit and then invite the young man to come to the station for a formal interview.'

'Do you think Lucy Green might be right about the yellow dress, that Sarah put it on as a celebration?'

'I think it's possible, but why not wait until she reached the hotel and relative safety? As I said, it wasn't a travelling dress

from the sound of it. No, I still believe she was meeting somebody. Somebody special, someone she wanted to impress.'

'Well, not Brewer, then,' Walker said wryly. 'Can't see him
being particularly interested in pretty dresses. And evidently
not Philip Maddison; he was interviewed at the time and has
an alibi for the day before Sarah was killed and also the evening
of her death. He was still away from home and attending lectures
all the day before.'

'And yet he mentioned nothing to you about her planning to
leave.'

'No, he did not. Perhaps he thought that would only bring
trouble down on his own head and on Lucy Green, and that
nothing would be gained by admitting he was helping Sarah
Downham to run away.'

'Well, perhaps our mysterious AH is this Aiden Hughes and
they were going to run off together. Do you have any knowledge
of the man?'

'If I remember, he was one of the men who confirmed Brewer
was at the Wharf the night one of the girls was attacked. I don't
recall that he has a record.'

'And he also knew Philip Maddison and Linus Green. And
yes, I understand, everyone seems known to everyone else
around here. But he's worth looking into. And where did the
carpet bag get to? We found only the skirt, blouse and cardigan
in the barn. Why leave those behind? She could easily have
packed them in her bag.'

'Perhaps because she didn't like them?' Walker suggested.

Henry realized he may have a point. 'Perhaps. She would have
been carrying a bag with her clothes and her shoes and presumably whatever money she could lay her hands on and whatever
Philip Maddison had sent to her – she would probably have been
worth robbing. And she was wearing her boots. So, we now have
more of her belongings to look for. Whoever attacked her must
have taken them away. It's possible they kept hold of them.'

'That would be useful,' Walker agreed. 'So where now?'

'To visit Elizabeth Brewer. I want to know if she was privy
to this plan to run away. If she was, then the chances are Brady
Brewer knew about it, too.'

TWENTY

Constable Cronin drove the short distance to King's Toll and pulled up outside Elizabeth Brewer's house. Henry immediately had the feeling of something being wrong, and when he knocked on the door, this was confirmed by a neighbour coming out to see who he was.

'But don't you know already that she's not here? She's in the hospital. Man, she was attacked last night, in her own home – surely you know that?'

Henry exchanged a glance with the equally puzzled Walker. 'Where has she been taken?' he asked. They were told that she was in Market Harborough, that the local constable had seen to things, whatever that meant. Then, asking if they could get inside the cottage, they were told to go round the back.

The back door hung loosely on its hinges; it looked as though it had been kicked open. Inside the previously neat cottage, furniture had been overturned and the deep reddish brown of blood stained the braided rug beside the now cold fire.

Henry knelt and examined the bloodstain. It was extensive and seeped through to the floor beneath. He realized from talking to the neighbour that she had survived only because they had heard the noise of the door being broken down. Whoever had done this had been confident they could attack quickly and be gone before anyone could see them. He had no doubt the intent had been to kill, but Elizabeth Brewer had apparently still been alive when they had fled the scene – although they may not have realized that. Looking at the amount of blood she must've lost, he did wonder if that was still the case.

'Why were we not informed?' he asked Walker.

'Different divisions within the county. Although geographically King's Toll is closer to East Harborough and even closer to Husbands Bosworth, it falls within the purview of Market Harborough, and to make it even more complicated, the local constable they mentioned lives in this village. Of course, he would be first summoned, and equally naturally he would report to his own station. It seems to me she is lucky to have survived at all.'

'Indeed. So that will be our next destination, and presumably we will need to speak to your colleagues in the local constabulary. If I leave that job to you, I will see what I can find out from Elizabeth Brewer, if she can speak to me. If she is still alive.'

They were silent on the fifteen-minute drive. Henry found himself regretting that this woman might be hurt or dead; he had liked her, even if he had not believed everything she had told him. Constable Cronin dropped him at the hospital and then took Walker the short distance to the police station. A few minutes later, Henry was standing beside Elizabeth Brewer's bed, struck by how much could change in so short a time. She was still alive, just, but had lost a great deal of blood and lapsed into unconsciousness. Her doctor was not sure if or when she would wake.

She looked like a shadow of herself, Henry thought, the powerful and somewhat squared-off woman now diminished and deathly pale.

'Can you tell me what might've happened to her?' he asked the doctor.

'From what I can gather, the neighbours heard the noise and the sound of a fight. Thankfully, they went to investigate very quickly and saw two men run away. Both had scarves tied across their faces, but one was tall and the other not so much. One of the neighbours gave chase; the man and his wife who live immediately next door went inside and found Miss Brewer lying on the rug beside the fire. They thought she must be dead, but then they saw her hand move. It is possible that she fought back. There was a poker lying close by, but she had no real chance against two of them. It was the stab wounds that were most serious.' He lifted one of the blankets and showed Henry the bandages wrapped around the woman's waist, thickly padded on one side. 'She was lucky; it's likely the blade went wide and there was no time for a second strike. She was lucky also that her neighbour had the wisdom to pack the wound and bind it tight.'

'Miss Brewer had nursing training,' Henry said. 'I wonder if she was conscious enough to instruct her.'

'I don't know, but it undoubtedly saved her life.'

'Has she regained consciousness since being brought here?'

'Intermittently. But there's no way of knowing when or if that will happen again. She lost a lot of blood – surgery was lengthy, and there was also the blow to her head, although whether that was inflicted by her attackers or when she fell, I can't tell.'

Henry nodded. 'If she regains consciousness, would you be so good as to inform me? If you contact the police station in East Harborough, they can likely get a message to me. This evening I will be at the Three Cranes Hotel, so you could reach me there.'

The doctor promised that instructions would be left at the nurses' station, and Henry figured that was all he could do for the time being. Why had she been attacked? Why now? What did her attackers think she had told him? What did they think she knew? What had she done to bring this rage down upon her?

He waited just inside the reception area until Cronin and Walker returned. Walker had been able to read the statements taken from the neighbours, but they added little to what Henry had found out, apart from the confirmation of his suspicion that Elizabeth Brewer had been just conscious and able to instruct her friends in how to bandage her wound. It had been the landlord of the pub opposite the house who had taken her to the hospital, laying her on the back seat of his car, wrapped in blankets. That, too, Henry considered, had contributed to her survival. Whoever had attacked her probably assumed that she was now dead and was no longer a threat, and Henry knew that could be to their advantage.

He remembered belatedly that they had intended to speak to Percival White that evening and made a mental note that he must contact the journalist when they got back to the hotel. He made a second mental note to ask about Aiden Hughes, and if Mr White had ever come across the name, but there seemed little more that could usefully be done this evening. The investigation into Elizabeth Brewer's attack was out of his hands, and there was a lot to think about. He found that he was eager to sit down with Mickey and discuss what they knew so far and plan what to do next.

Back at the police station, Walker announced that he would have to stay for a little while to catch up on some paperwork, and Henry and Mickey left to return to the hotel. Mickey was shocked to hear about the attack on Elizabeth Brewer.

'Whose cage did she rattle?' he wondered.

'I think we may be closing in,' Henry said. 'Someone clearly believes that Miss Brewer told us something, or more likely that she knows something she could tell the police. We just have to hope that she wakes up.'

TWENTY-ONE

L eaving through the back door at eight o'clock, he did not see the shadow in the flat cap following him, nor did he notice the soft and even footfall in his wake. In truth, he was so intent on his purpose that there was no caution in his movements or even keen observation.

He wandered for a while through the back streets, unusually quiet tonight. The threat of attack was keeping the women inside and the men close by. The mist and drizzle no doubt added to the sense that it was better to be by a warm fire. These were not ideal conditions; he preferred clear nights when he could see the moon and there was light enough to see their faces, but tonight the streetlights would have to do. His arm and shoulder ached from where that bitch had hit him with the poker. He smiled, though, at the thought that they had done for her good and proper. Teach her to threaten him! The truth was the violence of the previous evening had just heightened the desire for more of the same.

He spotted the girl as she left work, leaving by the shop door and shouting goodbye to someone inside. She looked left and right, clearly anxious, and then took off at a swift walk. He followed the girl. The shadow followed him.

It was not long before she became aware of him. She glanced back over her shoulder and then quickened her pace, and he could see her looking around and wondering where she could go to call for help. But the street was deserted, shops closed for the night, businesses shuttered and dark. This was not a residential street, and no one would hear her if she cried out for help. No one would respond if she hammered on the doors. He quickened his own pace to match hers, his pulse racing now, the anticipation burning.

She began to run, and he gave up all pretence that he was merely someone who happened to be in the same street. He ran after her, long legs eating up the ground; he could hear her heels clattering against the pavement, and she was whimpering, too frightened and breathless even to scream.

He reached out and grabbed her, first catching a sleeve and then her arm, swivelling her around, his free hand going to her throat, grasping and squeezing and pushing back so that she staggered and flailed her arms, fearing that she was about fall. He had glimpsed a dark space between two buildings that would be perfect for his purpose.

She struck out at him, pulling at his scarf, her gloved hands against his face not even leaving a mark. She reached wildly for his eyes, for his hair, but he could see the hope and the fight fading from her gaze, and he took a deep and satisfied breath. She struck him again, on the shoulder and upper arm, and he flinched as she made contact with the heavy bruising. He gripped her more tightly.

And then it all went wrong. There was a shout, words he didn't catch – just the sense of noise behind him. The sound of running feet and, worst of all, the sharp blast of a whistle. Police, it must be the police. In his heart of hearts, he knew it had been stupid, seeking out a woman in town and not in a more remote area, but this time the opportunity had just not arisen, so he had taken the risk.

He let go of the girl and took to his heels, vaguely aware that she had run off in the opposite direction. What if she recognized him? What if she knew him? He didn't think there was any possibility of that, but she might be able to give a description. His heart pounding and breath gasping in his lungs, he dodged down side streets and back alleys and through the back door, took a moment to compose himself and then walked softly upstairs. No one heard.

Neither he nor the girl stayed around long enough to see the shadow in the flat cap detach itself from the deep shadows between the houses and slip the whistle back into a pocket.

Half an hour later, two women made their way into the police station. The girl was visibly distressed. Her mother, arms folded over a faded brown coat, was simply angry.

'Decent people can't walk the streets,' she declared. 'And here you are, telling me you know nothing about this attack on my Mildred, when one of your constables frightened the devil off by blowing on his whistle. Loud enough to wake the dead it was, so my Mildred told me. She was too scared to stick around and see what happened after that. I told her the constable must have given chase and that she must come along now and tell you what happened. The devil might still be out there.'

Walker, standing in the doorway to the reception area, preparing to leave for the night, listened to this exchange and realized that his desk sergeant had no idea what the woman was talking about. 'Have any of our constables reported this incident?' he asked.

It seemed no one had. 'That would have been Priestley's beat, but he checked in not ten minutes ago, said all was quiet. He did mention having heard a whistle, but thought it was kids mucking about because when he went in the direction from where the whistle sounded, he could see nothing, just empty streets.'

Walker had been about to head for home; he was tired and frustrated, but this sounded at the very least a strange and possibly important incident.

He didn't see why he should be the only one to have his evening interrupted and so he told the desk sergeant to phone the Three Cranes Hotel and summon Detective Chief Inspector Johnstone and his sergeant to hear what the young woman and her mother had to say. Then he led them through to his little office and offered them tea.

Shakily, Mildred told her story, with many interruptions from Mrs Jones. Henry and Mickey arrived some ten minutes later and the story was told again, Mildred seeming a little more confident this time and Henry imperiously silencing the older woman with a raised hand. She looked outraged, but, to Walker's surprise, she shut up.

'Describe this man to me,' Henry demanded.

'I don't remember much; it was all so shocking.'

Mickey leaned forward and asked to examine the girl's throat. 'Have you seen the doctor yet?' he asked gently.

'The police surgeon has been summoned,' Walker said.

Carefully, Mickey moved the collar of her coat aside and

then turned her chin. The marks of a single hand were clear on her neck.

'Was he taller than you? Heavily built? When he was following you, how did his footsteps sound?' Mickey asked.

Mildred Jones looked puzzled for a moment.

'Well, answer the gentleman,' her mother said. She fell silent again as Henry's look was once more turned in her direction.

Mildred took a deep, shaky breath and then said, 'He was tall – taller than me anyway – but maybe not as tall as him.' She nodded in Henry's direction. Henry stood at six feet two. 'He wasn't that heavy built, or anything like that, just ordinary. But he was strong, really strong. He grabbed my arm first.' She pulled back her sleeve to show the marks on her arm where the fingers had bitten deep.

'He grabbed my sleeve and then my arm, and then he turned me around and he had his hand, his other hand, around my throat.'

'His left hand,' Mickey said.

She looked surprised and then nodded. 'Must have been. And then he squeezed, and I could hardly breathe. And everything was going dark, and then I heard something, and I realized it was a whistle, and I thought it was the constable. And then he let go; he ran away and so did I. I had a terrible time getting my breath, but I was so scared, I think it was the fear that helped me run.'

Mickey nodded. 'And how was he dressed? Well dressed, poorly dressed? Like a workman, like a gentleman?'

She frowned again, obviously trying to remember. 'He wore an overcoat, not a jacket, or workman's coat, but an overcoat, a proper one. He had his collar turned up and he was wearing a hat. A Homburg maybe or something like that. He had his scarf around his neck and pulled up over his mouth. I lashed out at him. I was wearing my gloves, so it didn't do much good, but I was trying to scratch his eyes out.'

'Quite right, too,' her mother approved.

'And you dislodged the scarf,' Mickey guessed.

'I must've done. He was clean-shaven – no beard, no moustache – but things were getting a bit dark by then, so I'm not really sure what he looked like. I'm sorry.'

'Can you guess at his age?'

'He wasn't young like me, but he wasn't really old either – maybe thirty?'

They questioned her further, but it was clear she couldn't remember much more. She was pale and shaken and, Mickey thought, incredibly lucky.

The doctor arrived and examined her, and then sent her home with a police escort.

She turned in the doorway and said, 'There was a funny thing. It might be nothing, but when I was flailing about, trying to find something to hit, I rammed my hand into his shoulder and I'm sure he flinched, as though he was in pain.' She shrugged. 'I didn't think about it at the time, but now, well, it does seem a bit odd, doesn't it?'

'You think it's our man?' Walker asked when she had gone.

'I think there are similarities, too many for this to be mere coincidence,' Henry told him. 'It is significant that the attack was in town and not out in the countryside. Which reinforces my sense that whoever killed the first two women knew their habits and knew where they might be found on any given night. One might have been an opportunistic killing, but not two. We know he now has a taste for killing, but perhaps he has no knowledge of other young women that are easily available, unless he knew that this one would be working late.'

'Or he walked the streets looking for a possible victim.'

'Which suggests a lack of caution. An eagerness perhaps. It suggests he can't wait for opportunity but is impelled to act. That makes him even more dangerous.'

'And the possible injury to the shoulder?'

'Could have been caused by anything. But it's an enticing prospect that such an injury might have been caused by Miss Brewer and her poker.'

TWENTY-TWO

I t was amazing how different it felt, dressed in the flat cap and heavy work jacket that had belonged to her brother. The boots felt stiff, and the cleats and hobnails struck sparks from the cobblestones, reminding her of when they had both been children and they had delighted in pounding their feet against the dark streets and sending small fairy lights behind them as they ran.

She had considered going to the police, now that she felt she knew for certain, and there would have been satisfaction in handing this man over and eventually seeing him hanged, except that she was sure that he would wriggle out of it. That there would be some way for him to escape, some way for him to seek help and disappear before the police could get to him or a case could be made. It would take time to convince anyone of his guilt, and that was time she didn't feel she had. The attack on Elizabeth Brewer – news she had heard by chance, overhearing servants' gossip – had confirmed her view of that.

No one gave her a second glance. The persistent drizzle that had characterized the last week meant that heads were down and those that could afford them were sheltering beneath umbrellas. She had the coat collar turned up, the cap pulled down and her hands thrust deep into the pockets. She was just another cold and miserable figure hurrying through the streets and trying to get home.

She slipped in through the back door, knowing it would be unlocked. She knew that the landlady encouraged her tenants to come in through the back, taking off their shoes before they went into the kitchen. She was proud of the state of her floors and the carpets on the stairs and the landing and the rugs on the floors in the rooms she rented. With some justification, she regarded her establishment as being better than the norm.

Softly, she mounted the stairs. Afraid they might creak, she was careful where she put her feet, keeping to the edges of the treads. He looked up as she opened the door, his face puzzled at first and then mildly amused. Then he must have realized what she intended because he had a knife in his hand and he was coming straight for her. As she swung the hammer, he caught her arm with the blade, just above the wrist and where the jacket fell back and left her arm bare. She was too focused and intent and determined to take any notice of it, beyond the faint sensation of being stung. But her own blow found its mark and he fell heavily to the floor. She hit him again, just to be sure, and then a third time, because the sensation of the hammer splitting the skull was oddly satisfying. It occurred to her, vaguely, that he did not seem as tall as he had in the street. Then she pocketed the hammer and made her soft way back down the stairs.

She had just reached the kitchen door when she heard the front door open. Breathing hard now, she opened it just wide enough to slip through and then scurried swiftly across the yard and into the alleyway beyond. To her relief, there was no one to see her and she slowed her pace, turned on to the street once more and pulled up the collar, hunched her shoulders and thrust her hands into the pockets of the jacket, glad that the colour was so dark and that no one would see the blood now staining the sleeve and running down to coat the fingers of her right hand.

TWENTY-THREE

'His name,' Walker said, 'is Aiden Hughes and he was a commercial traveller, selling cleaning products to hotels. And yes, it seems likely that he was the Aiden Hughes we spoke about yesterday. An odd coincidence, don't you think?'

'I dislike coincidence,' Henry growled.

'The landlady says he was often away for five or six days, but returned most weekends, picked up new stock and off he went again on a Monday morning. Occasionally, she said, he would do short weeks, only two or three days, but he would always be sure to let her know in advance that he would be needing dinner on those days. She described him as a very polite man, and a very considerate tenant.'

'Well, somebody took a great dislike to him,' Mickey said. He was kneeling beside the body with his camera. 'Whoever it was, they did a neat job – the first blow put him down, the second and third made certain he was dead – although I'm guessing the first was probably enough to kill him. I'm also guessing the blow was struck with a hammer of some description – you can see the indentation.'

'Next of kin?' Henry asked.

'The landlady didn't know of any. He went to work, he came back here, and he rarely seemed to go anywhere else. There were a couple of pubs that she reckoned he drank in, the Wharf, which we know about, and the George; someone there might know.'

'The George at King's Toll?' Henry asked.

Walker frowned. 'I had assumed she meant the George here, but that's a good point and I will double-check. It's the King George in town here, the George and the Dragon at King's Toll. Thinking about it, the George and Dragon makes more sense; the landlord has a special rate for commercial travellers, and there are spaces at the back for those that have vehicles.

He runs something of a taxi service between the train station for those that don't. Although it's a little out of the way, he's cheaper than most and cleaner, so I understand the pub gets a lot of repeat custom. If Aiden Hughes had friends in the same business, it's possible he might have met them there, I suppose. It's a bit of a walk back to town, but he's a local boy, so he knows the back roads and shortcuts.'

'Sarah Downham used to walk the route without difficulty, so I doubt a strong young man would see it as particularly onerous,' Henry commented.

They left Mickey at the scene to gather what forensic evidence he could and returned to the police station. The landlady had reportedly heard the back door close just after she had returned home at ten o'clock in the evening. This was something like a quarter of an hour after Mildred Jones had been attacked. She had only discovered that her tenant was dead when he had failed to come down for breakfast and she had gone to see if he had overslept. Were these two incidents linked?

Back at the police station, they found Sir Joseph Bright waiting for them. 'The bodies are rather piling up, aren't they, Henry?' Sir Joseph said somewhat sharply. 'I have to admit I did expect a speedier conclusion to all of this mess. Instead of which we have another murder. I hope you have some explanation for what is going on.'

'I'm surprised you have heard the news so quickly,' Henry said.

'I came here to speak to you on another matter, and the desk sergeant just informed me where you were. Have you identified the dead man?'

'A travelling salesman by the name of Aiden Hughes,' Henry told him. He was certain there was a flicker of recognition in Sir Joseph's eyes. 'Did you know the man?' he asked.

'I don't recognize the name. Besides, why would I know a travelling salesman, unless he'd come up before me in court?'

For the moment, Henry decided to let it pass. 'And what did you want to speak to me about?'

'It seems to me you clearly don't understand the sensitivities,' Sir Joseph said. 'The whole community has been affected by the deaths of these two young women. Do you really have to go around asking questions that have already been asked, pulling the scabs off wounds, if you will? I chanced to speak to Kerr yesterday, and the man was most upset. He's not the brightest of the bunch, and he's not long lost his wife; you can imagine how this must have distressed him, and you are asking more questions when all he did was find the body.'

'I asked about his observations,' Henry said calmly. 'I would do the same with any witness.'

'But it's not on, Henry. I understand the kind of people you are used to dealing with in the city, and no doubt they are more used to being questioned by the police, but these are simple people—'

'And two young women have been murdered. Now a third person is dead. Another woman attacked in her own home. I'm sure you would wish me to investigate this thoroughly.'

'Attacked? Who?'

'Elizabeth Brewer. Two men broke into her home; she was beaten and stabbed. It's not known if she will survive.'

'I had no idea. When did this happen?'

'The night before last. We only learned about this last night; it seems the local constabularies do not communicate with one another. And now we have three murders to solve and a possible fourth if Miss Brewer dies.'

'Did anyone see anything?'

'Fortunately, her neighbours heard the attackers breaking in and came to the rescue, but not before serious injury had been inflicted. They saw the men fleeing the scene. One tall and the other shorter, both with scarves tied across their faces. They were pursued, but not captured. And then, last evening, another young woman was assaulted only a few streets from here. Thankfully, the attacker was interrupted and frightened away. But it seems to me, Sir Joseph, that although we were brought in to examine one murder, there is more trouble in this little town and its surroundings than I would usually expect to find on the streets of London, and there are far fewer resources for dealing with it.

'The murders of Sarah Downham and Penelope Soper did not suddenly happen with no prior warning. There have been attacks, escalating attacks on young women, for the past two or more years, likely carried out by the same individuals.'

'Individuals? What do you mean?'

'I mean that there are likely at least two men involved. The descriptions are too dissimilar to be simply the result of witnesses being mistaken, even though the attacks are noticeably alike. One is tall and dark, the other shorter but equally strong. The pattern seems to have been missed, at least by anyone who could have done something about it. The local police forces seem not to have communicated as fully as they might, and the journalist who noted the pattern was summarily told he must not frighten the public. Poor Sarah Downham, who knew at least one of the victims; she and her friends tried, in their very clumsy way, to understand what might be happening. Now two of them are dead. And so, Sir Joseph, you'll understand that I have no sympathy with your demands for results. Not when opportunities for solving these crimes, before they ended in murder, have likely been missed.'

Sir Joseph's face had changed from milk-white to deep red and back again. He seemed at a loss for words because he plucked his hat from the sergeant's desk and walked stiffly from the police station.

'You think he'll still be content to pay your hotel bill?' Walker asked mildly.

Mickey worked slowly and methodically around the room. The body still lay where it had fallen, the police surgeon having not yet arrived to confirm the extinguishing of life. Mickey guessed, from the position of the chair pulled out from the small table, that the man had been sitting when his assailant entered the room. He had risen, been struck down, fallen beside the chair. Whoever had attacked him had done so very swiftly; a knife rested on the floor close to the man's hand, so he had been preparing to meet the attack. The three blows spoke of a determination to see him dead, but not, in Mickey's eyes, frenzy. The indentations were close together, oddly precise, as though whoever had struck them wanted to pierce the skull through to the brain. Certainly, they wanted to be confident that the man was dead.

There was little in the room that might give a clue to the man who had lived there. It was small and clean, with a neatly made single bed against the wall, a chest of drawers against the opposite wall and a blanket box set at the foot of the bed. Hanging shelves housed tobacco and matches and a pocketknife; the chest of drawers, some clean shirts and underclothes; the chest, two spare blankets. There was little that was personal: only a few paperbacks – cheap detective stories that looked to be well thumbed and bore pencil-marked prices that suggested they had been bought second-hand – sheets of writing paper and a dip pen and ink bottle with a scant amount of ink. A cheap canvas housewife containing needles, thread and darning wool, spare buttons and collar studs. Not much to show for a life, Mickey thought. Or maybe this was a man who did not care to own things. So, what did he spend his money on?

A heavy tread on the stairs suggested the arrival of the police surgeon, and he was not surprised to find Doctor Clark standing in the doorway. Something about the way he regarded the body caused Mickey to ask, 'Did you know this man?'

'An acquaintance of my son's. They attended school together when they were both young. Before I sent Roland away to board.'

He looked with evident distaste at the body, and Mickey asked, 'What sort of a man was Aiden Hughes?'

'I wouldn't know. I knew the boy, not the man. He wasn't a good sort – far too fond of tricks and mischief. Not someone I wanted my son to associate with.'

'Was the friendship why you sent your son away?'

Mickey was shocked by the immoderation of Dr Clark's reply. 'I sent him away for his own good. To a school where good morals and attention to his schoolwork were considered essential markers of a gentleman. I wanted my son to have a proper education. To be able to take his proper place in society.'

Mickey raised an eyebrow at the tone. 'You wanted him to become a medical man?'

Clark made a dismissive sound that Mickey found hard to interpret. He withdrew a pad from his pocket and, without even bothering to kneel and examine the body, wrote the certificate pronouncing that this man was indeed as dead as everyone thought he was. He placed this on the chest of drawers and then turned to leave.

'I understand he also knew Philip Maddison,' Mickey said. 'And Brady Brewer.'

Dr Clark did not reply. Mickey heard his heavy footsteps on the stairs and then on the tiles of the hall. The front door slammed.

'That,' Mickey said, 'is not a happy man.'

TWENTY-FOUR

I f Dr Clark thought that the worst of his day was over, he was soon disabused of that notion. He was told on returning home that Sir Joseph Bright was waiting for him; the maid had already brought him coffee.

Sighing, Dr Clark pushed open the door and stepped inside. Bright was pacing – and impatient, the coffee undrunk on a side table. With a slightly shaky hand, Clark poured some for himself. It was still warm, though not as hot as he would have liked.

'A girl was assaulted in the street last night,' Bright said without preamble, 'and the night before that, Elizabeth Brewer was attacked and stabbed in her own home. By two men. One tall and one shorter, and you and I both know who those two men were.'

'Well, one of them is dead,' Dr Clark said, his voice expressionless. 'Aiden Hughes was attacked with what the police assume was a hammer.'

'Apparently so. What the hell is going on? You gave me your word—'

'You don't *know* that my son was involved.'

'I don't? I've stuck my neck out for you. I've helped because of a long and important friendship. But no more. I wash my hands.'

'You helped because of what you knew I could expose, Joseph. Our friendship didn't enter into it. Apart, of course, from helping to salve your conscience. No doubt you kept telling yourself you were helping poor old Clark. Clark with a devil for a son. It was the least you could do. Doubtless, you told yourself that lie so often that you came to believe it. But it's not the truth, is it, Joseph? You helped me because you were afraid. I knew about your land deals, buying up property for a fraction of what it was truly worth, but making such a fuss over it that the poor sots who sold to you believed you were doing them a favour. I know about your women. For God's sake, man, I'm the one who treated you when you caught the damn pox. I knew about the bribes you took and the favours you cashed in. That was why you helped me. To keep your whiter-than-white image pure. But you and I both know that image is about as pure as snow that the cows have pissed on.'

'Did he kill the Soper girl?' Sir Joseph demanded.

Clark was silent. He had not been sure, had chosen to believe what Roland told him – but now?

Sir Joseph towered over him, his breath hot in Clark's face. 'Then say what you like,' he said. 'It will be the word of a man with a murderer for a son.'

He snatched up his hat and left.

TWENTY-FIVE

'I want a word with you, young Constable Cronin,' Mickey said.

The young man, having been unexpectedly summoned into Inspector Walker's office, looked anxiously at the senior officers. 'Have I done something wrong, sirs?'

'I don't imagine that you have recently,' Mickey told him. 'But I'm curious as to why you were mentioned in Miss Sarah Downham's writings. She recounts a particular incident with a catapult.'

'Ah,' Cronin said. 'That.'

'Take a seat,' Mickey invited, 'and enlighten us.'

Somewhat reluctantly, Cronin did as he was told. 'When we were all young – I mean, until we were ten or eleven – we were all at the same school. There was me, Mr Philip Maddison, though he was a bit older, Miss Sarah a couple of years behind me, with Miss Lucy and Linus, though they changed schools and went to the Husbands Bosworth one because it was a bit easier to get to in the winter. There was also Harry Aitken – Harry was in the year above me.'

'And Aiden Hughes?'

'Yes, he was a bit older, too, and then Doctor Clark's son. It's a small town, sir; it's not surprising we all went to the same school. Then as Mr Maddison and Roland Clark got older, they were sent away – they would have been about twelve or thirteen, I suppose.'

'And did you know them outside of school? Sarah Downham's journal entries suggest that you did.'

Billy Cronin looked a little embarrassed, but he nodded. 'When we were all little kids, it didn't make much difference where we came from. All bundled into the same classrooms, doing the same lessons and playing the same games in the playground. As the boys got older – I mean, Mr Maddison and Roland Clark – they got sent away to school, but me and Harry and Linus Green, we'd run into them in the holidays, and while we were still young – I mean in the first couple of years after they went away – it just seemed like it always had.'

'And then things began to change?' Mickey asked.

'Yes. I've not really thought about it in a long while. It was as though they realized there was a big difference between us and them. I mean, Mr Maddison wasn't so bad, but . . .'

'And the catapult incident?'

Constable Cronin's cheeks were definitely a little flushed. 'You know what kids are like, especially boys – always up to mischief. We'd play knock-door-run, especially if we knew it would really make someone mad. Go scrumping apples, throw firecrackers into people's yards – really stupid things. My mam would wallop me with a wooden spoon, and occasionally my dad would take a swipe with his belt, but to be honest, with five kids under her feet, it was my mam who was the disciplinarian. Anyway, as you get older, you stop being such an idiot. But when they were back, especially when Roland Clark was back home, it got more difficult not to get involved.'

'They were older?'

'And they were toffs. To be honest, sirs, I liked to be able to boast that they were friends – a doctor's son and someone as rich as Mr Maddison – that they still wanted to be friends with me.'

'And the Greens? And Harry Aitken?'

'Harry lost his job as a delivery boy, as you know, sirs. Then he was apprenticed. He seemed to grow up fast and, I don't know, become a bit wary of the likes of Roland Clark. I didn't understand why at the time. Linus and Lucy Green changed schools, and though they still saw Miss Downham quite a bit, I lost touch with them for a time. Roland Clark pallied up with Aiden Hughes and I, well, I suppose for a while I tagged along.'

'And the catapult?'

'It was stupid. They liked pranks. The sort we'd all grown out of, but more serious. They liked actually scaring people or doing damage. Not so much Mr Maddison, but . . .'

'What kind of things?'

'Well, it was one thing to chuck firecrackers into someone's yard, but not so good if you posted them through the letterbox. And they liked to follow girls, make rude comments, suggestive comments. And they liked to dare other kids to do things. The little kids especially. They'd promise them sweets and then laugh when they got into trouble. Stupid things like Mary Ellison. They promised her sweets if she'd drag her neighbour's washing off the line and drop it in the mud. She got seven shades beaten out of her by her dad, and although she told him Roland Clark had put her up to it, no one believed her.'

'And they promised you something if you'd break windows with your catapult?'

'A shilling. That was a lot of money. The window was an accident; I was aiming for this big old plant pot standing on the porch outside the Downham house. We all ran but we'd been spotted. Mrs Forsyth went spare. Roland and Aiden just stood there, laughing at me. Constable Smith gave me a clip round the ear and escorted me home. My mother knocked me into next week and back with a wooden spoon, and I had to go and sit on the back step and wait for my father to get home.'

'And he finished the job?' Walker enquired.

Cronin shook his head. 'Never laid a finger on me, sir, but he told me something that day that really stuck with me. He said that it might seem like fun now, playing silly buggers with boys who were richer and from a better class than me, but I was to remember that while they'd always have the right to call me Billy, once they were grown up, I'd always have to call them Mr or Sir – not because they deserved it or worked for it, but because of what family they'd been born into.'

'An important lesson,' Mickey said. 'And after that?'

'After that, I steered clear. Mam made me get a job after school as a delivery boy. I hated it, especially when Roland Clark saw me in the street and laughed at me. But she let me keep some of the money and that made up for a lot.'

Mickey thanked him for his honesty and then asked, 'And what does Roland Clark look like?'

'He's tall, dark-haired, not heavily built but solid enough. You know he's working for the Master of Hounds, Sir Joseph Bright?'

Mickey nodded. He glanced over at Walker. 'Constable Cronin, if you'd be so good as to get the car.'

To get to the kennels, they had to drive first past the stable yard, and Henry was reminded of Brewer's propensity for drinking and gambling with the stable lads. The narrow track turned away before reaching the kennels perhaps a quarter of a mile further on. As they got out of the car, Henry realized that they were standing on the ridge above Glebe Farm and upon which they had seen the hounds being exercised when they had spoken to Ronan Kerr.

He tried to get his more general bearings. They had passed the gate by which Penny Soper's body had been found a few minutes before arriving at the stables. He had seen the turnoff for Naseby just before that – although presumably the road would take a route into the village from the opposite direction to the one he had travelled with Cronin. Through the village, out the other side, the road would pass the spot where Sarah Downham had been killed. From there, the path led to the Greens' farm and on to East Harborough. *How far?* he wondered. Four, five miles?

The persistent drizzle that had characterized the past few days had cleared, and the pale grey sky seemed vast as it stretched out across the valley.

'It's a fine spot,' Mickey commented.

'It is indeed,' a voice behind them said. 'What can I do for you, gentlemen?'

Henry turned and regarded the man who had spoken. Tweed jacket, heavy boots, jodhpurs, he was tall and slim and had grey eyes that almost matched the still-irritable sky. He introduced himself as James Gresham, Master of the Hounds. 'Or Huntsman, if you prefer.' His smile was broad, but his eyes enquiring.

Henry introduced himself and Mickey and explained that they wished to speak to Roland Clark. The grey eyes clouded just a little, he thought.

'He's about somewhere. Ah, Roly, these gentlemen want a word.'

A young man crossed the yard. He was half a head taller than his boss and more heavily built, with very dark hair and even darker eyes. His gaze was fixed, Henry realized, not on them but on their driver.

'Well, Billy Cronin, as I live and breathe. Last time I saw you, you were riding a shop bicycle. And now you're driving a bloody great car. And' – he looked more closely – 'a copper, to boot.' He laughed as though this was the greatest joke.

'Afternoon, Mr Clark,' Constable Cronin said.

Henry was reminded of what Cronin had told them earlier about his father's advice.

'So, what can I do for you?' Roland Clark asked. 'A chief inspector and a sergeant. It must be important.'

Henry remained silent for a beat or two, just studying the young man. He was not, Henry gauged, a man who would be comfortable with silence. It was not something he could control. 'Where were you two evenings ago?' he asked eventually. 'For that matter, where were you last night?'

'What is this about, Chief Inspector?' James Gresham asked. 'Roly was here, as far as I know.'

'Mr Clark?'

'I was here. Both evenings. All evenings. Both nights, all night.'

'Can anyone vouch for you?'

'And why would I need anyone to vouch for me? Come now, Chief Inspector, what's all this about?'

'Two evenings ago, Elizabeth Brewer was attacked in her own home, beaten and stabbed.'

'Yes, we heard about that,' Clark said. 'Pity – she was a nice enough old girl. Did some work for my father from time to time, you know. That brother of hers put paid to all that, I'm afraid. Persona non grata, I expect she is now. In any decent house, at any rate.'

Henry ignored the tone. He continued, 'And last evening a young woman was assaulted in East Harborough.'

'Good Lord! Was she badly injured?' James Gresham asked.

'Thankfully, not. The assailant was interrupted. But only a little later, an acquaintance of yours was killed in his room at his boarding house. Aiden Hughes. I believe the two of you were friends?'

'Acquaintances, certainly. Well, poor old Aiden. What happened to him?'

'We believe that someone stove in his skull with a hammer.'

'Did they indeed!' The young man's eyes were hard, his smile now brittle. 'And this involves me because . . .?'

'Witnesses saw two young men run from Miss Brewer's house. The description we have could well have been of you and Aiden Hughes.'

Clark laughed, and Henry could see the relief in his eyes. He knew he had left no fingerprints. Knew he had worn gloves.

'And could have been any other two young men in the neighbourhood. Is that the best you have, Inspector?'

'Then you won't mind coming to the police station and giving us your prints,' Mickey said cheerfully.

'I would mind. I was here, and this is very close to harassment.'

'We are simply making enquiries.' Mickey's smile never faded. 'I'm sure you'd like to help us in any way you can.'

They were interrupted by the arrival of another car. Sir Joseph Bright, face like thunder, stepped out and crossed the yard to where they stood. 'And what's all this about, Henry?' he demanded.

'I follow where the investigation leads. I told you that already.'

'I welcomed you into my home. I've given you every assistance possible.'

'And I need to know where Mr Clark was last night and the evening before.'

Sir Joseph turned to the Huntsman. 'James? Do you know where he was?'

Gresham frowned, clearly not happy about being put on the spot. 'Well, last evening, I know he was here until I left, a little after seven. We were making plans for checking the coverts. Roly will be Field Master at the next hunt.'

'There you are, then.'

'And later in the evening? And the night before?' Henry persisted.

'I told you already; he was here as far as I know. But he's

not a child; he doesn't have to check in with me every time he leaves the yard.'

'There. He was here. What more do you want to know?'

James Gresham opened his mouth; it seemed to Henry he was about to object that this wasn't what he'd said. He could see the satisfaction on Clark's face.

'Sir Joseph, perhaps before you declare yourself so certain, maybe you should consider the consequences if that turns out to be wrong,' Henry said quietly.

'Is that a threat, Chief Inspector?'

'No, Sir Joseph. I don't need to make threats. I just follow where the investigation leads.'

He gestured to Mickey that they should leave.

'What do we do now?' Mickey asked. 'He's our man – or one of them at least. My bet is the other was Aiden Hughes.'

Henry nodded. 'Who killed Hughes and why? Does this have something to do with Sarah Downham and her friends poking about, trying to work out who assaulted those girls?'

'Or maybe suspecting but having no proof. We wondered if they'd confronted someone with their half-baked evidence. We should have brought Roland Clark in.'

'And we will. As it stands, though, Sir Joseph will make it difficult for us to get the evidence to stick. Which makes me wonder – what or who is he protecting? What's his role been in all of this? If we're bringing Clark in, then it would please me to have him accompanied.'

'By Sir Joseph?'

'And Doctor Clark. I'll bet you a damn good dinner that Clark senior knows what his son is capable of and at least suspects what he might have done. And that Sir Joseph, even if he didn't collude, protected Roland Clark. We know he gave him a job. A prestigious job, if you consider these things have status, which in these parts being some kind of hunt master seems to have.'

'That's the kind of bet I like,' Mickey said with satisfaction.

Back in East Harborough, they split up: Mickey, with Walker's help, to go through any juvenile records for Clark or Hughes;

Henry to the very belated meeting with the journalist, Percival White. Had these men come to his attention?

Percival White greeted him with enthusiasm. 'You've certainly stirred things up,' he said.

'How so?'

'I had a visit from the esteemed magistrate, Sir Joseph Bright, this morning,' he said. 'Apparently you cited a local journalist as having gathered evidence regarding attacks on young women. He came round, demanding to know what I meant by my claims, what evidence I had for making them.'

'And what did you tell him?'

'I told him he should speak to my editors.' He smiled. 'He seemed most aggravated. What happened with Aiden Hughes? Sir Joseph seemed to take the matter personally.'

'Did he now? When I spoke to him, he denied knowing the man. And do you have anything in your records pertaining to Hughes, or to Roland Clark?'

'Not much, I'm afraid. Anecdotally, Mrs Rogers remembers them being "little tykes", always making mischief and bribing or coercing younger children into dares and general mayhem.'

Henry nodded. It had been a long shot.

Somewhere, deeper in the house, a telephone rang. A moment later, Mrs Rogers herself came in. 'That was the police station,' she told Henry. 'Miss Brewer is awake and wanting to speak to you.'

Percival White was on his feet in an instant. 'My car is parked outside, Inspector. No time to waste, now, is there?'

TWENTY-SIX

On their second visit to the kennels, they arrived mob-handed in two cars: Mickey and Inspector Walker driven by Constable Cronin, and Henry in the company of the enthusiastic Percival White. James Gresham stared at them all in disbelief.

The hounds, maybe disturbed by the sound of the vehicles or perhaps just sensing the tension in the air, gave voice loudly and enthusiastically. 'What in heaven's name is going on?' James Gresham demanded.

'We've come to arrest Roland Clark,' Henry told him. 'Charges of murder and attempted murder.'

'Of what?' For a moment, Gresham stared at him in apparent disbelief. Then he seemed to make up his mind. 'I saw him in the office about an hour ago. I don't know where he is at present.'

A search of the yard and its buildings and environs soon showed that Clark was nowhere to be found.

'I'm told he received a telephone call from his father about forty minutes ago,' Gresham said. 'He seems not to have been seen after that.'

Henry swore in frustration.

'Not to worry.' Gresham seemed in his element now. 'He's on foot; can't have gone far. The dogs will soon find him.'

As the officers and the journalist looked on, Gresham marched to the office and came back with a brown overall jacket. He opened the door to one of the kennels. Dogs swarmed around him, tails and bodies wagging in excitement, bowling into his legs and licking his hands as he attached the leads. He dropped the jacket to the ground, encouraging the dogs to sniff and tear at the garment, noses buried deep in the heavy twill. And then they were off, Gresham holding the leash, Henry following, his long coat flapping behind him like grey woollen wings.

* * *

Mickey watched him go. He had seen Henry do this before – chasing a hunting pack, though on that occasion they had been bloodhounds – keeping pace effortlessly, seeming untiring. *He's still carrying his injuries*, Mickey thought. *He's going to pay for this excess.*

'What should we do?' Percival White was clearly itching to follow.

'Let them run,' Mickey said, 'while we bring up the rear at a more sedate pace. I'm not such an eager beaver that I wear myself out to no good purpose.'

About twenty minutes on, the voice of the pack in the distance seemed to change. 'They have him,' Mickey said. They hurried on and reached the spot where the dogs held Roland Clark at bay, Gresham keeping tight hold of the leads. The young man had backed up against a large tree, and although the dogs, to Mickey's eye, seemed merely to be enjoying their play, he could imagine how disconcerting the sight of half a dozen wide-open mouths, all sharp teeth and lolling tongues, might be.

Mickey removed his handcuffs from his coat and handed them to his boss. As the now deeply cowed Roland Clark passed by, Mickey grasped the young man's shoulder hard enough to make him wince. 'You thought you'd finished her off, didn't you, lad? But now she's awake and ready to tell all.'

TWENTY-SEVEN

'What exactly did she tell you?' Walker asked. He and Mickey had simply received the summons to meet Henry at the kennels to make the arrest.

'When I spoke to Elizabeth Brewer, she was able to tell me that she managed to pull the scarf from Hughes face,' Henry said. 'Clark then came in and used the knife on her, but she knew if her first assailant was Hughes, then the other must be Clark. She admitted that she was foolish enough to visit Aiden at his boarding house. She seems to have threatened him and I think she knew he'd try to shut her up. I asked her why she didn't come to us, but it seemed she wanted someone else to be informed first.'

'Who?' Mickey asked.

'When she left the boarding house she went to visit Sarah's aunt and told her what she knew. She then promised to hold her peace for a day or so and I think she was under the impression that the aunt would inform us – though there she misjudged the situation badly. I have to wonder if Sarah's aunt had seen the handkerchief marked with AH among Sarah's possessions but only made sense of the initials after Elizabeth's visit. And she confessed to something else.'

'What was that?'

'That you were right about her brother. She fell asleep, and when she woke up, the fire had almost burned down and Brady wasn't there. She knew that if he'd been home while she slept, he'd have put more logs on the fire, so, despite what he insisted upon as being true, he must have left at some point. He'd told her he'd just popped out for a drink, but she knew he lied because of the way the fire had burned down.'

'Then why lie to the police?'

'I'm not sure she knows herself. Maybe because it was hard to admit her brother really was a murderer. She had got used to defending him.'

'So Brewer killed Sarah Downham.'

'Looks that way,' Henry agreed. 'You were right all along.'

'So why don't I feel better about it?' Walker said.

From the moment he entered the interview room, Mickey wanted to wipe the grin from Roland Clark's face. Henry sat down opposite the man with Mickey beside him.

This might be the last time, Mickey thought. *The last time we do this. Well, it's not a bad exit.*

He waited for Henry to begin, but Clark was ahead of them both. He was proud, Mickey realized, of what he'd done. He fancied himself as a cut above.

'I was there when Brady did for Sarah Downham,' he said, the grin never faltering. 'We got wind of what she was up to. Meeting Aiden near the farm. Brady grabbed her and I got Aiden. We made him watch. He'd tried to talk his way out of it, told Brady that he was just having his fun, that the girl didn't mean anything to him. So when Brady got wind of them trying to run out on him, he figured Aiden should see just what happened to people when they got on his bad side. Scared to death he was, thought Brady was going to do for him as well. Cried like a baby, he did. I had to stuff my glove into his mouth to shut him up and Brady had to do the same to the girl. You should have heard her scream.' He leaned across the table towards Henry. 'Didn't scream for long, though, did she?'

Henry's voice was calm. 'And so *you* killed Miss Soper.'

'I did that. Saw what fun Brady had and wanted some of that for myself. Besides, it muddied the waters, didn't it? I had so much fun watching all you clever, clever folk rushing around like headless chickens.'

'My guess would be that you were relieved when Brady was hanged for Sarah Downham's murder. You couldn't be certain he wouldn't turn on you,' Mickey said.

For a second or two Clark's smile faltered and Mickey knew he had hit his target. 'A man like that, well, you could never hope to predict what he might do or when someone like you might have outlived their usefulness.'

Again that flicker of anxiety on Clark's face.

'So how did you persuade Aiden Hughes to go with you to Miss Brewer's home?' Henry asked.

Clark laughed, his confidence returning. 'He didn't take a lot of persuading, did he? That daft old bird had already gone round to his place and riled him. He sent her away with a flea in her ear, but I convinced him that she needed dealing with.'

'Well, it was you, too, wasn't it? Hughes and you, attacking women. My guess is you took turns and tried to outdo one another. It was Hughes last night.'

'Never had any self-control.' Clark was contemptuous. 'He got urges. That's what he called them. Said it was like an itch he had to scratch.'

'Unlike you?'

'Me? I didn't *need* to do anything. Whatever I did was because I liked it, not because I got some damned urge. And he nearly got himself caught, didn't he? Had to run back home double quick. He'd only just made it in when that other daft bird turned up. She'd seen him in the street, guessed it was him I suppose, or maybe she'd just followed him back.' He shrugged. 'Like I said, he took risks because he couldn't resist the urges. Me, now, I'm fully in control of mine.'

'And was Miss Downham going to meet Aiden Hughes that night? The night she died?'

Clark snorted contemptuously. 'Always fancied him, didn't she? And him – he liked the idea of having a woman like her. He'd never have to work again, would he, if he got hooked up with a girl like her. So he played her along, and Brewer helped. He'd been promised a cut of whatever came to the girl when she got her inheritance. She'd have been married to Hughes by then, wouldn't she, so what was hers was his. Problem solved.'

'So Brewer's attentions to Miss Downham were misdirection?'

'I think he enjoyed that. He thought it was funny. Worked, though, didn't it? No one thought twice about Aiden. And Sarah was just stringing Brady along. More fool him if he thought a girl like her would ever look his way.'

'But what I do not understand is if Brewer was planning to cash in on Hughes's good fortune, why kill the source of that good fortune?'

Clark frowned. 'Because Aiden was a damned fool.'

'Because Aiden Hughes decided he didn't want to share after all,' Mickey suggested.

Clark nodded. 'That's about the size of it.'

'And he was foolish enough to tell you.'

Clark's grin was back. 'Got it in one, Sergeant. I took great pleasure in telling Brady. Not a man you'd want to cross.'

TWENTY-EIGHT

They were at the Downhams' house. It was late evening, and the household was preparing to settle for the night but had been gathered for post-prandial bridge and brandy. Henry asked the father, Philip Maddison and the aunt, Mrs Forsyth, to go through to the study, so he could speak to them all together.

Philip Maddison and Mr Downham escorted Henry and Mickey through to the library. Mrs Forsyth had excused herself and gone upstairs, promising to return shortly.

Briefly, Henry explained that they had arrested a man for killing Penelope Soper and that they were certain Brewer had killed Sarah.

'As we all believed.' Mr Downham was clearly not impressed.

'You knew that she was leaving that night,' Henry said to Philip Maddison. He was, Mickey thought, a nice-looking young man – and from his expression, he had evidently been hoping that his part in that night's events would have gone undiscovered.

'I . . . I . . . don't know what you mean.'

'You know exactly what I mean.' Mickey could see that his boss had no intention of letting Philip off the hook. He guessed that things would never be the same between the Maddisons and the Downhams after tonight.

'Neither you nor Sarah wished to be married. You, no doubt, because you were not yet ready to commit, and Sarah because she fancied herself to be in love with someone else.'

'Brewer!' Downham was furious. 'She never had feelings for that man. It was lies, all lies.'

'No, not Brewer,' Henry said calmly. 'His attentions were simple misdirection, to divert you from her real suitor. He planned to benefit from your daughter's affections, but not as directly as you all thought. No, she thought herself in love with a young man by the name of Aiden Hughes. I believe she may

have met him at a dance. He professed himself in love with
her, and poor Sarah believed him. They planned to run away.
But,' he said to Philip, 'you knew this, didn't you?'

The young man sighed and looked down at his feet, unwilling
to meet anyone's gaze. Mrs Forsyth had now entered the room.
She stood in the doorway, something white clutched in her
hand. Mickey noticed her, but all other attention seemed focused
on Philip.

'I hoped to talk them out of doing anything stupid,' he said.
'They had agreed to meet me. I'd offered them more money,
just until Sarah came into her own.'

'Which just goes to prove I was correct.' Downham was
furious. 'Girls of that age have no idea . . .' He trailed off as
though realizing what a hollow victory it was, to be correct
about such a thing.

'She was to catch the train with him, come to me and then
decide how to proceed. I thought I might be able to make her
see sense. When she didn't arrive, I thought . . . I assumed they
must have gone off somewhere together. I thought about elope-
ment, not murder. I never believed, not for a moment, that she'd
come to harm. That was such an awful shock. He was a gold-
digger; anyone could see that – apart from poor, sweet Sarah.
I'd never have believed he'd do her harm. I knew him from
when we were all children.'

And before he had to call you Mr Maddison, Mickey thought.
But he held his tongue. His attention was drawn to Mrs Forsyth.
Sarah's aunt crossed the room and laid a white handkerchief
on her brother's desk. It seemed stained with red.

Mickey got up and unwrapped the little bundle. It contained
a hammer, the rounded head clumped with blood and hair.
'You killed Aiden Hughes,' he said, aware that he sounded
slightly awed. This small, plump, soft-looking woman in her
jet-trimmed dress.

'He killed my Sarah,' she said. 'I thought it was Brewer,
then I found some letters he had written to her and I knew. I
had to wait. I didn't know what I could possibly do without
completely ruining my Sarah's name. I thought with the new
investigation, you'd be certain to catch him. I was sure he
must have killed that Soper girl; Elizabeth Brewer had

confronted him about that and, lo and behold, he tried to silence her. She came to see me after she had spoken to him and told me that my Sarah and this Aiden had been planning to run away. I could hardly believe it . . . but what she said made sense of the items I had seen when I packed away Sarah's belongings. You didn't even look his way. So I did it myself.'

Oh Lord, Mickey thought. All these different groups of people, all known to one another, all in their own little boxes. If any one of them had spoken to any other, lives would have been saved and this mess solved long since.

EPILOGUE

'It's good to have met you both,' Inspector Walker told them as they prepared to leave. 'It's going to take the town a fair while to recover from all of this, though.'

Henry nodded. 'It's not the tidiest of endings,' he agreed. 'I imagine relations between Doctor Clark and Sir Joseph Bright will suffer after this. Sir Joseph will recover, no doubt. Men in his position learn early that their reputation can be patched up with a donation to this good cause or that. If Doctor Clark has any sense he will sell up and move somewhere he and his son are unknown. But that will not be an easy task.'

Mickey paused before following his boss into the car. 'Young Cronin would make a good detective,' he said. 'You should see what can be done.'

'The thought had crossed my mind,' Walker agreed.

The drizzle had set in again as they drove out of the small town and into the countryside. Most towns tended to peter out, Mickey thought, but this one seemed to end abruptly, whichever road you took.

'No one has come out of this well,' he said.

'Does anyone, ever, when murder has been done?'

Mickey was silent for a few minutes and then he said, 'A telegram arrived for me this morning. My promotion has been approved, with immediate effect.'

He saw Henry smile, suspected he already knew.

'Congratulations, Inspector Hitchens,' Henry said. 'I will miss you more than I can say.'

'We'll still be working out of Central Office,' Mickey reminded him.

'No, Mickey. I've been giving this a lot of thought. I no longer want to spend my days seeing the worst that humanity can do. I need to find something else to do with my life.'

Mickey regarded his friend fondly and shook his head. 'You may walk away, Henry Johnstone,' he said. 'But the need to solve puzzles and right wrongs is etched into you, body and soul. It won't leave you alone.'

They sat in companionable silence for the remainder of the journey. Mickey caught glimpses of field and sheep and farm through gaps in hedges and views through farm gates, and had the feeling that for both of them a new adventure was about to begin.

And that they were both somehow content with that.